USA TODAY BESTSELLING AUTHOR

Dale Mayer

the *Haven*

TIMBER 01

TIMBER: THE HAVEN, BOOK 1
Beverly Dale Mayer
Valley Publishing Ltd.

This is a work of fiction. Names, characters, places, brands, media, and incidents either are the product of the author's imagination or are used fictitiously. Any resemblance to actual events, locales, or persons, living or dead, is entirely coincidental.

ISBN-13: 978-1-778867-32-3
Print Edition

Books in This Series:

Timber, Book 1

Burke, Book 2

About This Book

Timber fulfills his dreams of opening an animal refuge, called the Haven, a sanctuary hidden from the chaos of society, where he and the animals he rescues can find solace and peace. Timber is a loner by choice, so his heart swells with joy each time he saves a creature in need. Yet he never anticipated the unexpected friendships that would blossom nor the overwhelming number of animals seeking refuge from the very first day.

Tiffany, a local veterinarian, is thrilled by the news of a new rescue opening. Always in search of foster homes, she see a new opportunity, if only she can persuade the reserved owner to collaborate. Despite Timber's ease with animals over people, she feels a spark, a challenge she is eager to embrace, hoping to bridge the gap between them.

As the rescue begins to thrive, Timber senses a growing tension. Not everyone is pleased with his mission; some are openly hostile. Yet, amid the challenges, a heartwarming bond forms between him and Tiffany, a connection that promises to change everything. Together they face the adversity, as their shared passion for the animals ignites a love that neither had expected.

Sign up to be notified of all Dale's releases here!
https://geni.us/DaleNews

CHAPTER 1

T IMBER WOODLAND STRAIGHTENED from his project, wincing at the jolt of pain, and reached for the old T-shirt hanging from a nail on the wood post beside him. He used it to stop the sweat from running down his face, then took a moment to wipe his hands before rehanging the rag. Even in shorts and a tank top, he couldn't stop the sweat from forming. It was New Mexico in the summertime, after all.

Stretching his arms out first, he next moved around a few steps to loosen up the joints in his legs. It was one thing to work outdoors all day long. It was another thing to work outdoors all day long and to feel every muscle screaming at him at the end of the day—something he wanted to avoid as much as he could. Yet still he pushed himself to the very limit, testing where that line was daily.

He sighed. His life had been broken in two. Before the accident and after.

Before, he had always been a fitness fanatic, easily making it into the Navy SEALs, plus adding field medic to his skills.

And afterward? Well, to be honest, his prosthetic tried to slow him down. He shook his head at that. He had too much to do, and the dream of the Haven, an animal rescue and rehabilitation center, drove him.

He smiled as he felt a sense of accomplishment, a sense of a job well-done. It was hard to explain if you'd never really experienced it, but, to Timber, life was meant to be lived. That meant to have a body that was well used too. It's just that *used* seemed to be a second cousin to *abused*, something Timber constantly kept an eye on.

It had taken a long time to get into the physical shape he was in, and the last thing he wanted was to lose it over carelessness now. Of course it could happen in a heartbeat if he injured himself or if he overdid it on a regular basis. It was hard not to. He was alone and doing everything himself. Therefore, he was overdoing it daily.

Yet he had healed enough to finally walk freely on his prosthetic, and doing construction work for Badger over the past many months had been better than rehab. Plus the added design work that he did for Kat had helped Timber and Kat to further refine his prosthetic. So each kind of work had also been a form of mental and physical therapy, but a program that he was sure his former physiotherapist wouldn't have expected or would even have allowed.

Regardless, moving heavy construction materials, swinging a hammer, and climbing timber frames on construction jobs, as Badger's crew worked to build houses for those in need, had helped Timber in so many ways, even after he had left them to put down roots here.

And now his body moved with a freedom he rejoiced in. He just needed to remember that tomorrow would be a whole different story if he didn't look after today.

How prophetic. If everybody would learn that simple lesson, things would be a whole lot easier. But people didn't seem to learn easily, and he was no exception.

He stepped back, took a look at his work, and nodded.

It was coming along. It was slow, and that was fine, since it was his and his alone. It was a dream come true, even if it was in a very dilapidated state right now. He was perfectly capable of fixing it. It would just take time, energy, and money. Doing it fast would be great, but he was just fine to settle on doing it well.

He took several more steps, kicking out his legs, readjusting his prosthetic ever so slightly, making note of where it was hurting and wondering whether he was doing something wrong or should really bring it up with Kat.

As a prosthetics designer and manufacturer, she'd been instrumental in getting his mobility to this point, and he appreciated it. Finding her and Badger had truly been a blessing in disguise, and, through that construction work for them, Timber had concluded that *this* was what he needed to do.

One of Timber's dogs, Kojack, a Heinz 57 mix but with a bit of Lab in him, raced over to Timber, then slightly detoured to chase a squirrel that had been keeping him company all morning. Timber quickly corrected the dog's behavior, as the squirrel was just as welcome here as the dogs were. Kojack had been badly abused in his early years and now had almost no hair on most of his body, but he had a heck of a good sniffer and was a great watchdog.

Even if he wasn't, Timber would have taken him in a heartbeat because Kojack needed a home, and that was what Timber was all about. If an animal needed something that Timber could provide, he was there for them.

He reached down to scrub the back of Kojack's head. He barked and rubbed against Timber's exposed legs. The animals didn't care about Timber's prosthetic, injuries, or scars. They just cared about the fact that Timber was here for them. They now existed in a world full of joy, contentment, peace, and even fun because they were out here playing on a regular basis. For Timber it was work, but, since his toil was for the dogs and for the future animals too, well, it was everything.

He laughed when Kojack raced over as Philly, a brown Malinois, got up and slowly moved toward him. Philly was an older shepherd, probably a K9 dog at one point in time, but her training had been a long time ago. Now she was much more concerned about where her next meal was than where the next villain of the story was. Timber was fine with that. She was a sweetheart, and she moved about gingerly, probably just as sore and stiff as he was some days.

He bent to stroke her forehead. "Hey, girl. How are you doing?"

While cuddling her, he surveyed his property. He had over sixty acres now and was hoping to get more from the owner of the ranch next door. It was land the current owner wasn't using, land that even now the family was trying to break up and to sell off in bits and pieces, just so they could get the money for other things. And the old man, Andy Killerman, was holding off as much as he could.

Timber didn't want to be part of the breakup of the Killerman family land, but, if any of that land was available to come his way, he was more than happy to negotiate. So far, Andy had been more than reasonable, and Timber appreciated that; but he also understood that the rest of the Killerman family didn't see it the same way. If Andy bent to their wills, they would want Andy to make a deal on the land. Timber knew that the prices would likely go way up too, and that was something he didn't want.

When it came to Andy though, it was anybody's bet. He

was a rancher through and through, and he knew what a deal was. He knew what the value of his property was. So, as much as he had been happy to let Timber have some acreage, Andy was still holding off on the rest of the property, and that was fine.

Sixty acres was more than enough for Timber to deal with right now. He'd hoped for ten, twenty, and it had turned into thirty, then doubled from there. In truth, sixty acres had been a godsend for him, particularly when it came with a watering hole on the side, which meant that chances were good that he would have a decent water supply.

He could always put in more wells, and he already had one for the main cabin, his house, but one never had quite enough water, particularly in this New Mexico area. Once again he grabbed the rag, wiped off his face, then reached for his water bottle and took a big slug. He would love a cold beer right now, but not until the day was done. Only then would he consider it. Right now, there was work, … hell, there was always work.

Feeling an odd sensation coil up his back, he shifted ever so slightly to see what his internal antenna had caught, whatever the hell that meant anymore. When he had been a US Navy SEAL, his instincts had been his saving grace many a time, and he had certainly kept them cultivated and fine-tuned, but what the hell that meant in his current life, he had no clue. His life was completely different than he'd expected it to be. That's what happened when you got injured on the job, particularly to the level of the injury that Timber had sustained.

He looked around once more, the warning tingles gone. So was the animal that didn't want to approach. At least not yet. If hurting enough, the animal would return to get some help from Timber, as Timber had done for himself. He now smiled down at his steel blue prosthetic. His prosthetic was top-notch, and that was due to Kat. He'd also helped her to build some jigs to make some of the processing of these individual one-off pieces a little easier for her, and, as a thank-you—and her hope for continued assistance from Timber—she had been helping him build these prosthetics for his own leg. This one was doing pretty well, and he was really happy with the way it had worked out. Still smiling, he quickly texted Kat just to share that. She deserved to know that things were going well.

She responded, **Good. I would like to see it in a couple weeks, just to assess how it's holding up against the hard work.**

He laughed at that, since he'd worked damn hard when he was on Badger's crew, but this personal work of Timber's was a little different, and he knew that she understood that. He sent her a thumbs-up, popped his phone back into his pocket, and reached for his hammer again. He'd replaced the boards on the outside deck already and the support beams for the roof that would go on top. There had been an old awning, but time and weather had completely destroyed that to the point where he'd ripped it down and reframed it for a permanent roof atop the deck.

Not everybody would see that as a priority, but he had certainly identified this project as something he could do fairly quickly and would have a big impact on his lifestyle. He was an outdoor boy through and through, and having a deck, particularly when the weather was up and down, would be a big boon. Not to mention that the animals thoroughly appreciated it. He laughed, reached down, and scratched Philly on the back of her neck. She just looked up at him, her tail wagging. "I know, girl. We're almost done for the day."

Kojack barked at him, and Timber picked up the ball on the ground nearby and tossed it for him. He knew it was a game that would never end because Kojack had a ball fixation that just didn't quit. And that was okay, as long as he understood that, when work had to be done, that took priority. The dog didn't understand in the least, of course, but that was all right too.

Timber laughed as Kojack dropped the ball at his side. Timber threw it a few more times while he had a few more sips of water. Then he returned to measuring and ensuring everything was level and plumb. With the new post up, his next plan was to get the ridge framework secured to each post and also to the existing roof on this main cabin. Then he would put up the rafters, followed by the plywood, some waterproofing, and, before long, it would be a permanent roof.

He had shingles nearby, and, as long as the weather held, he should be okay to finish off the roof in the next day or so. He needed to go into town and get more supplies, but he was holding off as long as he could. Town was just that, *town*, and that meant people, so not his favorite thing to do, but he also had to take Lucy in for her checkup.

He looked over where she was, in the basket beside her brother. Lucy and Bingo, both King Charles spaniels, had been rescues that came his way within days of his moving here. He just smiled as Lucy looked up, batted her eyelids at him, and stretched out. She was now missing a leg and was still adjusting to life without that extra support. She would take any affection and love coming her way, particularly if it meant she got to be carried around, something she was way too accustomed to.

The previous owners hadn't taken her to be checked until she'd somehow gotten an ugly infection that would cost her a leg. They wanted her put down instead, but Timber happened to be there, picking up Philly from her checkup, when he'd heard about Lucy. He'd talked to the vet Tiffany, a young woman he couldn't help but admire, and Lucy's surgery had been done, with Timber taking care of her ever since.

The owners, hearing about it, had given him Bingo, as the two siblings were bonded. Lucy was such a sweetheart, but she was currently one of the biggest financial draws on the place. She wasn't exactly a contributing member of the property, and that was all right too, as far as Timber was concerned. Not everybody had to pull their weight. Some of them got away with doing absolutely nothing but eating and sleeping and looking for love.

Her brother Bingo had somewhat adopted her lifestyle, sticking close by her side, as if understanding that her life had changed in ways that nobody had expected. Timber knew firsthand how that felt. He understood that everybody needed support at times, and right now Lucy was at the top of the list.

Yet surely she must sometimes think that all this was way too much. She'd been hard-pressed to even try to get up and walk, but something about being outdoors with the other animals had urged her to take a few steps, then a few more and a few more. Her balance was still terrible, and she fell several times, but she was improving every day. As long as Timber could get her to keep getting up and getting out a bit, life would be that much easier on her.

He walked over, bent down, gave her a quick cuddle,

then said hello to Bingo, who stretched out a paw right beside him. Timber had to laugh. "The two of you are the laziest dogs I've ever seen."

Lucy gave half a bark, high-pitched but excited. Any time he talked to her, she always had the same reaction, as if she was absolutely thrilled that somebody was taking a moment to say hi. He always wondered how animals ended up with some of the people that they did. He didn't blame the previous owners; Lucy had come down with a serious infection, and most pet owners would have chosen to put her down. Yet Timber saw the value in her and knew she deserved a chance to live, but that didn't mean everybody would.

He straightened up once more, then looked back and announced, "Come on. Let's get those timbers up, as long as we've got the crossbeams in place. These upright ones won't hold against the wind." And, with that, he got back to work, but his instincts once again had him looking around a few minutes later, a weird feeling prodding him. Frowning at not seeing anything still, he headed back to get more work done. Yet he was always aware of that weird sense of something off, something wrong.

Finally, with the crossbeams up and everything tightened down, he looked over at Kojack. "You haven't picked up on anything, have you, buddy?"

Kojack just wagged his tail.

That meant their earlier visitor wasn't human. Kojack had a very strong sense of anything human, with good reason, but that also meant it was an animal, probably feral. And Timber had just enough wounded animals around the place that, if this new visitor was a predator, that would make sense. Yet often Timber found that, even if a predator, it could still need help. He preferred to think that some automatic distribution system sent the animals in need to find their way to him, and then he would do what he could. His time as a field medic in the military held him in good stead for most things, on two legs or four.

When it was something more serious, he had a great relationship with the veterinarians in town, mostly because he kept bringing them so much business. But they also gave him a hell of a deal, and, more often than not, he ended up getting their services and their supplies for cost. He couldn't ask them for more than that because everybody had bills to pay.

When he was finally done for the day, he stopped, grabbed his water bottle, then slowly opened his sixth-sense gaze, focusing on his peripheral vision, trying to determine just what he had been sensing. Catching the barest hint of movement off to the side, he froze and saw a deer, staring back at him. Even from here, he felt the waves of pain coming off her. Ordering the dogs to sit, he slowly backed up in her direction, trying not to scare her, not at all sure just what he was looking at or why she was here. He didn't know whether she was injured or something else was going on. He hoped it wasn't serious.

As he got closer, he shifted just enough to take another look at her. She was standing on four legs, but holding her weight off the front. She stood between multiple branches, so it was much harder for him to get a clear impression of her, but, when he did see it, his gaze sharpened as he assessed the situation, and then the anger hit—and hit hard.

An arrow was sticking out of her shoulder, and it seemed to have been there for way-the-hell too long.

Knowing that he would now be tasked with the job of

trying to get even closer to see if he could do something for her, and then actually do it, he shifted as close as he could and then slowly talked to her, trying to keep her calm, while he took a careful look at the injury on her shoulder.

"Hey, girl," he whispered. "That looks mighty uncomfortable. Can I help you with that?"

She just stared at him through the wells of pain in her gaze, and he winced, knowing just how much pain she would be in. He'd been shot a couple times himself—never with an arrow, thank God—but, as he stared at it, he realized that the tip of the arrow was in but wasn't as deep as it could have been.

So, whoever was out there hunting with an arrow was somebody who also didn't know what he was doing. You never left an animal in pain like this, and the newbie hunter probably had no clue how to even operate the equipment he was using. This was a bow and arrow, not a crossbow, and, for that, Timber was grateful because this would be a little bit easier for him to deal with. As he walked closer, the doe stiffened and tried to move.

He froze and whispered, "That won't help. I need you to just stay where you are."

Talking calmly, he felt a hint of a breeze waft through the air. He watched the doe lift her nose and sniff. He did the same, checking for anything out of the ordinary, anything wrong. He noted nothing thankfully. As he stared at the arrow, it was hard for him to still the anger in his heart. That anybody would do this to an animal was just heartbreaking, and to leave her in this condition was even worse. He took another step forward, talking to her.

Just as he got close enough to reach out a hand, she caught sight of him, or maybe of Kojack at his side. He called Kojack to heel. Kojack stepped back and waited, giving him room. It wasn't the first animal they'd come across that needed help, and it wouldn't be the last one. But Timber could hope that, if he got to her and could help her, she would accept it. She slowly sank down onto her front legs, her back giving out underneath her, as she collapsed, staring up at him. There was hope in her gaze, also fear, but the hope itself was waning.

He finally managed to get close enough to crouch beside her. He took a look at the arrow and realized it had a screw-in head on it, so holding the head firmly against her flesh, he quickly unscrewed the long handle of the wood from the shaft. With that part out, he took a quick glance to see just how bad the injury was. It had penetrated enough that it was excruciating with every step she took, yet it wasn't anywhere near bad enough to kill her.

It had just caused her such pain with every movement that it was more than she could bear. It didn't take him much but one harsh pull to extract it. It didn't have a barb on the end and came out clean. She cried out with the pain, but then her pain was gone. She stared at him, and he wondered if he could run to the house and get his medications and return to find her here. He had to, so that he could clean up the wound and could put in a stitch or two.

He rose slowly to his feet, calling Kojack to his side. He moved swiftly to his house and inside to where he kept his medicine chest. He did an awful lot of rough medicine around this place, but sometimes that's all that was needed. Grabbing his kit, he slowly returned to the doe. As he got to the spot, she was still there. She seemed to be calmer and in a lot less pain and distress. He smiled as he crouched beside her again and quickly cleaned the wound. Then, grabbing the suture material, he stitched the muscle underneath that had been pierced and sliced, then slowly moved his way back out of the wound, until the skin itself was closed. And, with a final application of an ointment to fight infection, he stepped back and smiled at her. He murmured, "Looks as if you might be good to go."

She stared at him but remained quiet, not moving, just resting.

He nodded. "Rest for as long as you need to." And, with that, he stepped back, taking Kojack with him, slowly and steadily putting more distance between them. He hoped that she got the message. When he turned around the next few times, she was still there, just watching him. He smiled and added, "There's no rush. Take your time."

Almost as if she understood and heard him, she stayed quiet for the longest time. When he came out after dinner a little bit later to check on her, she was still there. He frowned, concerned there might be another injury he hadn't seen. Just as he was wondering if he should try to get close to her again, she slowly got up and started to eat the grass around her, and that was the sign that he'd been waiting for.

With that, he smiled and let her just rest and work her way through some food. He had water but none close by. It was on his lists of things to do, to get a water catcher system outside, but he hadn't done that yet. He had one for collecting rain, but he didn't have a trough yet. So he grabbed a bucket, filled it with water from the rain barrel, and moved it closer to her. Then putting it in plain sight, he backed off and let her have access to it, if that's what she needed.

By the time he made it back to his cabin again, he saw her drinking. He smiled, thinking that, as days went, today had been pretty decent. Now, if only he had an idea who the hell was clumsily hunting deer with a bow and arrow. Considering the fact that he owned all the acreage around here, it bothered him more than a little because this was private property. Not only was no hunting allowed, it was intended to be a refuge for animals, so no hunting of any kind would be tolerated around his place.

Perhaps he needed to go look around and find out who was causing this kind of chaos, although they may well be long gone since he couldn't kill an animal with a shot like that. Either way, it wasn't good for anybody. With the two dogs, Kojack and Philly, loaded up into the back of the truck, he slowly drove out of his place and down around the roads. He stayed to the paved road to see if anything was there. When he didn't see anybody, he moved slowly back toward the property.

He parked the truck, walked over to his pasture, where the deer had come from, and called over his gelding, Sparky. Timber slipped a halter over his chestnut face, buckled it up on the side, and, using a stump, he quickly clambered up onto his back and walked him bareback around the property. He kept an eye out for anything that was off, and there was always something off. It was just a fact of life.

As he moved slowly, he caught sight of something in the distance. He froze, wondering what it was, then moved a little closer and found a tent and several men, sitting around a fire, a case of beer between them as they laughed and chortled. When he came through the trees and stopped just at the edge of their camp, silence fell. He looked at them, his tone calm but dark, as he announced, "You're on private property."

One of the men hopped up and replied, "No, we're on

Andy's property, and we've got permission to be here."

"No," Timber stated calmly. "This isn't Andy's property anymore. This is my property. And you are trespassing."

"What the hell?" the one guy asked, glaring at him. "No way. We've been coming here for years."

"Coming here and doing what?" Timber asked, glaring at him. "Hunting?"

"What do you think?"

"Are you the one who left that arrow in the doe?"

The guy frowned at him. "Oh, she survived that?" he asked, then laughed.

Timber continued to glare at him. "Yeah, she survived that, and, as you've admitted yourself, you're hunting on private property."

"What then? You want a percentage of the kill?" he asked, with a mocking look in Timber's direction.

He shook his head. "No, you need to vacate the premises, or I'll be calling the cops."

"Oh, wow, as if we care," replied the head guy, a playfulness in his tone. "Seeing how this isn't even your property."

At that, the other two men started to laugh.

Timber smiled at them and repeated, "You are on private property, and that's not allowed. So, get your asses off my property now …"

"Or what," asked one of the men, with another laugh. "It's not as if you'll stop us."

"Really?" Timber replied. Moving Sparky forward, he came up closer and stated, "This is your final warning. Get the hell off my property now. If I see you here again, and you're using unlawful weapons and hunting anything on these acres, I'll feel free to shoot back."

At that, the men stopped and stared at him. "What the hell?"

Timber's anger built. "You come onto somebody else's posted property, you hunt an animal, and you don't even take care of the fact that you wounded an animal and left her to exist in pain, while you're sitting here drinking beer?"

"We couldn't find her," the main guy shared, without any shame. "We tried to track her, but we couldn't."

"That's because you don't know what the hell you're doing, and, because of your lack of skill, you shouldn't have access to weapons," Timber said, pointing toward the road. "Get your asses off my private property."

"It's not your place. It's Andy's, and we're not going anywhere," snapped the one young man who seemed to be their leader, and he looked pissed.

One of the others got up and added, "Look." He swung an arm toward his buddy. "Obviously he seems to think that this is Andy's place. We haven't been here in a while and just assumed it was still Andy's."

"He would have told us so," said the angry leader of this group.

"No, he wouldn't have," the second guy argued, followed by a snort. "Hell, you didn't even ask the last couple times you came here."

The one who had been talking out of his ass shot him a hard look and snapped, "You shut the fuck up."

"No, I won't," he said, glaring at him. "You told me that it was all cool and that we were allowed here." He turned to face Timber. "Sorry, man, I'm not trying to get in your way."

Timber raised one eyebrow. "Then you're leaving now, right?"

"We could leave in the morning," he suggested a bit sheepishly.

"No," Timber growled. "You're leaving now."

The guy flushed, looked at his two friends, and grimaced. "I don't think they'll go for that."

Timber nodded. "You're leaving now on your own, or I'll confirm that you do."

"Whoa, whoa, whoa, whoa, whoa, what the hell is all this trouble about?" asked the third man, finally speaking for the first time.

"Are you deaf?" Timber asked. "You're on private property. You're hunting without permission, and you're not allowed here. You've already injured one animal and left her to suffer, and now I want you to get the hell off my land."

"*Pfft.* You don't have the means to get us off here," the leader declared arrogantly, standing up and glaring at Timber. "I told you already, … this isn't your fucking land, so I don't care who and what you think you are—"

"Call him," Timber interrupted. "Call Andy and ask him."

The blowhard hesitated. Then his buddies looked at him, and he shrugged. "It's not as if I'll bother him at this hour of the day."

"Meaning that you don't have a clue if it's still his land or not," Timber pointed out, with a nod, "and you're too damn scared to ask him in case it isn't. I'm telling you right now it isn't, and now I'm calling the cops and the game warden." He pulled out his phone and was already texting.

"Whoa, whoa, whoa. … What the hell?" asked the second guy, jumping up. "We've been hunting here for years."

"I don't care if you've been hunting here for decades," Timber added, staring at him. "I told you repeatedly to get off my land."

The third man, obviously sensing that things were heading south very quickly, immediately got up and started packing up his gear.

The brash one looked at his buddy, staring him down. "No way. I'm not leaving," he announced, "and no freaking way this guy will make me."

The quieter one hesitated, then explained, "If it's his land, we're in the wrong, and, if we're in the wrong, he's in the right, and that means he can shoot us. You may be good with that, but I am not sticking around to get a load of buckshot up my ass."

"That's a really good point," agreed the second one.

"No, it's not a really good point." The leader sneered. "He doesn't have any right to kick us off. I told you before that this is Andy's land."

The quiet guy just kept packing up all their gear.

The second guy added, "And if you can't show us that Andy still owns it, then I'm not sure I believe you."

The head guy glared at his friends and asked, "What the hell?"

"Yeah. … What the hell?" the second guy repeated. "That's kind of how we feel too. We came here for a hunting trip, and, right about now, I'm not sure what the hell we have."

"What we have is some washed-up guy who thinks he's in the right," the angry young man said, and all of a sudden a rifle was pointed right at Timber.

He stared at the rifle, looked over at the young man holding it, and stated, "And now you've crossed the line. You've got about ten seconds to pull back and to get yourself on the right side of this."

"I'm already right where I should be," the man said, with a sneer. "This is not your place. This is Andy's place, and we are allowed to hunt here." When the bark on a tree just above his head exploded all around him, he lost his footing and slammed to the ground, his friends immediately backing up, their hands in the air.

Timber was a quick-draw expert and always carried a gun stowed in his waistband. He rested it in his lap as he studied them all. "I've warned you enough. Now get the hell off my land."

The other two scrambled over to their friend, who was struggling to his feet. He looked at Timber and declared, "I don't know who you think you are, but believe me that I won't forget this."

Timber nodded. "I've got a cross already made up with your name on it."

"You don't know my name, … so obviously you don't."

"Yeah, well, *Loser* will do."

And, with that, he moved Sparky back ever so slightly, giving them a little bit of space to pull back and to quickly get their tent down, so they could load up. The other two men didn't say a word. They were quick to pack up, and Timber waited until they were loaded up in their vehicle.

Still in shock, the head guy didn't say a hell of a lot, but it was obvious that he was steaming with a fury that would explode at some point in time. As Timber watched him, he knew he was a rattler in the grass. He knew plenty of men like that, but they weren't men he would allow to come back. "And just in case you didn't get the message, there's no hunting on my land."

"How the hell are we supposed to know which is your land?" he asked cryptically, snarling.

"I'm sure you noticed, as you drove in, that every mile has a sign posted that says No Hunting Allowed on Private Property." Timber smiled at him. "No way you didn't see them."

"We ignored them," the third man admitted. "He told me that they were just there to scare away people who weren't allowed to be here."

The second man, getting into the truck, glared at his angry friend and muttered, "I'll remember that."

The leader flushed, then looked over at his other buddy, the quiet one, who just shook his head at the others. Then he shrugged and added, "This is a bad deal, man. I'm going home."

"What do you mean, you're going home?" the leader asked furiously. "We came here to party, and I came here to hunt," he yelled, spitting fire. "You hear me? … Yeah, I think we'll hunt. Regardless of whose land he thinks it is." And, with that parting remark, he slammed the truck door and drove off in a harsh cloud of dust, leaving ruts behind.

Timber quickly took note of the license plate, pulled out his phone, and texted it to the game warden and the cops.

If he was lucky, somebody would give a crap enough to chase down these guys and to make an arrest. But Timber highly doubted that anybody would care enough. Most of the people here believed in live and let live, and that worked fine—until it impacted them and their property. But these losers were gone, at least for the moment.

Timber just wasn't sure how long that would last.

CHAPTER 2

TIMBER RODE SPARKY slowly back toward the main residence. A couple other buildings were on the property as well, which would give rise to so much potential. As the wannabe hunters drove off, Timber felt the waves of anger coming off them. Two of them didn't look to be a problem, but that third one? … Timber wasn't so sure about him. That guy was trouble, and Timber saw that a mile away.

When he got near to the paddock, he got off Sparky and quickly phoned Andy. When Andy answered, Timber heard a sleepiness to his tone that meant he'd been woken up.

"You doing okay?" Andy barked into the phone.

Timber laughed. "I just chased off some of your cronies who claimed they were entitled to hunt on your land. I wanted to let you know they didn't take kindly to being chased off, so you might be hearing from them."

After a moment of silence, Andy swore. "I haven't let anybody hunt on this property in a very long time," he snapped. "What did they look like?" Timber gave him a quick description of the three idiots, and Andy snorted. "Yeah, I know who they are," he muttered. "I'll have a talk with them."

"If I catch them over here again, there won't be any talking." He almost heard Andy wince.

"And you would be in your rights," Andy replied. "They aren't bad kids. They're just young and stupid."

"Which in my book means bad," Timber snapped. "They gave zero respect, ... and they left a doe out here with an arrow in her shoulder."

At that, Andy started to swear again. "God damn, I'm sorry to hear that. ... I mean it, Timber. Calm down, and let me have a talk with them."

"You can do that all you want," Timber noted calmly. "I've already warned them off and told them in no uncertain terms what would happen if they come back. Still, I get the impression that one in particular doesn't feel like listening to anybody."

"Yeah, I have a hunch I know who that is. He's always got a chip on his shoulder and likes to think he's somebody special," Andy said.

"You better help him understand that *special* in my books versus his won't be the same thing."

"Nope, nope, I hear you," he muttered. "Let me know if they come back again."

"Oh, you'll hear. One way or another, you'll hear," Timber declared. "I've sent the license plate to the ranger and to the sheriff."

Andy sighed. "No, you're right. I'll try to get them to stay away," he repeated and disconnected.

Timber walked Sparky into the paddock, took the bridle off him, gave him a good load of grain, and patted him. "Thanks, buddy."

And, with that, he headed back to the house. He still had work to be done, but he wouldn't do any more on the building for now. He headed inside, poured himself a cold glass of water, absolutely loving the taste and the temperature of the well water. Then he turned on the stove and tossed on the steak he had sitting at room temperature.

He tossed into the same pan a few sliced potatoes sitting in a bowl of water, then added some onions and mushrooms too. Very quickly he was sitting down to a meal. Then realized he'd been so thrown off by the drama of the day that he hadn't fed everybody else.

He swore because that was not like him. The rule was always that he fed all the animals before himself, and he quickly ate now, not enjoying it nearly as much as he could have. Then he bounced to his feet and headed out to do the rest of the chores.

He was still pissed at himself for having let those characters throw him off, and, by the time he was done, he was more than ready to sit down with his water and maybe a beer. Just as he did, his phone rang. He checked the screen to see it was Andy. "And?" Timber asked.

"He didn't answer, but I talked to his mom. He's apparently been on a real bender for the last little while. I guess his girlfriend broke up with him, and he's taken it pretty badly."

"What's that's got to do with me?"

The old man laughed. "It ain't got nothing to do with you. I'm just warning you that he's in a bad state."

"I hope you warned her."

He hesitated before he spoke. "I did, and I told her that he's playing with fire and that he better stay a long way away. Despite what he may say, he hasn't been allowed to hunt on my land in a very long time, and he damn well knows it. So, if I catch him, I'll have something to say about it too."

"How did she take it?"

"She seemed surprised, as if everybody was allowed to go out there," he shared, "and that is definitely not the message

I want going out there."

"I hope not," Timber snapped, bitterness in his tone. "The last thing I want is to be cleaning up after these idiots."

"How's the doe doing?" Andy asked.

"She's still hanging around, so I presume she's not all that great," he muttered.

"Did you get the arrow out?"

"Yeah, I was able to do that much and to get it stitched up," he added. "And you know how I feel about that."

"I know. I do understand that, and I'm sorry," Andy said. "It's been a long time since anybody caused that kind of chaos."

"I hope it'll be a long time before anybody else shows up," Timber muttered. "That's not exactly how I want people here to think of this place."

"No, I get it," Andy murmured. "I'll keep trying to get in touch with them to clear the air directly. In the meantime, if you see them again, just remember they're young and stupid."

"Yeah, … well, young and stupid doesn't bode well for growing old," he barked and ended the call.

He was extra careful checking up on the animals before he went to bed that night, but, even then, he slept with an unease that suggested he didn't have a good feeling about how these young men would handle getting kicked off his land. Not that he wasn't up for the fight, but he didn't want the rest of his animals stressed to that extent either.

Every one of them had been a rescue in one way or another. Every one of them had already seen the ugly side of life, and Timber didn't want them to see any more of it, not if he had something to say about it. He knew the dogs would jump in and would do anything they could to defend him, but they couldn't take on bullets. So, if this asshole was just using arrows, obviously he didn't know what he was doing with them. And that was a whole different story too. It was unfortunate because it seemed as if a large chunk of stupidity was involved, no matter which way Timber looked at these trespassing illegal wannabe hunters.

CHAPTER 3

TRYING TO SLEEP was difficult, so finally at 4:00 a.m. he gave in and just got up and sat outside. Watching the dawn arrive, listening to the birds sing, he felt this wonderful sense of peace. He looked over to see if the doe was anywhere around, but he didn't see any sign of her, which could be both good and bad. He didn't want to push her—to make her feel as if she needed to get up and go—not until she was ready. But he also couldn't be sure that these guys wouldn't come back and pop her for real this time.

As he walked out in her direction, he noticed a movement and stilled, just in time to witness one of the miracles of life. He watched as the doe gave birth. He hadn't even realized she was pregnant, and it was certainly later in the season than he would have liked for animals in this situation. He squatted and waited until she was done. Seeing how stiffly she moved, he was aware that she was still much better than yesterday, and that brought a smile to his face. He moved a little bit closer, talking to her, just checking that everything was okay.

The fawn managed to get to its feet in a fairly decent amount of time, and that was what counted right now. Timber went back into the barn, poured out a little bit of grain, and brought it over for the new mom. He put it down on the ground just a few feet away from her and stepped back. She was already protective about her baby but seemed to be tolerating his presence rather well. She stared at him, but she could smell the grain. He knew she could because of the way her nose twitched. He backed up a little farther, and she hesitantly took another step closer to the grain, then very quickly nibbled away at it.

With her gaze almost constantly on him, he just smiled and let her eat, happy to have given her a little bit of something to help boost her energy and to help her heal at a time when she needed it the most. Not only did she need it because of the injury, but giving birth would have zapped her of the nutrients she needed to recover too.

His heart was full of so much joy as he watched her. He took several photos with his phone. He would send them to Kat shortly. When he returned to his cabin and put on coffee, his sadness and restlessness was curbed just enough for him to enjoy the peace. It was hard to even imagine how full his heart felt. While his coffee brewed, he sent the photos to Kat. He got a phone call not long afterward.

"Sending me pictures of deer now?" she asked, with a teasing tone. "I'm glad to see you found another hobby."

"Photography has always been a bit of a hobby," he shared, "but, in this case, she's special." And he quickly explained.

"They just left her with the arrow in her?" she cried out in outrage.

"Yeah, but they're also very typical dumbasses. They couldn't figure out how to use the bow and arrow properly, and then, once they'd shot her, they didn't know how to find her, much less help her."

"They should be taken out and shot," Kat muttered into the phone.

He smiled at that because he was definitely on the same page, but sadly most of the world didn't see it their way. Regardless, anything and anyone who hurt an animal without any thought to the consequences deserved exactly what was coming to them, as far as Timber was concerned.

He spoke with her for another few minutes and then disconnected. She had invited him to come by and visit sometime soon, which she always did. He just smiled and didn't say anything. *Soon* meant a different thing in his world than it did in hers. But he understood that he was always welcome at her place, and that in itself was something he hadn't felt in a very long time. Working for the two of them had been a godsend. Right now, it just seemed as if time alone was something he needed. He needed space to grow and just a chance to breathe, but still understood it would be a temporary condition for him.

With a cup of coffee in his hand, he stepped out onto the front porch just in time to watch the doe settle back down with the fawn at her side, both of them resting after the ordeal they had just been through. They were hidden enough in the bushes that they should be safe, even if somebody drove up unexpectedly. However, if somebody was looking for her, she wasn't safe enough. Timber hoped she had the wiles to pull away and to get herself and her baby to safety before something happened.

Tugging on his work belt, Timber got back to roofing the deck. He'd already stripped off part of the roof on the house, so he needed to get the plywood finished there first. Then he would get the tar paper up. At least that was the plan. Hours later he took a break, wincing at his sore muscles, yet smiling because he was further along than he'd expected.

He kept working steadily until he heard a sound off in the distance. He tilted his head to focus on the noise. When he heard the dogs barking followed by the definite sound of a vehicle coming, he frowned, stepped back, and took a look around to see just who was approaching. He was still wary enough that he didn't trust anybody. Right now he couldn't tell if this would be friend or foe.

Honestly, in this place, at least at this point in time, he looked at almost all of them as foe. Badger would always be welcome, of course, as was Kat, Badger's partner, and quite a few guys Timber had worked with, while constructing houses. Otherwise, Timber had a few civilian and ex-military buddies here and there, but, for the most part, he was left alone, just the way he liked it.

When the vehicle arrived, Timber recognized Andy's truck. Timber walked over to see the old man struggling to get out of his vehicle. Timber smiled at him. "Hey."

"Hey," Andy replied. "Did they come back?"

"Not that I've seen yet."

"I'm really hoping they don't," Andy muttered. Timber didn't say anything, just nodded. Andy faced him and stated, "I really don't want them shot."

"Keep them off my place then," he snapped.

Andy nodded at that. "You're right. That's exactly what should happen … but the one kid? He's a bit of a hard case."

Timber remained silent, just waiting for whatever Andy had to say.

"And I know you'll say they'll only get what's coming to them, and you're right," Andy conceded, with a raised hand, "but just because they're stupid doesn't mean we should be knocking them off."

"Then he better stay away from me," Timber declared,

his tone hard.

"How's the doe?"

"She's doing better," he noted, "and she delivered a fawn this morning."

He looked at him in shock, then growled. "They shot a pregnant doe?"

At that, Timber nodded and added, "Exactly my point."

"Shit." Andy shook his head. "I talked to one kid's mom last night, and she doesn't appear to be really worried, but …"

"But?"

Andy shrugged. "I'm guessing she is really worried—not so much about what you might do, but what those kids might do."

"How much trouble are they getting into?"

"Lately … apparently a lot. I just don't know quite what that means, and nobody was too willing to give me any real answers."

"They better provide some answers," Timber stated, thinking it over. "If those kids are a really bad crop, you know there can't be any give."

"I know," Andy admitted, "but I need a bit of give. I really don't want to tell her how bad of a deal they've got."

"The only bad deal they'll get is a bad deal that they started and earned."

Andy sighed. "I understand where you're coming from, and a lot of days I would have been right there with you. All I'm asking is that you just try not to kill him."

Timber raised his eyebrow at that. "I wasn't planning on killing anybody." At that, Andy sighed again, this time with visible relief. Then Timber continued. "However, if somebody shoots at me, I won't miss."

Andy winced. "I get it, and I'm sorry. I'm just really hoping it doesn't come to that."

"So am I," Timber said. "The last thing I need is to get tied up in that deal. If the parents won't rein them in, they are just asking for me and the sheriff and the ranger to step in. Somebody needs to rein them in."

"Yeah, well, the other kids are just followers, but this one? Well, reining him in …"

Timber nodded. "I hear you. It's not easy, and it's apparently not something that anybody seems to be doing right now."

"No, and that's the biggest challenge. This kid seems to have it in his head that he can do what he wants and that nobody can stop him."

"He's wrong," Timber declared, "and he or anybody else who comes up against me here on my own damn property will have the same issue."

Andy nodded. "You might find that his mother will come out here to see you."

"She better not," he replied sharply. "You know I don't like company."

"I know, and I did tell her that, but she seems to think that she could appeal to your senses."

"What she needs to do is get control of her son and leave my senses out of it," he snapped. "Then the stupid kid won't be an issue for anybody. I don't really want to deal with this issue."

"I told her that, but she's, *um*, … what can I say? She's a mom."

"Not for long if she doesn't get that one under control."

"And she can't get him under control," Andy shared, "so I don't know what to say."

"It's very simple," Timber explained, "as long as he stays away from me and my property, he's fine. The minute he comes back here again, he's not."

Andy nodded, headed back to his truck, and lifted a hand to wave goodbye. "Just keep it in mind."

"Nothing to keep in my mind, Andy," Timber stated. "I'm not pushing to get into a fight, but, if the fight comes to me, I won't back down."

Andy turned to him. "I know, son. I know. I can hear it in your tone and can see it in your body language. I know you'll protect your own."

"And you haven't allowed them to come hunting here in a very long time?" Timber asked.

"Never," Andy declared, rubbing the back of his head. "The one kid's father used to come back in the day. When they were short on food, I let the father come in and cull a little bit of what needed culling," he shared, "but it was very judiciously done. I didn't realize the kid was coming back to help himself, but if he's running around with the ringleader, it makes more sense."

"And apparently has been doing it for quite a while," Timber pointed out.

Andy stared at him and shook his head. "Yeah, that's what happens when you help people."

"Exactly," Timber muttered. "Keep that in mind."

Andy laughed. "I'm good," he said, still chuckling. "I can live with it, but I need you to go a little easy, if they come back."

"I'll be as easy as I can be and not harder than I need to be, but I will not walk away from it."

"No, of course not. Anyway ..."

As Andy slowly walked back to his truck, belatedly Timber called after him, "Do you want a coffee or something?"

He stopped, then looked back at him and shook his head. "Another time maybe. This old body of mine is starting to feel its age."

Timber just nodded and didn't respond.

After a moment, Andy added, "I do need to sort out what I'm doing in terms of the rest of the ranch." At that, Timber stiffened, and Andy nodded. "What are your plans for this place anyway?" Andy asked. He looked up at the cabin and pointed. "You've already done a crap load of work around here."

"I don't know that I've done much of anything yet," Timber acknowledged, as he walked closer. "It's a whole lot less than I want to get done, but I'll get there."

"And you're still stuck on the refuge thing?"

"I'm not stuck on it," Timber clarified, "but that was always the plan, a place for those in need of refuge to come and find it."

"Two-legged and four?"

Timber nodded. "Yes, two-legged and four, depending on the issue."

"Right, because of course ..."

When he didn't say anything more, Timber nodded. "Because of course ..."

Andy laughed. "It's not that I doubt you've got things happening here that'll be good for everybody," he began. "I just hope the word doesn't get out that you're offering a *human* refuge. I'm afraid that would bring in the wrong kind of people."

"Maybe," Timber agreed, "but unfortunately I've seen an awful lot of the wrong kind of people be the right kind of people, but society had labeled them the wrong kind."

Andy thought about it and shrugged. "I guess that, once you've got people who are in trouble, there's no such a thing as the wrong kind."

"That'll be one of the questions to handle on an individual basis," Timber noted. "Still, I'm not looking for trouble."

"I know. I know." Andy held up his hands. "You're not looking for it, but if it comes your way …"

Timber nodded. "If it comes my way, you can bet that I'll be ready with a quick response."

CHAPTER 4

LATER THAT DAY, somewhere around two o'clock, with the heat from the sun beating hard on his head, Timber heard the dogs and commotion followed by a vehicle arriving. He swore because for him to get company twice in one day meant that something was going on, and he didn't like anything about it. He watched as a sheriff's car drove in slow and steady, before coming to a stop at the edge of the driveway onto the property. Then again, Timber had a lot of equipment and building materials sitting everywhere, so coming any closer could have potentially been a problem. Two men got out and walked toward him. He reached for the rag and wiped his face, taking off the sweat, as he dropped his hammer and strolled over to meet them.

As he got closer to the one, Timber stopped and stared.

The other man looked at him in shock, before a big grin crossed his face. "Jesus Christ, *Timber?*"

Timber nodded and reached out a hand. "Richard, we meet up again."

That wasn't enough for Richard, who wrapped him up in a great big bear hug, chortling in sheer delight.

The other deputy just looked on.

When the reunion hug was over, Richard stepped back, looked over at his partner, and announced, "This is Timber Woodland. I served with him overseas."

The other deputy appeared to be surprised. Pointing at Timber, he asked Richard, "So you know him?"

"I do know him," Richard stated, "and he's one hell of a good man too."

Timber smiled at him. "It's good to see you, Richard."

Richard laughed. "It's more than good to see you, good God," he declared, staring at him. "It's absolutely unbelievable, mate. It's been what, four or five years? I heard you got blown up." Timber, wearing shorts, gave him half a smile and pointed at his exposed legs. Richard's expression shifted as he took in the prosthetic. He shook his head. "I'm sorry, man. I didn't know."

"Doesn't matter." Timber shrugged. "I'm on the other side of it now."

Richard smiled and nodded. "That's what I would expect from you. Nothing ever knocked you down and kept you down for long."

"It knocked me down pretty hard," Timber admitted, "but it'll take an awful lot more than that to keep me down."

"Yeah, that's the truth."

Timber smiled, then asked him, "And what the hell are you doing out here anyway?"

At that, the other man stepped up. "We heard some complaints."

Timber chuckled. "Oh, yeah? What kind of complaints and from whom?"

"We're not sure how valid the complaints are," Richard interjected. "So, let's just have a nice quiet conversation." Richard turned to face his partner, who snorted.

Timber asked, "Are you're talking about that kid and his cronies who were out here yesterday?"

Richard stared at him. "Yeah, what do you know about that?"

"I know that they were hunting on my posted land," he stated, "and you know how I feel about that."

Richard nodded. "Of course, but they say it's not your land and that you chased them off with gunfire, and you shot at one of them."

He smirked. "Yeah, after one of them pointed their rifle at me and cocked the thing. You know full well that if I'd been trying to hit him, I would have. I can't believe he went whining to you about me, when he was the one breaking more than one law."

Richard winced, and the other man glared at him. "What the hell does that mean?" the other man asked Timber.

"It means that this is my land. You no doubt saw all the No Hunting/Trespassing signs on your way here. You can check on the proper sale with Andy, and, chances are, you've already done just that. So I'm not sure what you're even doing here right now, unless"—his gaze hardened, as he turned to look at Richard—"unless you guys are in cahoots with some club I've not yet earned a membership in."

"It's not that we're in cahoots with anything," the other guy said, "but we have to check out every complaint."

"That's fine. You check out every complaint," Timber replied. "Did you not get my phone call yesterday, reporting the incident?" Timber paused for an answer that he never got. "*Right*, so I should go into town and put in a complaint of my own."

"For what?" the other man asked.

Timber just stared at him for a long moment, then deliberately ignored him and turned to Richard. "Because those three men were hunting on my property, trespassing, and they shot a pregnant deer and left it wandering around with an arrow in her shoulder."

Richard winced again.

Nobody who'd served in the military would understand more than Richard would just what that would do to an animal.

"That was really shitty," Richard muttered.

"Not only really shitty but, when I told them to get off my land, they got very aggressive and told me that it wasn't my land and that they had every right to hunt here."

"And do they?" the other man asked him.

Timber faced him with a scowl. "You're more than welcome to talk to Andy, which I already did last night, and, in fact, he was out here this morning. The truth of the matter is that he *never* gave them permission, even when he did still own the property. Andy gave the one kid's father some leeway many years ago, when the family was short on food, and allowed him to come and take out a young buck. That was a long time ago, and nobody ever gave any of these three idiots permission to hunt here, much less to shoot a pregnant doe."

"And how would you know she was pregnant?" the other man mocked.

Richard turned on him angrily, as Timber stared the other guy down and snapped, "Because I watched her give birth this morning. And I've got the photos to prove it." When Richard looked at his sad excuse of a partner in delight, Timber nodded. "It seemed the rough first aid of yesterday that I gave her may have done her some good, and she came through the night strong enough to have her fawn, at least."

"You were always a hell of a field medic," Richard muttered.

"Yeah, well, it's not exactly something I thought I would need down here already, but obviously I do," Timber noted.

"I think that's a skill you'll always need," Richard muttered. "And, even if you don't, it's always a good one to have," he pointed out.

"I agree," Timber replied, "but I won't be here taking arrows out of animals from punk-ass kids who don't know the meaning of trespassing."

Richard repeated, "And Andy told you that they hadn't been given permission by him either?"

"That's what Andy told me," Timber confirmed, still ignoring the other deputy. His name tag read Foster, but the way he acted, he was a loose cannon on the wrong side of the law, so was to be watched. "Andy also talked to the one guy's mother, who was hoping I would go easy on him next time I saw him."

At that, the other deputy turned and asked plainly, "Did you threaten him?"

"Threaten him?" Timber repeated. "What are you, related in some way?" Foster flushed and Timber nodded. "Interesting to send some relative of the kids out here," he noted, frowning at Richard.

"We're incredibly short-staffed," Richard explained. "Honest to God, if I'd known you were here, I would have been more than pushy about getting you to come onboard." When Timber just stared at him, Richard shrugged. "I know who you are inside and out," he shared. "So believe me, if you want a job, I'm pretty sure I can get you in."

At that, Foster snorted.

Timber turned to him. "And yet you're the kind of guy who doesn't want me onboard, even though you don't know me, and why is that?"

Foster snapped, "Because Richard can't say that about you because you couldn't pass the physical."

At that, Richard turned on him and said, "Hey, that was uncalled for."

"He won't, will he?" Foster repeated.

"Aren't you about forty pounds overweight, Deputy Foster?" Timber asked, pointing to the rather hefty midsection he sported. "I highly doubt you would pass a physical either, and, in fact, I kind of like my chances."

As Richard just smiled, Foster glared at Timber. "Yeah, that sounds like you, taking a cheap shot below the belt."

"What do you expect me to do with those idiot kids?" Timber asked, still and calm. "I was in the right to order this punk kid and his two buddies off my land when he came in here, trespassing and hunting on my property, which as you saw was clearly posted. I doubt any of them even have a valid hunting license, but I guess that doesn't really mean anything to you, *Deputy* Foster, does it?" Timber asked, his gaze not leaving the other man.

"It does mean something," Richard interjected. "Obviously in small towns, everybody is heavily connected, so it's easy to ruffle feathers and all that."

"Ruffled feathers are one thing," Timber clarified. "Shooting animals for fun ... on my posted property is a completely different thing."

"I agree with you there." Richard looked at his partner and asked plainly, "And what are your thoughts on it now?"

"I think we have to confirm his story. We've got two people saying very different things."

"Yeah, we're saying very different things," Timber confirmed, staring at him. "And yet it doesn't matter to you who's in the right here because you'll make sure it's not me."

"I didn't say that," Foster declared.

"No, but you implied it." Timber stared at him with a hard look. "I don't threaten easily," he said, looking from one deputy to the other. "So, I'm not sure what your purpose was in coming here, but I've got to tell you. If those kids come back again, they will see the wrong end of my rifle."

"Hey, hey, hey, no threats, man, that won't help," Richard stated.

"You're not the one who spent a lot of time with an innocent animal that was suffering so badly that she let me pull an arrow out of her shoulder, scrub it clean, and stitch it back up, were you?"

"Right," Richard muttered. "And, if that's what those kids were doing, then obviously that's got to stop."

"But we don't have any proof that that's what he was doing," Deputy Foster pointed out. "And we don't know this character." He pointed at Timber.

"That's not true," Richard snapped. "I do know Timber. I didn't know it was him when we came out here, but now that I know who we're dealing with, I definitely hold the story those kids told us in question."

His partner frowned at him. "Seriously?"

"Yeah, seriously," Richard stated, with a hard look. "You don't understand what it's like out there overseas and what we go through in the military. You get to know the true mettle of a man when you walk a mile in his shoes. And believe me that I've walked in Timber's shoes, and he's walked in mine," Richard declared, his tone hard. "No way he would have done something like what that one kid described."

"You haven't seen him in how long, and he's crippled

now," Foster added, his tone almost mocking as he looked at Timber. "You don't really know who he is at all."

Richard's face turned dark red, as he asked Foster, "*Deputy Foster*, did you just call him a cripple *again*?"

He flushed. "I don't know what you expect me to say."

"I expect you to be decent and respectful. That's what I expect," Richard snapped at his partner. "And I think you may be forgetting who you're talking to, *Deputy Foster*."

As the other man flushed, Timber watched the play-by-play curiously. He figured Richard was pulling rank, making Richard the Chief Deputy. Timber tried to hide his smirk.

Richard turned back to Timber. "Look, if he comes back, just chase him off and let us know, will you?"

Timber didn't say anything.

Richard hesitated and added, "Please, Timber, don't shoot the kid if you don't have to."

Timber shrugged. "Don't need to shoot him at all if he doesn't come back. So, if he comes back, you know the rules as well as I do."

Richard nodded and sighed. "I do. Anyway, it would be nice to catch up one day." He looked around as he walked to his car and then back at him. "Do you ever come into town?"

"Sure. I go in for supplies." As Timber walked with them, the sunlight hit his prosthetic leg, illuminating it.

Richard noted it and shook his head. "Damn, that's a mighty-fine leg."

"Yeah, and a mighty-fine artist designed it for me."

He stopped and asked, "Kat?"

"Absolutely," Timber agreed, with a smile. "I worked for Kat and Badger for a good … I don't know. Ten months? I still go in and help every once in a while," he murmured.

"Help them with what?" Richard asked curiously.

"Building, trades, whatever, you know?"

"I do know." Richard smiled. "It's a hell of a good group there." He turned and looked at his partner, who was looking a little less antagonistic. "You know Kat and Badger as well as I do."

He nodded. "I do." He turned to face Timber. "Do you think they'll vouch for you?"

"They don't need to, since I can vouch for myself, but, yeah, I'm sure they would."

Foster frowned at that, since it was obviously not the answer or the turn in circumstances he wanted to hear. "I guess we need to go back and talk to those kids again then."

Timber didn't say anything, but he nodded and waited as they got in their car. When they were gone, Timber turned and looked around at his place and groaned. "Of course that's the kind of shit I'll have to deal with now."

And, with a headshake, he got back to work.

CHAPTER 5

F IRST THING THE next morning Timber pulled up and parked at the vet's office, then hopped out and walked inside to talk to the receptionist.

She looked up and smiled. "Hey, I'm glad you got the message this morning."

He nodded. "I'm glad the drugs are in."

"I'm still surprised you even know how to use these," she admitted, as she went to get his order.

"Ranch first aid sometimes deserves … a little bit more in the way of treatment."

She shrugged but didn't seem to really understand what he was saying, and that was okay too.

The veterinarian came out, and Timber smiled at her. The vet had a glorious lot of red hair that never seemed to stay pinned. Young. Beautiful. Talented. As usual Tiffany looked preoccupied, the glasses on top of her head sliding off her hair as she was looking for something.

When she stopped and saw him, she smiled. "Hey, Timber. How are you doing?"

"Good. How are you?"

She sighed. "I'm fine. A little scattered as usual, but I'm here."

"*Scattered* is not an issue as long as you're not scattered when it comes to the actual surgeries."

"No, no, I'm always right there for that," she acknowledged, with a laugh. "But some days, it's a challenge."

"Everything going okay?"

"Yeah," she replied, with a smile. "How about you?"

He shrugged. "I was hoping to pick your brain for a minute."

"Sure, go for it. What's up?" He explained about the doe, and immediately she frowned and gasped. "I really wish people would be more concerned about the animals they hurt," she declared crossly.

"You and me both," he agreed. "We also know that some people will just be bad people and not give a crap."

"I do know," she replied, "but there's always hope."

He smiled, then he showed her the pictures he'd taken of the wound and the job he did. "Anyway, I was wondering about trying to get her a shot of antibiotics."

She looked at the picture of the wound again and asked, "Any idea how long the arrow was in there?"

"No, but I suspect not very long, since I caught the trespassers still on my land that day," he said. "And she did come to me fairly quickly."

"The fact that she even did that is huge," she murmured.

"She also gave birth right afterward."

She looked up at him and then nodded. "She came to you for help, and you gave it." She smiled warmly at him.

"And I want to confirm that whatever else she needs right now, she gets," he explained, "so I'm open to suggestions."

She pondered it for a moment and nodded. "I can give you a shot to take with you, if you think you can give it to her. It would definitely help her, since she needs every bit of her resources just to recover from the birth and to get back on her feet right now." She chewed on her bottom lip. "Anything we can do would improve her chances."

He reached out and tapped her arm, pointing to her mouth.

She sighed. "I know. I know. Bad habit. I don't even realize that I keep chewing on that lip."

"It's making it puffy," he murmured.

She shrugged. "I should be used to it," she declared, with a smirk in his direction. "I would love to see the work you're doing out there sometime."

"*Sometime*." He smiled.

"I'll give you a shot for the doe. So, how is Lucy doing?"

"She's slow," he noted. "She doesn't really want to get around very much yet, still preferring to be picked up and carried, rather than walk."

"Oh, I get that." Tiffany laughed. "Smart girl. Still, that's not really an option."

"No, it sure isn't," he agreed. "If I had nothing better to do than sit around and look after her all day, that would be one thing, but I can't. I'm in the process of putting a new roof on the cabin and the back deck."

She looked up in delight. "Now that would be huge progress. I haven't seen that property in a very long time, but those buildings were not in great shape even back then."

"They're still not," he conceded, with a laugh, "but that is something I can fix."

She looked at him intensely. "Are you good with a hammer?"

"Very," he stated. "I'll get it fixed up in no time."

She beamed at him. "Okay, hang on. Let me go get the additional medicine." With that, she dashed off. She came back a few minutes later, handed it to him, and noted, "One shot. Give it to her all at once."

"Got it," he murmured.

And, with that done, he headed back home again.

CHAPTER 6

THE NEXT DAY, midmorning, he heard another vehicle pulling in, although the dogs had alerted him, they were quieter about it. He just finished nailing the tar paper on the roof and was ready to start putting down the asphalt shingles. He stood up and took a look to see who was coming, wondering at the constant visitors he was having versus a few weeks ago, when nobody ever came by, something that he kind of preferred.

He watched a small pickup move carefully in, but, instead of bouncing from rock to rock, they drove as carefully as possible, trying to minimize either the damage to the truck or the pain to the actual driver itself. His eyebrows shot up when he recognized Tiffany, the vet he'd spoken to yesterday.

He made his way off the roof, as she parked a little bit away from the house, keeping clear of all his tools and equipment, which he had to admit were scattered around still.

As he walked over to her, she hopped out with a hesitant smile. "Hey."

"Hey," he replied in delight. "I'm surprised to see you here."

She gave him a self-conscious smile. "I have to admit I was worried about the deer."

He looked at her in surprise and then smiled. "I'm glad that you care enough to worry about a patient you haven't even seen."

She winced. "I know, and I have no right to be here. I get that."

"It's not that you can't be here," he clarified. "I just wasn't expecting to see you."

She nodded. "And I get that, but I had the day off, and I was thinking about her last night and just wanted to confirm she and the baby were doing okay."

He wasn't sure what to make of that, but he motioned in the direction where the doe was grazing. "If you want to come this way, we'll take a look, but I don't know how she'll handle another person."

"Right, and not being in an office setting means it's a whole lot different trying to get close to her," she noted, with a half laugh. "Not exactly something I gave much thought to."

"Not a whole lot of thought required," he stated smoothly, "and I'm happy you're here regardless. It's just nice to know that somebody else cares."

"Did you ever find out more about the guy who shot her?"

He shook his head. "No, not yet," he replied, his tone deepening. Even though he was doing his best to deal with the outrage, it still came up and hit him every once in a while. "I have to admit to struggling with the whole anger thing over it."

"Who wouldn't," she said, looking at him. "I'm pretty pissed about it myself, and I don't even know the details."

He smiled at her. "That makes sense, considering you are a vet."

"And looking after animals is what I do," she declared, interjecting smoothly. "And more than that, you're doing something that I always wanted to do, which was to have a big rescue outfit," she shared, with a half laugh. "So, if you're willing to take in all kinds of animals, I would be willing to help out, if you need it."

He raised his eyebrows, pushing some of his hair back. "That's a really kind offer."

"I know of a lot of rescues," she began, with half a smile as she looked around at his dilapidated cabin and the tools everywhere, "but not a one that doesn't need the assistance of a veterinarian."

"We all need vet assistance," he agreed. "For anybody working with animals, that's a given. And, while I'm sure you guys thoroughly deserve the pay, it's a huge drain on anybody's resources."

She nodded. "I know. That's why I'm here." Her gaze scanned the area around them, and he knew she would see his old truck on one side and an older horse trailer parked on the other. … He had a flat-bed trailer backed up to the deck, where he had been working. That was just the big items. "Sorry, I know it doesn't look like much yet," he noted.

Her gaze immediately switched to his, and she shook her head. "I wasn't thinking that at all. I was thinking that the potential is huge. How many acres do you have?"

"Sixty at the moment, but I hope to get more at some point."

Her eyes widened at that, and she whistled. "Now that really gives you some scope, doesn't it?"

"That's what I'm hoping," Timber said, "but, as you can see, most of it is just untapped land at this point."

"Sure, but it's still land, and some is still pasture. It's still space," she noted, "and, when it comes to rescues, space is what you need." She walked a few steps toward him and then stopped when she caught sight of the doe. Her hands went to her hips as she studied the doe, now staring at her intently. "Has she settled in here?"

"It seems maybe she has. I really expected her to move on, but, so far, she's sticking right here," he admitted.

"It means she feels safe."

"She might feel safe, but you know there are just enough problems here that I'm not sure I feel safe for her."

She looked back at him and frowned. "And you're thinking about whoever shot her in the first place?"

"Wouldn't you be?" he asked.

"I can't imagine anybody coming up here into your own personal space and trying to shoot her again," she admitted. "You're not exactly somebody people think they can just steamroll over." When he frowned at her, she winced. "Sorry, I guess I could have probably put that a little more politely."

"I'm not sure quite how you meant it in the first place," he pointed out.

"Just that you're a little ... intimidating," she replied, "and I think that most people would do their best to avoid you."

He laughed. "I could hope that was true. I've spent weeks out here working on this place and never seen anybody. However, since this happened, it's like I can't get rid of people." She flushed and he winced. "And I don't mean you, not at all."

She snorted. "I did come unannounced and without an invitation."

"Yeah, ... well, the world shouldn't require an invite

every time you turn around either," he said. "Come on. Let's go take a look at her, and then I'll put on some coffee."

"Oh, I don't want to take you from your work," she protested, as she followed him toward the doe. The animal didn't move, just stared at them calmly, as if trying to assess whether Tiffany was somebody to run from or not. "She really is beautiful, isn't she?" she whispered, with a happy sigh.

"I guess you don't get many wild animals in your clinic, do you?"

"No, not many," she admitted, with a smile. "And we have various refuges that take animals like this, so I was kind of wondering just what your plan was."

She spoke almost absentmindedly, as if that wasn't really on her mind at all. Yet he couldn't stop feeling as if maybe a hint of a question was in there that he wasn't sure how to answer.

She looked over at him and added, "And, if you don't have any plans, that's fine too."

When he burst out laughing at that, she frowned at him. "That laugh sounds a little rusty."

The laugh cut off midsound, as he nodded. "It was rusty. Hasn't been a whole lot to laugh about in my world for a while," he admitted, "but this has been good. There's something very …" He stopped, trying to think about how to phrase it, and still he wanted to find the right words for her. "There's something very freeing about working the land, building up a place of your own, and helping others," he shared.

She smiled. "I'll never argue with that," she murmured. "And helping others, especially when it comes to the four-legged variety, will always be at the top of my list." She gave him a big smile. She walked a few steps closer and then bent down, as if studying something ahead of her.

Timber took a step closer to where she was and saw the fawn curled up, sleeping. "She appears to be doing fine," he noted.

"That's good," Tiffany said. "I wouldn't want to deal with both the fawn and its mom."

"The mom is a little stiff when she moves, so she's a bit sore still, but, as you can see, she's on her feet, bright-eyed, and keeping a bead on us quite clearly."

Tiffany chuckled and then stepped back so that the doe would feel a little more comfortable about her presence. "Now that I know the fawn is okay, I want to see her mom walking around, but I don't want to chase her or to send her into a full-blown gallop. That wouldn't be a good thing right now. I just was hoping to see her walk a few steps, so I could take a look at that shoulder. Were you able to give her the shot?"

"I did, and that was an interesting scenario too," he shared, with a laugh, "but she let me get up to her and check the shoulder and the stitches. She wasn't too thrilled about my touching any of it, so I just got the needle in quickly, though that has also made her a little spookier today."

"Of course," Tiffany murmured. Just then the doe moved several feet off to the side, bent down, and chomped on a bit of grass. "Oh! her head's moving fine," she noted, studying her movements. "You're right about the stiffness, but it looks to me as if she's doing okay." She took several more steps backward, and the doe just watched her. "It would be nice to know that this wouldn't happen again, but there's no guarantee on something like that."

"No, there sure isn't," Timber stated, "but I'm hopeful

that we've seen the last of it."

She just nodded.

"How long have you lived around here?" he asked her.

"*Hmm*, a few years now," she said. "I think I've had the practice for about … three years."

"It's been a while then."

"I bought it from somebody who was ready to retire, but I had been working for him for … I don't know, maybe two years before that. So five years total," she replied absent-mindedly, as if it really wasn't important.

And maybe it wasn't, but he wasn't sure whether that meant she knew the locals or not. "So, some of the locals you might know, and some you don't."

"I'll know the ones who look after their animals," she replied with a smile, as she turned to him, "because those are the ones who come into the clinic. The other ones? … Either those don't have animals or those won't give the animals the care that they need. So those are the people I won't see very often. And then there's a certain group where everything is fine until it comes to the end of time, and then they need help saying goodbye," she stated calmly.

"That's the part of your job I don't think I could do."

"Sometimes it's one of the hardest parts of the job," she agreed, with a nod. "We definitely have issues with that, but who doesn't? My real problem is the people who bring in an animal they just don't want anymore, so they want it put to sleep. That's when I get angry."

"That's when you call me," he stated, "and I'll take it."

She looked over at him. "That's an interesting concept," she replied. "Have you thought about what and how?" She frowned, as she looked around.

He sighed. "So, we're back to the fact that I'm not quite

set up yet."

She turned to him and flushed. "Believe me that I'm not judging you in any way. I'm just trying to picture how you think that'll work. Will you put in some kennels and runs? You'll need fencing if you'll take in something larger."

"When you say larger, like what?" he asked curiously.

"Horses?"

"I could do horses," Timber said. "I was raised with horses."

"And they certainly need space," she pointed out.

He nodded as he looked around the land. "I do have a map of what I've got here," he muttered, "and I've kind of got a rough drawing of what I was thinking of."

"I would love to see it," she said.

He looked at her and then shrugged. "Well, … come on in. Let's get some coffee on, and I'll show you some of what I've got planned," he suggested, with a wry smile.

"*Some*, meaning that you need money to get it done?"

"No, meaning that the plans may change as I move on from one project to the other," he clarified, with a wry smile. "Because, even though I think I know what I want, when it comes down to it, plans change. So, I'm open to all animals, but some will require more space, more care, more special needs than others," he pointed out, with a smile. "Obviously dogs and cats are a given. Horses are fine, but I'm not set up for the water yet."

"Do you have water here?"

"I do. There's a watering hole, and I have a really good well at the cabin. There's a barn, but it's in sad shape," he admitted, with a sigh. "So, I was trying to get the house reroofed, so we would be good going into fall, and then I could get some of the work done on the barn," he explained, looking over at her.

"You'll need to bring in a crew if you can," she suggested, giving him a smile. "If you don't, it'll just take longer."

He smiled at her. "I have people I could ask. I'm just not the best at asking."

"But you're not asking for yourself," she pointed out. "You're asking for the animals."

He hesitated and then nodded. "When you look at it that way, it seems foolish not to ask."

"Exactly," she agreed in a light scolding tone. "It's foolish *not* to ask. And, if you're talking about Badger and his group, if you've done any work with them, you know perfectly well that they would be very happy to come out and help you too."

He frowned at her. "Do you know them?"

"I do," she stated, with a smile. "Kat helped my cousin get a prosthetic, and there has been the odd occasion," she added, with a laugh, "when I've gone to her myself to ask for help with an animal. We've devised a prosthetic or two for a couple of my patients."

He stared at her and nodded. "I can absolutely see Kat doing that."

"She's just that kind of person, and honestly, she kept the cost low enough that we could do it, in order to keep the animal in good shape and enjoying life," she shared, as she looked around. "Although right now you may not have what looks to be a very polished place, still—"

He broke up laughing at that. "That's putting it kindly," he said, still chuckling.

She smiled. "I was trying to avoid insulting you."

He just waved a hand. "Insult away. I'm really not sensitive about it, and I've only been here a few weeks."

"Okay, that makes me feel better."

He burst out laughing again and waved her in toward the front door. "Come on in. We can at least get some coffee."

"Coffee would be good," she murmured, as she stepped inside.

CHAPTER 7

TIFFANY STARED AT the massive interior that appeared to be just one big open room except for the big wooden staircase off to the side. "How on earth is that roof being suspended with such an open room?"

He pointed up to the huge log rafters. "That's how."

She shook her head. "Outside it looks like absolutely nothing, but, when you step inside," she admitted in amazement, "it's a completely different story."

"It still looks like nothing," he countered, with half a laugh, "but that will change very quickly, once I get started on the inside. But I won't do any work inside as long as the roof needs work."

"Patching or reroofing?"

"I'm reroofing this half, where the sun created the most damage. The other side is not too bad," he said, with a casual glance in that direction. "So, the actual house itself will be at the end of my list of repairs. I'm just trying to make it livable enough that the damage doesn't continue."

She nodded as she surveyed the well-worn hardwood floors and the interior walls that were half logs, half drywall. "I'm surprised drywall is in here."

"I think somebody got it in their head at some point that this would be a really good location for a home," Timber guessed, "but either they ran out of money or ran out of

"

support, or who knows? Maybe they couldn't stand the loneliness."

"It's not very far from town though," she replied, looking at him. "It didn't take very long to get here. That surprised me."

"Maybe," he conceded, "though this week, I've been thinking maybe I should have gone farther out."

She smiled. "If you're looking to have a rescue, you need to be close enough to get supplies and help, but far enough out that you're not dealing with too many pissed-off neighbors."

He winced at that. "Isn't that the truth," he muttered. "I was hoping I was out far enough to avoid hunters too, but that hasn't worked out too well."

"Yeah, I was hoping that would be the case too," she muttered, with a sad smile. She walked back to the doorway and took another look outside, but the doe was happily eating, staying close to her fawn. Often they would take off and leave them hidden and come back for them later, but, in this case, the doe wasn't allowing very much space between her and her baby.

She walked over to the single stretch of kitchen counter, saw that he also had a big table set up as an island, serving also as a makeshift dining room table, office, and apparently tool storage.

He looked at the table and sighed. "Yeah, obviously a bachelor's abode," he said, with a groan, "and clearly I'm still in work mode."

"But that's what you're here for," she stated. "Don't worry about how I feel about it. I'll always be rooting for anybody who's putting time and effort into doing something for animals."

He just smiled at that and nodded. "So, what about the doe?" he asked her. "Do you think she's okay?"

"She's looking fine," she replied, as she glanced back outside again, "and that's really good news. I'm very happy to see her up and moving as much as she is."

"Good," he muttered.

After he put on the coffee to brew, they shared more small talk, until he poured them both a cup. She watched as the squirrel he'd befriended, one he'd named Dodger, sat on the deck outside looking in the kitchen window. He scooped up a few peanuts from a container he kept nearby and placed them on the window ledge through the open glass. She chuckled. "Did Kat send you?"

She frowned at him and then laughed again. "Nope, she sure didn't. Although, if I'd told her that I was coming, I might have been given the third degree, particularly if you haven't been very good at letting them know how you're doing."

He winced. "Yeah, well, … that's probably true," he admitted. "I did promise her that I would keep her posted. I text her every once in a while, but I guess the communication has been a little slim."

"Did you really think she would send somebody out to check on you?"

"In a heartbeat," he declared.

Tiffany burst out laughing. "I'm glad to hear you know her so well. At the same time, it does mean that she cares."

"I know she cares," he agreed, with a smile. "Her heart is as big as New Mexico."

"Ah, that's a nice thing to say. Kat and Badger both have been a godsend to a lot of people."

"And I'm one of them," Timber admitted, "and don't worry. I haven't forgotten that."

She sighed. "I'm really not trying to get off on the wrong foot here, and I'm not here because of them. I'm not here at their request or anything like that," she shared, with a gentle smile. "I was just concerned about the doe and her baby, plus interested to see how you managed to get close enough to work on her."

"I'm glad to hear that," he said, "and I'm glad that you came on your own and not after a push or a shove from them."

She burst out laughing. "I don't push and shove that easily. I'm too small to get into a battle physically, and honestly, enough really good people are out there that, if they want to have battles, they can have them without me."

He smiled and nodded at that. "You do appear to have a big heart."

"I do," she agreed, "and trust me. It's got me into trouble more than once."

"In what way?" he asked.

She looked over at him and smiled. "I bought a dying rural veterinary clinic for one thing. I can keep those animals I already had treated safe and sound, but, in the meantime, some of those pets have passed, due to age, and a lot of those people never got new pets," she shared. "So I'm not sure that buying the clinic was the best move." Then she shrugged. "But we don't always make business decisions for the right reasons."

"Sounds as if it was the right reason to me."

"If the business grows, it will be fine, but there are always challenges." She didn't want to get into all the details about the accountant telling her to raise prices and to stop doing work for free and all the other issues he kept going on about.

"If you're talking about accountants and pencil-pushers," Timber noted, "I've got a few of those naysayers myself."

She looked at him, startled, then nodded. "That's exactly what I was thinking of." She gave him a smile. "I've had more than a few arguments where they've told me to sell."

"It's that bad?" he asked.

"Not right now, no," she noted, "but it's hard when you can't pay staff, so you have to get lines of credit to cover payroll, when business is down or whatever." She shrugged. "Still, I would rather deal with the debt and keep everybody employed, so I don't have to lay anybody off. When you need staff, you need them," she stated, "and I'm happy to report that the last six months have been better."

"That's good to hear. I would hate to think of your closing down."

"Me too," she said, "and I don't know what I would do after that anyway. I could always work at another clinic, but, after having my own, working for someone else is not quite the same."

"No, it's not," he declared. He turned toward the doe. "You also seem to be far more interested in helping animals than dealing with paperwork."

She laughed. "Isn't everybody? Paperwork is for a *special* kind of person," she declared, with a shrug, "and that is definitely not me."

He grinned. "That's why we have pencil-pushers," he said, "but we also have to remember that they are who they are, and that's what they do. They don't understand the animals, and they don't understand the need to have another water trough or power in a barn or to dig a second well as a backup. They don't think about carrying spare medications just in case you have an outbreak of something, and you're sure it'll be worse this next week. All of that kind of thing costs a lot of money, and, in their eyes, it's just inventory sitting there, not producing."

"And they don't understand why you can't just buy it when you need it," she added with a nod, as she interrupted him.

He smiled. "Yep, on the other hand, they do keep our taxes in line and keep us moving forward in whatever direction it is that we think we're going."

"Ah, it's that *think we're going* part that gets me," she admitted, with a smirk, "because, Lord knows, sometimes I'm not sure."

"One step forward," he suggested.

She nodded. "One step forward. That's the trick, isn't it?"

"I think so, and, if you look at what's right in front of you, and don't worry about all the details all around you," he offered, "it makes it easier. Once you're committed, confirm you're committed."

"Oh, I'm committed," she declared, "and I certainly won't be backing out anytime soon. It's just dealing with, … you know, accountants."

"And when there's a shortage of clients, what do you do?" he asked.

She looked at him and sighed. "If I don't need to be in the office because of the schedule, on my days off I volunteer."

He nodded. "Volunteer where?"

"The Birds of Prey Sanctuary."

"Right, of course you do." He laughed. "And they don't pay you either."

"No, they … can't afford to pay, and, as long as everything else in my world is covered, I don't ask them too. That's what volunteers are all about, right?"

"But it sounds as if you need to get paid."

"No, I don't. Business is just fine and has been doing much better these last few months," she clarified. "So, with any luck, I've turned the corner and now have established a reputation, and people know I can do the job. It's always tough when you take over from somebody who's been there for a very long time. Even though you worked with them and have seen these people before, all of a sudden you're the stranger left in charge of the business, and it's not the same," she shared, with half a smile. "It's taken quite a while to win people over, and that is something I didn't expect. I should have, I guess, small towns and all."

He laughed. "No, I think *all* people are that way," he chided her comfortably, "and it makes no sense in many ways, but, I guess to them, they just needed you to prove yourself."

"And yet having to prove myself even after they've seen me with their usual vet for two years before I took over doesn't make any sense and is kind of hurtful. But I think I've turned a corner, and I should be fine from here on out," she declared cheerfully. "Regardless … I'll be fine." And she refused to elaborate further. No way she would go more into that. "Now, what about you?" she asked. "What's your time frame for bringing in other animals?"

"I need paddocks, and I need to repair the barn. Of course, if there's an animal in need," he pointed out, "that's a whole different deal. However, as far as what I plan to be doing, I do have an idea roughed out." Then he gave her the rundown of what his next six weeks looked like.

"That is a lot," she muttered in amazement. "Can you

really get that much accomplished? Especially all by your-self?"

"I'm hoping so, but you're right. It is a lot. I'll do what I can do, and, at least for the moment, that is the plan."

She nodded. "You still need help."

He shrugged. "I do need help, and, if help is available, then I'll use it, but, if the help isn't, I'll get there in my time."

"And is it important that you do it in your time?" she asked.

He stared at her. "I'm not so sure that it is," he admitted. "Getting this place has been a big part of it, but, once I did, it didn't take very long to understand that I've bitten off a lot."

She smiled. "Yes, I can see that. *Bitten off a lot* is right. Might it be a bit too big of a bite, especially for just you to work on?"

"No, it's not too big. It'll just take a little longer to get where I want to go," he said. "That's more of the challenge."

As they sat here having coffee, he heard a series of shots fired. He bolted to his feet and raced outside, and she followed him, just a hair behind.

Timber was out in the yard, as a vehicle spun off in the distance, with crazy laughter coming from the driver in the vehicle. But it was too far away and going too fast for Timber to catch up to it.

"Do you know who that was?" She gasped at his side.

He looked at her, all in a rage. "No, but I'm afraid I have a good idea." He turned, looking for the doe.

"What are you looking for?"

"The doe."

"Why?"

"I'm afraid they've shot her."

She bolted into the yard, running as she looked for her. He was right behind her. They found the fawn, no problem, but the doe was smart enough and had gone into hiding.

Timber muttered, "I hope they didn't get her."

"I didn't hear it hit anything," she noted, "but then I guess I would feel better if I'd heard the bullet hit somewhere."

He stared off in the distance. "So, that's one of the things I'll need to get now—cameras."

She turned to him and winced. "That's probably something you never thought you would have to deal with, is it?"

"No, not something I wanted to deal with at all."

"You think it's the same guy?"

"Oh, it'll be related, I just don't know how." He sighed. "I just don't know to what extent."

"I thought this was Andy's land," she said, turning to look at him.

"It *was* Andy's land, and then I bought it from him, and I'm still looking to buy more from him, when he's ready to sell."

"Oh, wow," she murmured. "In that case, you'll be here for a long time."

He looked at her and smiled. "This is where I'm putting down roots. And, if anybody thinks that they'll chase me off this land, they've got another think coming."

CHAPTER 8

TIFFANY SLOWLY MADE her way back to her clinic, deciding it was time to get a bit of paperwork done. Honestly, she didn't really want to go home after that fairly unsettling visit with Timber. She really liked the man, but whatever that shooting was about, it was enough to scare anybody away. Yet she saw no reason for it. He was doing everything he could right now to get set up, and obviously he had a long way to go.

She pulled into the clinic and parked. Then unlocked the security system and headed to her office, when her phone rang. It was Kat. She sat down, smiled into the phone as she answered it. "Wow, it's almost as if you have strong instincts where I'm concerned."

"I do. Where were you?"

"I was just over checking up on our mutual friend."

After a moment of silence, Kat noted, "I'm not sure who we have in your neck of the woods."

"How about Timber?"

"Oh my gosh," Kat exclaimed in sudden delight. "How is he?"

"He's bitten off an awful lot, and he could really use a hand. Just for the record, he is too stubborn by far." At that, Kat started to laugh, even as Tiffany continued her tirade. "Plus, there's definitely some unsettling business going on, and, while I was there, shots were fired near his house. It doesn't appear any damage was done, but something is definitely brewing in that neck of the woods that shouldn't be."

"Shots fired?" Kat repeated in sudden seriousness.

"Yes," Tiffany murmured, "and he looked pretty pissed about the whole thing."

"I'm sure he did. I presume they took off?"

"Yes, they took off, and he muttered how it's just typical of a coward."

"Maybe," she murmured, "it's also typical of people who don't want to face Timber."

"Absolutely. I wouldn't want to face him either right now. He's pretty scary when he's pissed. I left soon afterward but more to give him a bit of space because it's obvious he was already figuring out what his next step was."

"And nobody saw anything?"

"No, I certainly didn't. They took off. They didn't even come fully into the yard," Tiffany explained. "It's as if they were hiding around the corner and then took potshots at the house, the barn, you know, … but deliberately avoided shooting somebody."

"That's a good thing," Kat spat, fury in her voice. "That's not something any of us need."

"No, Timber didn't look very happy about any of it. I did ask him if he had any idea who it was, and he nodded, but I got the impression he thinks that nobody will care and that the law won't do anything."

"I don't know about that," Kat declared. "I know Andy pretty well, and I can't imagine that he's tolerating any of that."

"I know Andy too, but haven't seen him in quite a

while. I realize that he's aging, and I'm sure that's having an effect on whatever hold he had on things."

"That's always a sad stage, isn't it?" Kat murmured. "Look, good talk, but I'll speak to Badger about this."

"If you end up telling Timber that I sent you, he might get pissed off at me."

"That's not part of the plan," Kat assured her, "but I definitely need to keep an eye out and to confirm he's okay."

"He can't be under your wing all the time," Tiffany pointed out to Kat.

"Yeah, I know that," she conceded, "and it's always hard to let them go. He's been here, part of the family off and on, at least as much as he would let me drag him into," she admitted, with a half laugh. "There's something very special about him, and I know he's been planning this rescue of his for a very long time."

"And I'm all for it. As you know, anybody who helps animals is right up my alley," Tiffany shared. "But honestly, I don't feel comfortable putting any animals over there, not until the shooting stops."

"No, that's not something we want. Did you see the doe?"

"Yes, and she looks to be doing pretty well," Tiffany replied. "I went over to take a look for that reason, but she appears to be responding to the antibiotics, and she's staying very close to Timber."

At that, Kat laughed. "You may not know it, but Timber has one of those uncanny abilities to relate to animals. Even those that would never come close to people and vice versa."

"I've always sensed a very calm stillness to him," she admitted. "And he is a fascinating character."

"Ah, *fascinating*," Kat repeated, with laughter.

"Oh no. Don't even go there," Tiffany murmured.

"I didn't go anywhere," Kat declared, with a chuckle. "That was all you."

"Nope, and while I might consider spending some time with him, it's because I'm quite interested in making sure the rescue becomes a reality because I always need places to put animals."

"I'm right with you there," Kat agreed.

"He needs a lot of help though, and I think he's a little too stubborn to ask for it." Tiffany wasn't sure she should be telling Kat that, but the work needed to be done to make it a working rescue. Left on his own, it would take a very long time.

"A little too stubborn?" Kat murmured. "That's definitely an understatement. He's definitely got a thing about not asking for help."

"Presumably there was a time when he needed it and it wasn't there for him?" Tiffany suggested.

"Oh absolutely," Kat agreed. "But he still has to get to the point where he's okay to ask for help and to accept it now."

"Oh, I don't think he's coming to that point anytime soon," Tiffany noted, with a snort. "That's not something I really see him doing. On the other hand, if you guys were to go out there and make an assessment of what he needed, maybe you could get a gang together."

"Oh, I hear you." Kat laughed. "Let me talk to the boss, since it sounds as if we may have bigger things to be worried about out there first." With that, she disconnected.

Kat left Tiffany laughing because, if there was one boss on that place, particularly when it came to the hearts and souls of the people who came through their orbit, it would be more Kat than Badger.

Badger was all about getting the guys back on the good side of life, fixing them up, helping them to give back to the world that they left. But that didn't necessarily mean that he was up for animal shelters or any other number of projects that his wife got herself involved in. And Tiffany certainly didn't blame him because, if Kat had hundreds of dollars or millions, she would be putting it out there, helping anybody and everybody she could. That's just the way the world was for her. Something the world needed more of.

The two of them were special, and Tiffany was absolutely thrilled to call Kat a friend. She and Badger understood that other people had needs too, not just those who were there in front of them.

When her phone rang not very long afterward, she looked down, surprised to see a number she thought she recognized but wasn't sure. She answered it cautiously. "Hello?"

"Are you okay?" Timber asked, his tone harsh and deep.

Enough concern was there that she realized how worried he was. She smiled. "I'm fine. There just didn't seem to be any point in sticking around when you were obviously on the hunt."

"If I was on the hunt, I wouldn't have left you behind," he stated. "I definitely wouldn't have left you alone with that going on."

"I'm sorry that happened," she began, "though I'm not sure I understand because you seem to be angrier than … I don't know quite how to say it."

"I'm pissed because it's a kid, a few young men who think they can run around ragged, disrespecting everything and everybody. I had already talked to Andy about it days before, and he said he would try to put a lid on him, but, as you saw earlier, that attempt didn't exactly work."

"No, not at all," she murmured, "and that's not good news for anybody. We can't have that kind of behavior."

"No, we sure can't," Timber agreed. "So obviously I have some work to do."

"Will you talk to Andy again?"

"I don't know," he replied bitterly. "It didn't do much good the last time."

"I can appreciate that," she said slowly, "but I think he would probably want to be kept in the loop, if for no other reason than keeping track of whoever is causing all this chaos."

"I don't know that keeping track of it will do any good," Timber grumbled, "and there's also a limit to what I can do within the law."

"Of course. Have you talked to the sheriff's office?"

"*Right*. They came out here the other day and paid me a visit because the kid thought that I should be charged for the way I treated him when he was here trespassing on my land, shooting a pregnant deer."

She gasped. "Seriously?" she cried out. "How is that a thing?"

"That's another issue entirely," he noted, with half a laugh. "Anyway I've already spoken to a couple deputies, and, as it turns out, one of them is an old military friend of mine, and that was really nice to see."

"So, you trust him?"

"I trust him, within the capabilities and confines of what he can do, but his partner was definitely not a member of my fan club."

She smirked at that. "And I can't imagine why," she

quipped, with a touch of mockery.

After a moment of silence, he asked, "Am I really that unapproachable?"

She thought about it and then said, "Yes."

He gave a snort of laughter. "At least you're honest."

"I am honest, and it's not so much that you're … I'm not even sure what it is, but I get the impression that you don't suffer fools easily and that you've already put the bulk of the world in that category. Close enough?"

"I'm not so sure I'm quite that harsh," he conceded, "but I see people out there doing stuff that's not very smart, and, as long as everybody stays away from me, I'm fine. But these kids were hunting on my land," he stated, "so I'm sure you can see how that didn't go over well."

"Agreed. I'm right there with you on that," she declared.

"But, according to them, they had permission, and I was far too rough on them."

"I doubt it." She snorted. "But I can see how anybody who has grown up unchecked with an entitled attitude might think they can cause you trouble by saying whatever they want to say."

"Exactly," Timber replied, "and the trouble is, it's my word against theirs, and … I'm nobody, and he's a …"

"Somebody."

"Yeah."

"No way," she argued. "You're not a nobody at all, and you have a lot of people with substantial standing in this area backing you."

"You mean Kat and Badger?" he asked, with a note of humor.

"Yes, Kat and Badger, plus people you may have worked with while you've been here."

"Sure, but I don't know how many of them would go to bat for me."

"What about Kat?"

"Kat would go to bat for anybody," he stated.

"And you also know that you're on that immediate list."

"Sure, but they shouldn't have to."

"I get it," she said, "but life isn't always as peachy keen as we want it to be."

"No, it isn't," he grumbled.

"How is the roofing coming along?"

"I took my temper out on it today," he shared, "so it's coming along just fine."

Just enough humor filled his tone that she could see it. "In other words, you got up there, and you worked your ass off, doing the work of ten men."

"At least six," he corrected, "and sometimes that's just the best way to handle life."

"Maybe," she murmured, "and sometimes it's a little hard to do."

"Not when you're pissed off and frustrated."

"Did you contact the sheriff's office?"

"I planned on it but worked on the roof instead. I'll text them in a bit."

"Well," she muttered, with humor in her tone, "I'm not sure I believe you, but I thought you told me how he was a good guy."

"He's a great guy. We served together and got through a lot of things. I'm just not sure he's in a position to buck the tide where he's at." And, with that, Timber disconnected.

It was a simple *click* of the connection, but it had such finality to it. If there was one thing Tiffany could say about him, it's that he was a straight shooter. She didn't know how he would handle this back-and-forth interaction with the sheriff's office, but probably with the attitude that everybody needed to stay away from him. And that was likely to be as good as anybody got. She also knew several of the local deputies, and one of them in particular for sure. She didn't know if that's the same one Timber had spoken to or not, but she found her fingers automatically calling him up.

When Richard answered the phone, he said, "Whoa, whoa, whoa, what does our local vet want with the sheriff's office?"

She smiled into the phone and asked, "Hey, Richard. How're you doing?"

"I'm doing fine," he replied, "and it sounds as if you're okay, at least I'm hoping so. I can't say we get many calls from you."

"No, and usually there's trouble when you do," she began, with half a laugh. "However, I was just out at Timber's place."

"Timber?" he repeated. "I didn't know you even knew him. I just found out he was here myself."

"Yeah, he came for some antibiotics for an injured doe out at his place."

"Right," he muttered, his tone calm but a little on the quiet side.

"Are you guys doing anything about that?" she asked him curiously.

"It's under investigation," he sighed. "Not a whole lot we can do though, and we don't even know for sure who it was." When she snorted at that, and a long moment of silence followed, he finally spoke up. "Unless you're trying to tell me something."

"I know perfectly well that you know who it was, and

Timber's spoken to Andy himself," she stated calmly. "Don't treat me like I'm a fool, please."

"I wouldn't do that," Richard replied, "but obviously we're still investigating."

"I don't know that Timber will say anything about it, but, when I was there, somebody came up through his property, very close to the house, but not up into the driveway, and started firing rounds into the barn and the house."

"What?" he roared.

"Yes, and then they took off, driving like a bat out of hell. It was a truck, and I can give you a basic description, but not more than that. I left soon afterward, but he just called to confirm I made it home safe."

"Why didn't he call me?" he snapped.

"Maybe you should be asking yourself that question," she declared. "I'm calling you because I was a witness, plus I also felt traumatized and attacked at the moment. I want to know whether it's safe to be in this town right now or we've got some vigilante garbage going on that'll make it dangerous for good citizens like me," she snapped.

"I'll look into it," Richard declared.

"If you *looking into it* means going out there and giving Timber a hard time," she stated, with a groan, "that won't go over so well."

"Hey now, that's not what we're about."

"Say what you want, but he's already got a distrust of the authorities now," she declared, "and I know that came from your earlier visit. So, I don't know what happened there, but, as a concerned citizen and somebody who was at the property and in the house that was shot at, believe me that I am very concerned."

"Of course you are," Richard agreed. "I assure you that we will get to the bottom of it."

"You mean, now that there's been a shooting, or now that somebody other than him is involved?"

He sighed. "Honestly, he isn't the problem."

"Oh, I know he isn't the problem," she stated. "At this point, because of the care he's given her, that doe will make it, but rest assured that I will take it personally if somebody goes in there and tries to take her out. The fact that anybody was brazen enough to shoot at the dwellings in broad daylight ..."

"And you're sure that the shots hit the buildings?"

"Let me say that they didn't go into his dogs or me or the doe, and she was hiding right there in the bushes."

"That's good that she wasn't hit."

"Yes, and she also has enough smarts to stay away from humans, but Timber has quite a way with animals apparently."

"Apparently?"

"Yes ... apparently," she repeated. "I just got off the phone from talking to Kat, and she mentioned it, but just consider the situation. Timber was able to approach a wild animal, who had been shot by a human, while she was pregnant. That doe allowed Timber to remove the arrow, to clean and stitch up the wound, and then to come back and give her an injection of antibiotics. And by then she had a fawn at her side, when she would be at her most protective."

"Wow."

"Yes, and you know that Kat and Badger know who Timber is as well. I told them about the shooting too."

"It would have been nice if you had called us," he said in a testy voice.

"I just did," she pointed out cheerfully, "because I can tell you one thing. Timber probably won't."

And, with that, she disconnected.

CHAPTER 9

T IMBER MANAGED TO retrieve two of the bullets, but the others eluded him, at least for the moment. He needed a metal detector on hand now, but it wasn't something he could just dredge up out of nowhere, and it wasn't something he was willing to invest his time or money in when it came down to it, not right now anyway.

He needed his money for other things. He had a pretty decent-size bank account and an investment account as well, but he also had some significant expenses coming up on the property, and that was without the budget for the animals themselves. It was clear that he would have to step up his plans to take care of his rescue business in a big way, and he never would have imagined that this attack was something he should have planned for.

He was grateful that Tiffany was okay but was also pretty pissed that it happened in the first place, especially while she was here. He also couldn't be sure who she told and what she said, but, a few hours later, he got an answer to that, as he watched as yet another vehicle pulled up into his driveway.

He stood here glaring, as Richard got out of the sheriff's vehicle, and matched him glare for glare. "It would have been nice if it wasn't Tiffany who called us," he snapped.

"Would have been nice if you guys had done your jobs

and had stopped those punks from coming back out here in the first place."

Richard stared at him, "Did you really expect me to do that right off the bat?"

"I don't know," he replied. "All I can tell you is that they were here."

"But you didn't get a good-enough look to recognize them, did you?"

He grimaced. "What do you think?"

"I think you have a pretty good idea, but, if push came to shove, you would struggle with lying about seeing the driver."

Timber crossed his arms. "I've pulled some bullets out of the cabin."

"They really shot up your place?"

"They really shot up my place," he stated, with a nod. "As far as I'm concerned, that's a declaration of an all-out war. If they come back, they'll get the same treatment."

"Look, buddy. I get it, but please don't do anything hasty."

"I'm not doing anything hasty," Timber declared, glaring at him. "But I am also not taking that shit from anybody."

Richard winced. "I get it. I hear you. I just wanted to come out and confirm that what Tiffany told me was true."

"That depends. ... What did Tiffany say?"

He glared at his old friend and muttered, "Come on, man. I'm not the enemy here."

"Neither am I," Timber spat. "I came here peaceably, and everything's been fine, until I find trespassers shooting up animals on my land," he repeated, "and it's just gone downhill from there. I didn't start it, but you can damn-well bet I'll finish it."

"Jesus Christ, don't be such a hard-ass," he roared.

"I'm not being a hard-ass," Timber countered, "but you better get a handle on this, or I will. Now, if you've got nothing else for me, I've already lost a bunch of time on this crap."

"I didn't even hear what happened," Richard said, cutting him off. "I need to take a statement from you."

"Why? At least you came alone this time. Thank you for that."

He groaned. "I know you didn't think much of my partner, but Foster isn't a bad guy."

"No, but he is somehow related to the little felon who's running around shooting things up, isn't he?"

"I'm really hoping that's not the case," Richard muttered, raising a hand, "but, if he is, action will have to be taken."

"Yeah, but it won't be action fast enough to stop this, will it?"

"It should, yes."

"*Should*," Timber repeated, staring at him. "Jesus, don't tell me the little asshole is related to the judge too."

"What do you expect? It's a small town in a rural area."

"And they're all okay with this?"

"No. Nobody is okay with it," Richard replied in frustration, "and I can tell you that Andy will be livid."

"According to Andy, he's already livid, but nobody seems to care anymore."

"What do you mean?"

"I suspect, with age, Andy's already lost any control he had over these people, at least regarding the use of his property," Timber shared, "and they'll just keep running roughshod over what they perceive to still be his land and to do what they want regardless."

"That shouldn't be happening," Richard noted, staring at him. "He's well known and highly respected in this area."

"I'm sure he is, and I don't know if the little shit giving me trouble is related to Andy, but I suspect he is, and, either way, he is one entitled and arrogant waste of space."

Richard winced at that. "Let's not judge him too harshly just yet."

Timber stared at him. "Did you have another reason for coming here?"

"Yes, damn it, I need a statement." Then he quickly pulled out his recorder and said, "Now, tell me what happened."

It didn't take much, a few short words as he described what had happened, and then Timber stated, "And that's it."

Richard nodded. "That certainly aligns with what Tiffany reported."

"So, hang on. You thought Tiffany lied?" he asked curiously.

"No, I wasn't thinking she lied," Richard said in frustration. "I was just hoping that maybe she got something wrong."

"It was pretty hard to get anything wrong in this case. And I get that you'll say they were just out on a lark—"

"No, that's way past a lark," he stated, as he stared at his old friend, "and you and I both know it. This is where the danger comes in, and that is something we both know too much about."

"We also know what happens when bullets start flying," Timber added, "and neither one of us are up for getting caught by one of those."

"No, damn it. There have been way too many bullets in both of our lives."

"Exactly, so if they come back on the property again …" Timber left that sentence hanging.

Richard groaned. "I'm asking you not to kill them."

"I might not set out to kill them," Timber began, "but it depends what they're doing. I will defend my land and the animals on it, and myself if need be."

Richard sighed, then looked around. "Tiffany mentioned the doe was doing okay."

"The doe is doing okay, but she has zero trust for man, believe me."

"No, of course not," he agreed, with another sigh. "And what was that about her being pregnant? Tiffany said she saw her foal?"

"Yes. She dropped a fawn the very next day after that kid shot her with an arrow."

"Stupid-ass kids," he muttered.

"Yeah, they didn't care though, did they? It's all about getting out and being big men, shooting things, and killing things for fun," Timber said, his tone hard.

Richard winced but nodded. "I know, and I get your frustration. Both of us have seen way too much of that shit for real. But we have to remember the younger generation hasn't gone through the same lessons."

"No," Timber agreed in a bored tone of voice. "At the rate they're going, those are lessons they may not live long enough to learn either." When Richard just glared at him, Timber laughed. "Just had to add that."

Richard looked at him with enough relief on his face that Timber realized his friend really was afraid Timber would go off half-cocked. "Just listen to what I'm saying," Timber explained. "I'm not looking for trouble, but they've already had their warnings. If they come back yet again, we'll have trouble. I won't wait and get shot at a second time. So you deal with them first, or I'll do it myself. You might want to tell them personally that's how I feel about it and that I mean business and have the ability to back it up."

Richard winced and then nodded. "Yeah, I hear you." He walked back toward his truck. "Are you sure you're staying in town?" he muttered, as he looked over at him.

"I'm staying. I'm putting down roots, good roots," he stated calmly. "That's what I need to do for myself. There shouldn't have been an issue. I've just been out here, minding my own business."

Richard walked over to his vehicle and took one last look around. "What have you got, four or five acres here?"

Timber looked at him, a small smile playing around the corners of his mouth. "I've got sixty, looking to get more."

"Sixty? Jesus, man," he muttered.

"Animals need space," Timber pointed out.

"You're really stuck on the animal thing, *huh*?"

"I'm really stuck on the animal thing. Yes, that's correct."

Richard looked at him sadly. "I presume that's due to your lack of love for humans."

"Let's just call it an abundance of love for non-humans."

Richard nodded. "Point taken." With that, he got into his vehicle and drove off. Timber stared out into the tree line for a long moment, wondering if he should call Tiffany, when his phone rang. He looked down to see it was her.

"I called him," she admitted right up front. "I don't know that I should have, but I felt as if somebody needed it."

"There was a good reason why I wouldn't," Timber admitted, "though I did tell you that I would message him."

"I know, and I'm not sure whether I did the right thing or not, but I called Richard, and I do trust Richard."

"As it turns out, Richard is the old military buddy of mine," he shared, "but I also think he's between a rock and hard place. Apparently I've moved into an area that everybody took to be theirs. He did ask me how much land I had and was quite surprised when he found out. I'm hoping for more," he added, with a chuckle, "but that would put a crimp in my actual budget for fixing up the place."

"If you accepted help from some people, you might make that happen."

He snorted.

"Right, back to that whole *you don't like people* thing."

"It's more than not liking people. It's more about that kind of thing usually has strings attached."

"But not always," she replied. "So maybe get off your high horse and talk to Badger."

He snorted again. "I suppose you're good friends with them too."

"Certainly with Kat anyway," she shared cheerfully. "We go way back. Even before getting her help with a couple patients."

"Of course you do," he muttered, followed by a sigh. "Will I have them interfering now too?"

"Maybe," she admitted, with a cheerful voice. "If so, you can thank me later." And, with that, she abruptly ended the call on him.

He stared down at the phone, but instead of being pissed off and angry at somebody else butting into his life, he felt a sense of humor and surprise that she had potentially done something he may not like, yet he found himself not pissed off at her the way he would have expected. And, with that, he got back to work.

CHAPTER 10

TWO DAYS LATER Timber had another visitor. This time he smiled when a big military jeep drove in.

Badger stepped out, looked around, and whistled. "Jesus, when you mentioned rough, you meant rough."

Timber walked over and went to shake his hand, but instead Badger punched him hard in the shoulder. Glaring at him, Timber asked, "What the hell was that for?"

"Just had to knock the chip off your shoulder," he snapped. "What the hell are you doing all this shit for without looking for anybody else to give you a hand? You know we've got a ton of manpower over there."

"Yeah, it's typical you would send it over here when you know damn well you need it for other projects," Timber stated, glaring at him as he rubbed his shoulder.

"Yeah, it might be typical of me," he snapped, "but this shit is also typical of you."

"So, we are who we are," Timber announced, as he glared at him.

"You're about to get some help, whether you like it or not. My question is whether or not we can set up a plan, so we can make the best use of the manpower, or will we waste time arguing about it?"

"What kind of help am I getting?" Timber asked warily. "And when?"

"Not today. I wanted to confirm I caught up with you first, so we could get some idea as to what you need," he shared, as he looked around, his gaze landing on the house. "You working on a new roof?"

"New roof, new supports," he replied. "The barn needs work. The house needs inside work too, but that's the last to be done. I need dog runs, paddocks. I need electricity in the barn and running water. Another well would be nice. Kinda want a clinic set up here too, for some emergency ranch medical attention. There's just no end to it," he muttered.

Badger stared at him. "And you planned to just do it one piece at a time?"

"Yeah, I would do it one piece at a time. You got a problem with that?"

Badger snorted. "No, you're just as knot-headed as everybody else."

"Apparently you know an awful lot of knot-headed people," Timber declared, glaring at him.

"I do, and, at the moment, you're taking the cake on that one."

He shrugged. "At least I'm on top of something."

At that, Badger burst out howling with laughter, slapped him a whole lot lighter this time, and added, "Now, show me what you've got for plans, and let's figure out how we can help you get something done, moving this thing forward."

"Yeah, it'll take a lot, which is why I didn't want to involve anybody."

"Right, not involving anybody, that makes sense. If you've got twelve weeks' worth of work here with you doing it all alone, it's about what, one week with twelve guys?"

He stared at him and said, "You don't have twelve guys

to spare. And it's more like nine months of work, so far."

"I have as many guys to spare as I say I have to spare," he snapped, glaring at him. "So don't piss me off again. Don't you dare piss me off."

Timber laughed. "I wouldn't dare because you might punch me again."

"Damn right I will."

Timber glared at him. "I need that arm to swing a hammer."

Badger nodded. "Glad to see you're back to normal. So let's have some coffee and see what you've got going."

They went inside, and Timber showed him what he had partially worked out in terms of work on the buildings. He pointed out, "The thing is, something new has come up, and I'll need the property fenced and to get a security system in place."

"Why security?"

With that, Timber told him about the unlawful hunting, trespassing, now the latest shooting. At that, Badger paled and asked, "Are you serious?"

"Yeah, I'm serious, and, worse yet, Tiffany was here at the time."

"Tiffany, as in the vet, Dr. Tiffany?"

"Yes, Dr. Tiffany," Timber confirmed, "and she went and told the deputy about it."

"And what did they do?"

"Richard—"

"Oh yeah, I know Richard," Badger interjected, "good man."

"He came out with a partner the first time," Timber shared, as he stared at him, glaring at the interruptions, "and he stopped by the second time alone, but I haven't heard anything since."

"Let's sure as hell hope he doesn't need to come out a third time," Badger muttered. "What about Andy?"

"I talked to him after the first incident, but I haven't bothered after the second."

Badger nodded. "We'll take that one step at a time. You ended up with quite a few acres."

"I did, but he's still got another piece that I want. It's 120 acres, and it lines up between his place and mine."

Badger didn't say anything at first, just nodded. "If it's nothing but land, it might go for something reasonable."

"It's nothing but land," Timber stated, "but I'm running into trouble since too many people are related or have those influential types of relationships in town. And now that I'm causing all kinds of trouble in town, *according to some*, I don't know whether I've got a shot at getting the rest of the land or not." Then he stopped and shrugged. "And that's not even fair to the people in town since I haven't spoken to anybody else. I'm just pissed and assuming the worst because somebody is a bad seed in that one family, and I figure they've probably turned everybody against me."

"I know small towns," Badger noted. "Some of them are good, but, like all families, some aren't so good. Generally we have no trouble with anyone, and Andy is a good guy."

"He is, and I probably just need to talk to him about maybe not selling off that piece, so I can buy it at some point in time."

"You do that, but, in the meantime, let's go over where you're planning on putting those fences and pastures, plus getting some paddocks set up. Let's take a walk through that barn," Badger added, "and, as far as the house goes, man, there's a lot to do."

"I know. I could have dropped it, and, at some point in time, I probably will," he admitted, with a smile, "but that's not today's issue."

"No, it sure isn't," Badger agreed. "That's a bigger job than we can help with right now, but, in a couple years, that's a different story." And, with that, the two men took a partial tour of the property, with Badger sorting out the scope of the jobs and what they could do and when. He nodded. "Okay, we need to get the materials, since you can't fence in anything without fencing materials, and we'll need a post-hole digger." Badger started rummaging through his mind, listing all the things they would need. And when he finally ran down, he looked over at Timber, who was staring at him.

Timber shook his head. "I don't know what the hell you were even thinking about to get involved in this," he admitted. "Kat will have a conniption fit and will be pissed at the both of us."

"Are you kidding? She's the one who sent me out here," he shared, "and, if I don't come back having helped you and helped you *a lot*, believe me that my marital life won't ever be the same."

Timber looked at him and started to laugh. "I always knew I loved Kat."

"Yeah, … well, you can't have her. She's mine," Badger snapped.

"Oh yeah, I know, and a dozen guys would line up as soon as your body is cold in the grave."

"Honest to God, they're already lining up, just in case," Badger muttered. "The good news is, she loves me, and she's not like a lot of other women. She's loyal to the core," he stated, "so I don't have to worry about that."

"Nope, and you've got the kids too. You are a very lucky man."

Badger looked at him and nodded. "And don't I know it," he stated. "I really do, and I want the same for you, but first we've got to get you a place to actually sleep."

"I'm sleeping here just fine."

Badger rolled his eyes. "Yeah, and that's why you put the roof on first, so your bedding doesn't get wet, and so you don't wake up soaking wet too, right?"

Timber shrugged. "I figured that it didn't make any sense to put too much money into the house, if I need to drop it in the end."

"Maybe not," Badger conceded, "but you do need to have some kind of a decent shelter for yourself, and, when you start bringing in more animals, you'll need a place to nurse them and to bring them inside where it's warm. You can't do that without some facilities. And, yes, … you can do it on your own, piece by piece over time," he admitted, waving his hands. "However, if we can give you a step up, a step up is what we will do."

"What do you have in mind?" Timber asked, frowning.

"I'll go back and figure out some stuff," Badger replied, "and then I'll be in touch." And, with that, he tossed back the last of his second or maybe his third cup of coffee, and walked out.

"Drive carefully," Timber said. "I don't know if those idiots are still out there on the roads."

Badger turned and frowned at him. "Point taken. I think I need to talk with Andy."

"Yeah, you do that," Timber muttered, "but I think he's pretty tired and fed up over this."

"Of course he is. Nobody wants to hear about that kind

of thing going wrong. But when you feel responsible, it's way worse," he muttered. "Are you thinking they are related to Andy or just somebody he helped out once upon a time?"

"I'm not even sure at this point," Timber shared, "but that one deputy, *Foster*, he sure as hell is related to that punk kid."

And, with a wave and a nod, Badger was on the road and heading out.

CHAPTER 11

S OMETIME IN THE middle of the night one of the dogs woke Timber. He sat up straight, his senses already on high alert, as he listened. He heard sounds, some nickers from Sparky in the barn, a little bit of unrest but nothing too unduly. From over where the doe was, there was nothing, but he would expect her to be hunkered down close to her fawn somewhere, and, if she were smart, she would have moved farther away, where people couldn't get at her. He wasn't sure what he heard until it came again.

It was a hard crunch of a boot on the ground, but something was off. He got up, quickly pulled on his prosthetic, his jeans, grabbed his rifle, and, with the two bigger dogs, Philly and Kojack, he headed downstairs. Lucy and Bingo were both huddled in their baskets.

He just smiled at them as he walked past and whispered, "It'll be fine."

They just looked at him, the fear in their eyes already bigger than he wanted to see, but then what would you expect from animals that knew nothing but mistreatment, and now they hear something out there moving around? That was not cool.

As he moved downstairs and stepped outside into the night, he stilled, his senses widening as he used an old trick from his military days to seek out any intruder. The sounds of the night echoed in his brain as he listened, until it came again off to the side, a little bit more toward where the doe was but still not close enough. His eyes had slowly adjusted to being outside. He wasn't exactly sure what he heard, but definitely something was moving out there.

He waited a little bit longer, took several slow cautious steps in the direction of the sounds, then called out, "Hey, visiting hours are in the daylight."

In the moment of silence that followed, he could almost sense the shock. Absolutely nobody responded, not a peep, not anything, yet he heard the catch in the back of the throat, the breathing of somebody who didn't expect to be seen or heard, somebody who didn't expect to be caught out here right now.

He waited and then added, "Just so you know, my gun is loaded. I'll count to three, then I'll start shooting."

Again no response.

Timber shot one bullet in the air. He wasn't the kind of guy who would shoot blindly out into the wild, not when his whole goal was to help these animals instead of letting them get shot up by these assholes or getting injured in any number of other ways. As he stood here, it was hard to suss out what was going on, but definitely something was.

He stepped into the night and slowly walked over to where the doe was, or at least where he'd last seen her. He was pretty sure she wasn't there now, which would be a good thing, considering what Timber was coming up against. He moved as silently as he could, but still the ground was dry. Where it was hard packed, it would be fine, but where it wasn't, the leaves would crackle underneath his feet. He knew that whoever was out here was still as the night, deliberately not moving and hoping to avoid detection by staying still. But Timber had played this game for a very long time in far more desperate situations, so he had learned a few tricks. As he moved toward his adversary, he could almost sense the palpable fear.

"I don't know who put you up to this, but they didn't pay you enough for it," he said in a conversational tone, "and, if you have any doubts about it, you're about to get proven wrong. You shouldn't have come out here. You shouldn't have taken money for this job."

And again, more shock came, more of a reverberation of shock. Nobody moved or said anything, but Timber could feel the shock reverberating all over his intruder.

He smiled as he sensed it. "If you come out now, I won't shoot."

Still no response.

"I might have a whole lot more to say to you, but I won't shoot," he explained. "You're on private property. You're trespassing, and you've got yourself caught up in the middle of something ugly that's already brewing. So, depending on which side you think you're on, you sure as hell better show yourself while you can."

Just then his eyes adjusted to the dark, and, out of the trees, a donkey bolted toward him. He wasn't sure where the hell it came from or what was going on, but he heard human footsteps running away. He looked at the donkey and realized it was injured, bleeding from fresh cuts down its side. He thought he saw older wounds as well, and it looked as if there was a rope around its neck and around one hoof.

He suspected somebody had ridden it in and then cut it loose. No way he would take it to go after whatever asshole had done this. Even now he heard footsteps racing away hard. He hopped onto the quad, the dogs joining him on the seat, turned on the engine, and raced down the driveway.

He got down to the corner where he figured he was probably just ahead of his intruder. Then he called out to the dogs to go get him. With that, the two bolted and worked toward flushing out whoever was in the trees. He knew they would move fast, but he could only hope that whoever was out there didn't understand that the dogs would corner him, and it would be up to them to try and talk their way out of this.

When the dogs hadn't returned, hadn't barked either, just as he thought that maybe nothing was out there, they both set to barking, hard and fast.

They had cornered something. Timber didn't know what, and maybe they didn't either because there was definitely an odd sound to their calls. So he raced to them on the quad, his gun in hand.

As soon as he got around the corner, he stopped to see a man on the ground, the dogs snarling above him. Timber called out to them to heel, then cocked his gun and walked over, pointing the barrel at the intruder. "Who the hell are you?" he snarled.

The guy looked up at him with a snarl on his face.

"You again," Timber said. "What in the hell are you doing back here? And how did that animal get hurt?"

"That thing's been a pain in the ass for my family since forever. I should have killed it a long time ago."

It was all Timber could do to not shoot him on the spot, but he'd seen assholes like this before, and sometimes there was just no other way to deal with them.

As he quickly pulled out his phone, the kid on the ground asked, "What will you do, call the sheriff?"

"Nope," he said, and, with that, he made a phone call.

When Andy picked up, as if he'd come to from a long slow sleep, Timber said, "You better get your ass over here." And he disconnected.

"What's the matter?" the kid asked in a mocking tone. "You can't do your dirty work yourself?"

"Not trying to," Timber replied in a calm and collected tone. "I was hoping to bring this to a peaceful end, but I can't be bothered about that now."

"Oh, wow," the intruder muttered in a mocking tone. "It's not like anybody will give a shit. You're nobody."

"Apparently you think you're somebody," Timber murmured. "Just look at you, running around in the dark, injuring whatever you think you can hurt just because—"

"I told you, that donkey's been a pain in the ass all my life."

"Right, and that's why you made a point of hurting it."

"It'll be fine. It's taken way worse."

"Then I guess I'm grateful that you brought it over to me," Timber replied. "It will live just fine now, and that'll be the irony of it," Timber shared, with a laugh.

"You're welcome to it. Jesus Christ, that thing just never shuts up."

"It won't now either." He heard it in the background, braying in distress. "Only a coward hurts an animal like that."

"I'm not a coward," he snapped, snarling at him, "but I don't like animals."

"So, you kept this one for what, to torture it?"

"No. Hell no. I couldn't be bothered."

"So, whose is it?"

"It was my grandmother's," he said, "but she's passed on, so I don't know whose it is."

"So, that would make it your granddad's?"

"Yeah, I know it's my granddad's, but it's not as if he's looking after them very well now either."

"And you are?" Timber asked, staring at him.

"Nope, I'm sure not, but somebody's in between us."

"Ah, you mean your father?" At that, the kid shifted nervously. "Your dad wouldn't like your being out here, I suppose?"

"He might not like it, but not for the reason you think," the kid said.

"What's your name anyway?" Timber asked. "Brian or something?"

"Yeah, Brian," he said, "don't wear it out."

"Wasn't planning on it and hope I never have to use it again, but I'll need it for the gravestone."

At that, the kid stared at him, not sure whether Timber was joking or not.

Then Timber fell silent as he studied him, knowing that Andy would be hightailing it over, and it was a draw as to whether he would give a shit about this or not.

When a truck barreled in, the kid heard it and muttered, "Oh, look at that. The cavalry to the rescue." But when he heard Andy's voice, he paled and asked, "What the fuck? You called my grandpa?"

Andy spat, "Yeah, he called me, you little piece of shit. What the hell are you doing over here again? I told you to stay away from this man."

"I don't give a shit what you told me," he sneered. "You're nothing but an old man."

Andy stared at him in shock, as Timber looked over at him. "You sure you want to save this one? Why bother? He's already a lost cause."

The old man sighed. "Yeah, but unfortunately he's my lost cause."

"He appears to be afraid of his father."

At that, Andy winced. "That's partly why he's the way he is, I suspect."

"No excuses, not now, not anymore." Timber declared, staring at Brian hard.

"I almost didn't find you," Andy said at his back.

"You couldn't miss us with my quad sitting right here, its lights still on," he stated, without turning to look at him. "But I've got to tell you, your grandson came over on a donkey, and he left it in pretty rough shape at my place. He told me that it's been a pain in the ass, and all he wanted to do was kill it. But leaving it here is much better since that animal has taken a hell of a lot more from him than just tonight's torture." He turned a hard gaze at Andy. "Is that the kind of shit you're running over there?"

"No, it's not," he snapped. "What do you want to do with him now?"

"I've already called the sheriff's office."

"No, you didn't, you only made one phone call," Brian interrupted, still glaring at him.

"Yeah, I only made one in front of you," Timber explained, with a sneer. "The minute I stepped outside of my cabin, I called the deputy, already had my phone recording and on Speaker, so you can bet he's on his way."

Andy interjected, "I'll take it as a personal favor if you would let me just take him home."

"Taking him home didn't work last time, did it?" Timber declared, turning to Andy. "He'll be charged with animal cruelty if nothing else."

"You can't prove nothing," Brian said, "and, besides,

nobody around here gives a shit about that animal. That donkey is just fucking useless."

Timber stared stony-eyed at him, then he turned to Andy. "Well, Andy, I'm sure finding out a whole lot more that I didn't want to know."

"Yeah, I can see that, son, and I'm sorry, but not everybody will be quite so happy to have you here if you'll just cause trouble."

"And is this me causing trouble to you?" he asked, giving Andy a hard glance.

Andy frowned at that. "I guess it depends if you'll let him go."

"I won't let him go because he'll just keep coming back," Timber stated, shaking his head at Andy. "The fact that you want me to let him go with the way he's talking to you and with the way he's acting is completely against everything I would have expected you to stand for."

"It's not that," Andy said, "but his father's around somewhere."

"Meaning?"

At that, the kid laughed. "Meaning my father is a snake in the grass, and he would just as soon shoot you where you stand, and even good old Andy doesn't want to cross him."

"I didn't say that," Andy replied. He turned to Timber. "My boy's a little touched in the head. He went to war and came back not in very good shape."

"So abusing animals is okay?"

"No, … it's not okay," Andy said in a hard tone, "but he ain't overlooking putting his boy in jail."

"Really? And what will he do about it?" Timber asked.

Then a shot was fired that hit a branch just above Timber's head. The branch snapped and landed right beside the kid.

Brian hopped to his feet and swore. He yelled out, "That was a little too close, thank you."

Andy sighed. "That'll be his dad," he muttered in a low tone to Timber. "And now we've got real trouble."

Timber frowned at him and asked, "And this is seriously how you want to play it?"

"No, it's not how I want to play it. I would prefer that my boy got the help he needs, but there ain't no way now," he muttered. "He's on the wrong side of the law, and he isn't even supposed to be here. I wasn't even expecting him. He just showed up."

"But he's here now."

"Yeah, he's here now all right, and that is not good for anybody. He needs help."

"I do not," declared the man striding toward them in the dark. He had his rifle up and aimed it at Timber. Timber kept his pointed right back at him.

"Look at that," the man noted, "We've got a standoff."

"No, we don't," Timber said steadily, as he eyed the newcomer. "Apparently you're Andy's son, and your son Brian is petrified of you."

"I am not," Brian argued crossly. "Why the hell would you say that?"

"Because it's the only thing that started to pull you into line. You sure don't give a crap about your granddad here, but apparently your dad is somebody you don't want to get crosswise with."

A hard gaze went from his son, Brian, to Andy and then back to Timber. "I hear you bought yourself some land."

"I did," Timber confirmed. "All signed and sealed and perfectly legal."

"You'll need to give that back."

"That ain't happening," Timber replied. "It was legal, signed, sealed, delivered, and I've already been working on it."

"Yeah, … so I heard, but you're also causing my boy trouble."

"Really? Seems to me your boy has been causing me trouble."

"It's his land."

"His land?" Timber repeated, shaking his head.

"No, it's not," Andy snapped in a hard tone. "It's my land, and I sold it to Timber because I wanted to."

"Then you'll buy it back, won't you, Papa?"

"No, I will not."

And quick as a wink that rifle went up against Andy's head, and a soft voice said, "Tell me that you'll buy it back."

Andy turned and looked at Timber.

Timber studied the other guy. "Wow. Old men, animals, and what? … Do you beat up women and children too?"

The son looked over at him and stated, "I don't have to beat them up, but I don't have a problem doing so if they need a tune-up."

"A tune-up." Timber snorted, his gaze narrowing. "I hear the local authorities are looking for you."

"They'll never find me," he stated, but the rifle never moved from Andy's face. Slowly he turned to Timber and said, "You'll sell that land back to Papa."

"No, I won't," Timber declared.

"I sure hope you've got your will all nicely written up because you won't live to make all the improvements you want on it."

"Maybe not," Timber conceded, "but I can guarantee

"It had to do with Kelly being upset at something I shared about Brian."

Katie rolled her eyes at that. "Oh God, that Brian is a major loser," she stated, with disgust in her tone. "Plus, he's vindictive and mean to animals."

"That's where the quitting part came in," Tiffany noted. "It's just as well because if Kelly was okay with his hurting a donkey the way he just did, or is in complete denial about it, I'm not okay with her being here."

Katie hadn't heard anything about the donkey, so Tiffany quickly filled her in. Katie gasped with shock and outrage that Brian would do such a thing or that Kelly defended him on it.

Tiffany nodded. "Keep in mind now that I may have potentially made an enemy out of the both of them too."

"Yeah, that's pretty normal for her. She goes off in fits and has only held a few jobs over the last couple years, so I wouldn't worry about it."

"Her résumé was a little on the skimpy side," Tiffany admitted sheepishly, "but we needed the help."

"Yeah, but we don't need that kind of people, not if they're okay with animal cruelty," Katie declared in a firm tone.

Tiffany smiled. "Thank you, Katie. I'm glad you agree with me on that one."

"Absolutely. You're only as good as the house you keep," she shared. "And I not only need the job, I already know what that Brian guy is like. So, no, I'm not quitting over a loser like him, that's for sure."

"We could be short on staff for the next few days."

"That's not a major deal. Kelly only worked couple days a week, and she was forever taking time off anyway, so it's not really that great of a loss."

"I wasn't aware of that," Tiffany noted, frowning at her.

Katie nodded. "Other things were always going on in Kelly's world that she was trying to change shifts for."

"And she is also young and still on the immature side."

"Yep, young and, dare I say, a little on the *stupid* side," Katie added, with a laugh. "But it is what it is."

And, with that, everybody got back to work, even as Tiffany realized she would have to put out an ad and hire somebody new to help out. The thought filled her with anxiety and stress because trying to find the right people for her clinic was important, but it was just as important to find someone compatible with the employees she already had.

And, with that thought in mind, she called Elizabeth, who had worked part-time for her in the past. As soon as Elizabeth answered, Tiffany explained the situation. "Hey, I just wanted to ask if you're interested in filling in on some shifts at the front desk. I've got a vacancy."

"Who left?" she asked.

She quickly told her about it, and Elizabeth groaned. "Oh gosh, yeah, that's fine. No surprise really, as Kelly never seems to hang on to a job longer than a few months at a time anyway."

"She's been here for about that long, but she got upset over something I said about Brian, who she is apparently friends with."

"That kid is in need of some tough love, if you ask me," Elizabeth shared, with a chortle. "Yet he's a choir boy compared to his father."

"Apparently Max's back, so that's a word of warning I'll take to the wise."

"What do you mean Max's back?" she cried out. "He's

supposed to be dead. I just meant the kid comes by it naturally."

"You might have been joking, but Max is not dead and has been hiding out over at Andy's for these past several days."

"Andy wouldn't have him there if he had a choice in the matter, so that won't go well and might explain why the kid's lashing out."

"Maybe, but the bottom line is that I'm short on staff," Tiffany added, with a sigh.

"Not a problem," Elizabeth said in a casual tone. "Honestly, I've been thinking about checking in to see if I could pick up a few more shifts anyway."

"Done," Tiffany declared. "How many do you want?"

"How many was Kelly doing?"

"Two full days a week, I think."

"Perfect," Elizabeth said, "I can handle that."

"Are you sure?"

"Yeah, absolutely sure, so, in a way, good timing all around."

Feeling much better, Tiffany explained the new schedule to Katie and asked her to email that to Elizabeth. Katie was all in favor, and, with that problem solved, they settled into a routine for the rest of the day. As the last patient left, and they closed up, Tiffany headed outside to her vehicle and looked around, realizing that everything felt different today.

Whether it was the events of the past few days, her interactions with Timber, or Elizabeth's reaction to the return of Max Killerman, Tiffany didn't know, but an odd sense of waiting filled the air. She wasn't sure why but couldn't believe it had anything to do with someone she'd never met or had even heard of before this. Still, it was a little disconcerting to think that somebody was around town with that kind of history. Plus, the last thing Tiffany wanted was trouble from anybody, and yet it seemed as if she'd put herself smack dab in the middle of it.

When it came to her former receptionist Kelly, that was a completely different issue altogether, but it seemed as if a solution had presented itself. So, for now at least, that was handled.

CHAPTER 14

A S TIMBER DROVE slowly back home, he stopped periodically to put up battery-operated cameras, hiding them in the trees, small but with a decent distance for recording. Now he had some semblance of security around the place. He'd planned on doing it right from the get-go, but there was also such a thing as time and money and importance to consider. Still, he should have made it a higher priority in all three terms. But he was here now, getting everything back on track, as he worked his way through the camera installations on his property and finally got back home. He was surprised to see Badger there, with two other men.

As Timber pulled up and parked, Badger walked over, his face grim. "Kat told me about Max Killerman."

Timber winced. "Yeah, I wanted to ask you about him."

"We already know all about him," he stated, with a snort. "For every bunch of good guys in the military, it seems there's one bad apple. Max received a medical discharge, but it was a mental disability, and I've got to tell you, he's not all there."

"I would definitely agree with you on that," Timber confirmed.

"You've talked to him?"

"I did, and, for whatever reason, he seems to think that

Andy selling me this place broke some deal between them."

Badger shook his head at that. "Max has known that Andy's been looking at selling for a very long time. Andy just didn't want to confront Max about it or to fess up and move forward with it. Andy's not getting any younger."

"No, in fact he looked pretty beat up last night. I think Max tried to convince him with his fists." Timber shrugged. "Then I put some additional pressure on Andy over the grandkid, Brian."

Badger nodded. "Probably what the kid needs."

"Sure, but that's where the father should come in, right?"

"So, Andy's probably afraid Brian will turn out like his father."

"Afraid is what both Andy and the kid are. They're clearly terrified of Max."

"They're not wrong to feel that way. It seems Max had a bit of a history before he went in the military to begin with. It sounds as if he went in, full of joy."

At that, Timber winced, because anybody who went in with that kind of attitude was probably looking forward to the killing part, and that was never a good combination.

T IMBER AND HIS two new helpers were still outside working, when dusk started to fall. He looked over at Dwight and Toby, the two men Badger had left behind, and said, "Sorry, but Badger didn't exactly make it clear. Are you guys staying here, or are you heading back somewhere else?"

"We're staying here for the duration," Dwight stated calmly.

"Okay, thanks for the help." Timber thought about it for a minute and then added, "Good thing I got some burgers thawing for dinner."

Toby nodded. "Yeah, that sounds great. We'll be here until we sort out what's happening with Max Killerman. That guy needs to be found."

Hearing something in his tone, Timber faced him and asked, "Do you know Max Killerman?"

"I do," interjected Dwight, the older of the two, in a hard tone. "And there's nothing good about him."

"That bad?"

"Yes, … that bad, the worst."

Timber didn't need to hear any more because that basically told him everything he needed to know. Anybody who'd been on missions with somebody like Max knew what that would mean. As the trio trouped inside, Timber announced, "I'll get started with dinner in a minute, but I've got to go deal with the animals first."

"No," Dwight stopped him. "We'll all go deal with the animals."

Wondering whether that was a deliberate act to keep them together or something completely different, Timber followed Dwight's lead, and they headed over and quickly fed Sparky. He checked out the donkey, who was doing just fine now, the cuts mostly superficial, which also made Timber wonder if it was more for show than anything. Even at that, it wasn't a good combination.

Toby stopped at the sight of the donkey, his jaw working as he examined the cuts. He grabbed a brush and started to curry the donkey's back, staying well away from the injuries.

Timber watched him for a moment and shared, "He'll be just fine in no time."

Toby nodded. "Damn good thing." Toby didn't say anything else.

Yet it had been enough. Timber was of the same opinion as the rest of them—that it was a really crappy deal.

As he headed inside, he quickly got the burgers started, wondering just how much he would need to feed everybody and whether he had enough groceries on hand for the duration, however long that would be. He hadn't planned on feeding extra people, but then he hadn't known a couple extra hands would be staying around.

He needed to talk to Badger about that too. Was somebody paying these guys their wages, or what was the deal? Timber knew a certain number of men in Badger's world would come just because help was needed, no payment expected, except for room and board. Timber definitely appreciated that, but he also needed to get up to speed on the details, and he hadn't had a chance to ask Badger while he was here.

After dinner that night, the other two men took their bedrolls and went upstairs, grabbing rooms. The upstairs had four bedrooms and two bathrooms. While the men were upstairs, cleaning up and getting ready for the night, Timber called Badger.

"How did it go?" Badger asked.

"We certainly got a hell of a lot more done than I can do by myself in one day. We've still got a way to go, but obviously we're getting somewhere now."

"Good."

"These men," Timber asked, "am I paying their wages?"

"No," Badger said. "Dwight and Toby both volunteered, and neither wants wages, but, if you can feed them, put a roof over their heads, that's fine."

"Yeah, absolutely," Timber agreed. "I'll talk to them about it. I just wanted to check in to find out what the deal was before I did."

"Sorry, I should have filled you in before I took off," Badger noted. "Any trouble?"

"No, not yet, but you know it's coming."

"I do, and so do Dwight and Toby."

"What's the story on Dwight?"

Badger sighed. "I probably shouldn't be talking out of turn, but Max took out Dwight's pregnant wife on a whim."

"On a whim?" Timber repeated in shock.

"Yeah, more or less because the woman chose Dwight over Max," he explained "and Max decided that, if she didn't pick him, nobody would get to live. Dwight had been attacked too but survived. Understandably he's never been quite the same. Toby is also military, went to war, survived some pretty rough duty. He's a good man to have in your corner."

"Yeah, I got that message already," Timber stated, with a chuckle. "They're both workers, that's for sure."

"Of course. If there's one thing about the men who are here, and you and I both know it, is that they all know how to work. If you need another hand immediately, let me know. Otherwise I'm getting together a large group, who can come move your projects forward, enough so that, when they leave, you're capable of carrying on."

Timber snorted. "You know I'm not *incapable* of doing what needs to be done here."

"Jesus, I know you are very capable," Badger grumbled. "But you need to get things dried in, you know, the roofs and barns. You need to get shit done and not just be sitting on the sidelines, knowing it needs to be done, plus distracted by this other bullshit going on. So … we'll be there with a bigger crew. I just don't know how quickly or how many total." And, with that, he rang off.

Not a whole lot Timber could say to that, but it was a hell of a deal when your friends stepped up in this way, just to help out. As soon as he had the place tucked down for the night, he walked upstairs to the bedrooms and saw the men both still had lights on.

He stopped at Dwight's door, knocked, opened it a tad, and asked, "Do you need anything before I turn in?"

"I'm good," he said, looking over at him, "just some sleep."

"Let's hope we get that too."

Dwight patted the rifle he had beside him.

Timber nodded and didn't say anything. He didn't even ask about it because really that would just insult the other man. Timber also trusted Badger. If he'd sent these men, it was because they expected trouble, and Timber knew it himself.

As he headed to his room, his phone rang. He looked down to see it was Tiffany. "Hey," he answered, a smile in his tone. "You're checking up on me now?"

"Yeah," she snapped. "You've been on my mind all day."

"Hopefully in a good way," he teased.

She sighed. "I just can't stop thinking about how messed up everything is over there."

"Oh, it's definitely messed up, but we're hoping that we'll get past that point soon."

"Yeah, you might be, but, if Max Killerman is around, that doesn't mean shit. Everything I hear about him is, … well, he's just plain bad news."

"Yeah, and that's the trouble. When these guys get those reputations, then they have to stick to it in order to keep others in their little corners," he murmured.

"And you don't think he deserves his reputation?"

"Oh no, not that. He probably does," Timber admitted, "but people like that, they just shoot first and ask questions later. In his case, I don't think he's too bothered about asking questions. I think he just likes the shooting part, probably way too much."

"I guess the military does breed that to some degree, don't they?" she asked.

"We can't blame the military for all of them because, in many cases, it's not the military as much as the work that attracts men such as Max."

"I hadn't considered that, but I guess you're right. For anybody who's drawn to violence, that would be a good place for them, or at least they think so."

"Exactly," he agreed, "and that's what ends up happening. It seems to be a good place for them, so they show up. Next thing you know, there's all kinds of chaos."

She sighed. "I just hate to even think of you being alone out there."

"I'm not alone anymore," he shared, and then he laughed. "What? Kat didn't update you?"

"No," Tiffany declared crossly, "and I've been hassling her so much already that I didn't want to call her again."

"You can rest easy. Nothing to worry about," Timber replied. "I have two men here to help me."

"Really?" she cried out in delight. "Oh my, that's much better."

He laughed. "I should be insulted over that."

"No, don't be insulted," she stated, with a groan. "Somebody like Max would shoot you in the back. He won't stop and talk to you or give you a chance. He'll just kill you."

"I know that," Timber admitted. "I do understand the kind of person who I'm about to tangle with."

"I just keep having horrible visions of the two of you ending up in a gunfight."

"Yeah, then I better be the one who comes out the other end," he stated, "because an awful lot of animals need me."

"There is that," she muttered. "There absolutely is, but it's never really clear in my dreams who wins," she noted. "So, I suspect it's just my fear talking."

"That's absolutely what it is. On the other hand, it's nice to know you care," he said.

She sighed. "I don't know why I do. I hardly even know you."

He laughed. "We're well on the way to getting to know

each other," he stated. "So, anytime you want to come out and check up on me, you're welcome."

"Seriously?" she asked. "I figured you wanted me to stay well away."

"From a safety point of view that's true, although I can't really see Max shooting up anybody else, since I'm the one he's after. And now that I'll be buying another big chunk of land off Andy, that'll really piss off Max."

"Do you need that land though?"

"No, not now, but, if Andy sells it to somebody else, I won't get it or won't have any control over who my neighbors are. This will give me a good buffer."

"Oh, that's true," she added grudgingly. "I hadn't really considered that."

"That's the problem. When life gives you that opportunity, you take it," he stated, "even if it bites into the budget a little sooner than I'd hoped."

"Of course you were looking to get a lot of work done on the place first."

"With these two men here to help out," he noted, "I'll get a lot accomplished, so don't you worry about that."

"Yeah, … well, that's another reason why I'm calling. I've got a dog here that needs a home rather badly."

"So, bring him on out," Timber suggested. "He can hang out with the other two."

"Don't you mean the other four?"

He snorted. "Oh shit. I have to go find Lucy and Bingo." He walked back down the hallway and stopped at Dwight's door. He poked his head in and asked, "Have you seen two small dogs, one that's missing a leg?"

Dwight looked at him, then sheepishly pointed at the corner of the headboard, and there were Bingo and Lucy, curled up on the bed.

With a smile, Timber walked back out with a wave.

Shaking his head, he returned his attention to Tiffany. "I guess we don't need to worry about those two. Bingo and Lucy are curled up on Dwight's bed."

"Is he okay with animals like that?" she asked, half anxiously.

"Yes, they'll be fine."

"That's good," she muttered. "I put a lot of work into keeping Lucy alive and giving her a second chance."

"Don't worry. She'll have a second chance here," he stated calmly. "And the guys know what they're doing, so no worries there."

"I hate to worry," she admitted, with a groan, "because, once I hand them off, I'm supposed to stop all that, you know? ... Worrying?"

"It doesn't work that way," Timber declared, with a laugh. "Once you start putting time and effort into helping somebody, you always have an invested interest in making sure they're okay. So don't ever judge yourself for coming from the heart."

"Coming from the heart is one thing," she admitted, "but, when you get it beaten up a time or two, it makes it that much harder. Anyway, we can talk about the dog later. I'm so glad to hear you've got some help out there. Good night." With that, she quickly ended the call.

Timber frowned. Something had been so intensely private about that little bit of extra information he'd gotten from her this time, and it made him wonder about her own history and about what had brought her to this corner of the world. Five years ago, she had told him, and then she'd bought the business herself. She was probably in a situation similar to what he had been. Either buy it now and invest yourself in pursuing your dream, even though you're not quite ready, or move on.

With the phone in his pocket, he closed up the downstairs for the night, grateful that it was at least summertime, and they didn't need heat, since he wasn't really set up for that yet. An old stove was in the front room, but he didn't think it would do very well over the winter. So, once they got everything patched and a new roof on that section, he would need to pop in new stovepipes and put a new stove in.

But that wasn't today's worry. With a bit of a smile on his face and fatigue in every ounce of his body, he crashed for the night. Sometime in the middle of the night—after he'd gone to bed, exhausted yet happy—he heard the donkey braying. He was up and out of bed and racing down the stairs, as he heard Dwight at the doorway.

"Easy, I think he's okay. Go easy. I'll go out right now myself."

And behind him, Toby added, "I'm going north."

"In that case," Timber replied, "I'll go east." And, with that, they all split up and moved silently out into the night, confirming that whatever had startled the animals—at least the donkey in particular—wasn't a problem. As Timber moved closer and closer to where the doe was, or had been, he heard movement in the shadows.

He froze and waited to see what would come out of the darkness. What came out surprised him, yet maybe it shouldn't have. The doe was there, still hiding off to the side, yet he was delighted. Her fawn was tucked up in the tall grass beside her, and she watched everything going on silently around her, as if waiting for something to happen, knowing she might need to run. Yet she was calm, and her composure calmed him down.

He watched from the shadows as a black bear rumbled through the bush and passed him. It stopped, catching his scent, but, with an age-old wary look in his direction, kept on moving. Timber smiled and let the old guy go. Yet that bear wasn't so old that he couldn't fend for himself, which is when the bear would become more dangerous around the livestock. However, this bear was definitely at a stage in life where he was starting to slow down a little bit.

It was possible there wouldn't be another winter for him because the infirmity of age in the wild came quickly. And it happened to everyone, not just to the people around you, but also in nature. Still, this particular bear wasn't quite to that stage yet.

As the bear walked slowly past Timber and past the doe, hiding ever so slightly in the shadows, Timber relaxed and took a deep breath. And that's when he saw an arrow in the tree above the doe's head. He didn't know how long it had been there, but it looked to be the same as the one he had removed from her shoulder earlier, and that was not something he wanted to see.

It was also pretty clear that it was a sign, a symbol from somebody or a warning that Max was out here, that he was always around and could do what he wanted, and Timber and his friends couldn't stop Max.

When footsteps moved his way, he slipped back into the shadows again and waited to see what came out, but it was Dwight, moving cautiously and yet not as worried as Timber would have expected.

When Timber stepped out of the shadows, Dwight stopped, noted the arrow above his head, and asked, "Did that just arrive?"

"I'm not sure," Timber admitted. "I didn't see it the last time I was in this area, so I'm afraid it's new."

Dwight stared at it and nodded slowly. "That's not good."

"No, it's not good, but it's very typical."

"Aye, that it is," he murmured, studying it.

"I don't think it was there before, but it matches the one I took out of the doe."

Dwight added, "I recognize it."

If Dwight recognized it, Timber was more than ready to believe him. "Max?" he asked.

Dwight nodded. "Yeah, just a warning, a warning that he's here, a warning that he can come and go at will."

"He can. It's not as if I have the place fenced, and, even if I did, that won't stop anybody who really wants in," Timber admitted.

Dwight nodded calmly.

"Do you have a personal relationship with Max?" Timber asked Dwight.

"Nope, ain't nothing personal about it. He's just bad news."

"And did you know him before?"

At that, Dwight gave him a hard look and replied, "I don't think anybody ever really knows assholes like this. If you're asking if I know him, yes, I do. He's somebody I've been keeping an eye on for a very long time."

"Your family?"

Dwight stilled, looked over at him, and slowly nodded. "Yes."

"But no vigilante motives, right?"

He shrugged. "Doesn't matter," he muttered. "Right now, you've got bigger issues, and that's keeping this man off your own family. And believe me, when it comes to Max, he doesn't care for anything. And, if he finds out there's something you care about, he'll confirm that goes first."

"*Nice man,*" Timber muttered, frowning at that.

"Yep, so you might want to keep that vet girlfriend of yours off the property for the moment."

"She's not my girlfriend," he said instinctively.

Dwight looked over at him and shrugged. "If she ain't, she should be."

"You know her?"

"I know good people."

And that was so typical of him—minimum verbiage, and everything stated in such a way that you knew he meant whatever he said and said whatever he meant. So he wouldn't elaborate on any of it.

Slowly the two men walked back, leaving the doe staring after them. Timber wished he could reassure her, but, if he showed any affection or extra love to this one, he knew Dwight was right. Max would take out the doe and her fawn in a heartbeat. She'd already been through enough, and the last thing he wanted was for her to suffer anymore.

As they walked back, Dwight asked, "Have you got any way to trap him?"

"I figured you might have that covered," Timber replied, with a mild laugh.

"It's not that I'm getting soft," Dwight replied, "but it's about staying on the right side of the law. Almost everything I think up would have worked, depending on where I was stationed, but not so much for the here and now."

"Yeah, that's the problem, … trying to stay legal," Timber muttered, "but we need some defense. Otherwise he could take us out in our sleep. Yet I don't sleep that heavy."

"Neither do I," Dwight shared, "but this isn't a normal circumstance. This guy is like a ghost, and, like a lot of ghosts, he's got some vendetta. And even if you knew what it was that he wanted, he won't give up just because he gets his revenge. That's not who he is. He'll confirm that he gets what he wants and that you pay." At that, Dwight turned and strode into the house.

Timber stared after him for a long moment. Something was uniquely comforting and also terrifying about Dwight. Comforting in that, as long as you're on the right side, he was there for you every step of the way. But he also had an agenda, and, as long as you were on his side when it came to that agenda, it was all good, but God help you if you crossed him. Timber wondered if he had traded a snake in the grass for a different kind of snake altogether.

With those thoughts heavy on his mind, he headed upstairs to grab a few hours of sleep himself. God knew he would need it to face whatever was coming.

CHAPTER 16

TIFFANY HAD ABSOLUTELY no reason to head back out there to the rescue center, but she just couldn't stop herself. She realized that this was more than she had expected, and she had no idea what was going on inside her head. Still, the fact remained. She was worried about Timber. She needed to go just for her own peace of mind and to confirm everything was okay. As she finally pulled up in front of the main house, she stopped and stared because they had made some serious progress. She hopped out and walked over to the deck.

When Timber came over, she offered him a bright smile and an apology. "I know. I know. It's not my place, and I shouldn't be here."

He frowned at her and shrugged. "You're welcome to be here."

She frowned at him intently. "Really?" she asked, with a wry look. "I seem to be pushing myself into your world all the time now."

He gave her half a laugh. "If I didn't want you in my world, I would have pushed you right back out."

For some reason that made her feel a lot better, and she laughed. "Good to know. I brought you some fruit from one of my trees."

"Fruit from one of your trees? What, are you a farmer too?"

She shrugged. "I have quite a few fruit trees on my place—apples and pears, although it's a bit early for them. I also have vegetables in the garden. I'm a bit of an animal and a plant person."

"That's good to hear," he replied, "because I'm not very good at growing anything."

She laughed. "I don't know about that. You're doing a heck of a job growing this place."

"Oh, now that's a different story," he stated. "I can build anything. It just takes time."

"If you can build even a fraction of this," she noted enviously, "it's way more than I can do. That's something I've always wanted to do, but it's not as if we, as women, are actively encouraged in the trades."

He shrugged. "I think you have to get over that and just do whatever you want to do."

"You're right there," she agreed, as she walked toward the front door. "You've already got the roof up."

He pointed toward the barn and added, "That's where we're working right now."

"Can I see?"

"Sure," he said, and he led the way over to the barn.

Yep, the very large structure was just as rundown as the last time she had been here. At least the original part in front. These guys had doubled the size of the shelter, putting up new supports and building a new back half, now with a brand-new roof over the whole thing. It had already been big to begin with. She whistled. "Now, this is a barn."

"That's what I'm hoping for," he said, with a bright smile. "I needed a full-size barn, a working-ranch barn, since you never know just what I'll end up with for animals in here."

She laughed. "I think you're planning on filling it pretty quickly," she murmured.

"Hopefully we can also move out some of the animals, if they can be rehabbed and rehomed."

She nodded. Entering the barn, she saw the donkey. Timber called him Danny, and he was paying close attention to an older man. He was rubbing his ears, and the two of them were basically hitting foreheads. She stopped and stared, then she laughed. "That's somebody who clearly likes animals."

Timber introduced her. "This is Dwight."

She looked at him in surprise and asked, "I know you, don't I? From Kat's place?"

He nodded. "Yep, I'm pleased to see you again."

She smiled at his old world charm and looked over at the other man, who smiled at her.

"Hey, Doc, I'm Toby."

"Nice to meet you, Toby."

The two men immediately got back to work, though she wasn't sure whether that was out of politeness or they were just anxious to get back to work. She shook her head as she looked around. "It's pretty amazing."

"Good," Timber declared. "That's how we want it."

She laughed. "I can't imagine how you guys got so much done already and so fast."

"Sometimes you just have to buckle down and get the job done. Of course it helps a lot to have two extra pairs of hands," Timber added. "Good timing too for Dwight and Toby to show up, as I needed this barn repaired pretty quickly, just in case the weather changed."

She pointed to the men and said, "You did mention you had two guys here but hadn't realized they were like living here."

He raised his eyebrows at her. "I blame you for that."

Astonished, she turned and stared. "What? How is that?"

"You told Kat. Kat told Badger. Badger was out here very quickly. The next thing I knew, he dropped off these two guys, and they've been with me now for several days. Next week Badger's sending a larger crew, but I have to get the supplies in first."

Just then they heard a truck rumbling out front, and he nodded.

"That's got to be the supplies I'm expecting."

"Am I in the way?" she asked anxiously, as she turned to look at where she'd parked.

He shook his head. "No, you're just fine there. A lot of the materials will get dropped right here by the barn, so we can continue building. Then we'll work on fencing some pastures, digging holes for fence posts and related things. When the crew comes next week, we'll be that much further ahead."

"Fences would be good." She turned and asked, "How is the doe?"

"Last I saw her, she was doing just fine."

"And when was that?"

"Couple nights ago," he shared, "in the middle of the night, oddly enough. Something disturbed us, and we got up. I found her, lying down with the little one not too far from here. While I was checking on them, a big old bear trotted on through."

She looked over at him and smiled. "Yeah, you're just far enough out that you'll get all kinds of wildlife."

"And that's fine by me," he said, waving his hand. "I don't intend to chase away a bear just because I moved into the neighborhood. That's not my style."

She laughed as his tone of voice adopted a drawl. "How's Andy?"

"Now that I don't know." Timber frowned, as he looked over in the direction of Andy's place. "I'm hoping he's okay, but our last meeting wasn't exactly the easiest."

She nodded. "I'm a little worried about him."

"Have you heard from him?"

"No, not recently, and I know people are saying that he's really struggling, but I don't know exactly why." When he hesitated, she added, "I gather you do."

"Maybe," he grumbled, with a frown. "He asked me *not* to press charges against Brian, but I wasn't too interested in letting the kid off the hook."

"Of course not. Brian hurt two animals, that we know of," she declared in outrage.

"More than that, he was also causing all kinds of chaos on my property, not to mention shooting at my house."

"That's right. He can't just get away with no consequences."

"The problem is that everybody has let him get away with anything he's done for a very long time," Timber pointed out, "which is why I couldn't let that happen again."

"So, what did you end up doing?" she asked, frowning at him. "I hope something happens this time, or Brian will never stop."

Timber looked over at her. "Oh, I did something all right, and you may not like what I suggested either."

"I won't know if you don't tell me," she replied, with a smile. "What did you suggest?"

He hesitated, then shrugged. "I think Brian needs to go into the military because he has zero respect for anybody and anything. I believe it's the best chance he has at changing his life."

She stared at him in shock, which quickly turned to delight. "Oh my, that is perfect."

He frowned at her. "For some reason I thought you would be against it."

"No, I'm not against it at all," she stated. "Brian needs to learn some respect. He needs to grow up and to see the true cost of hurting animals or people, because it's such a small step from one to the other."

He nodded. "It absolutely is. Anyway, I haven't heard back from Andy over it, but that was one of my conditions. The kid goes into the military, and Andy's sells me the rest of the land I want."

"You didn't ask for it for free?" she teased.

"I'll pretend you didn't just ask me that, but no," he clarified. "That wouldn't be right. I won't force him, but I do want the opportunity to buy it, if he's willing to sell."

"I think that's fair," she said. "I don't know that Brian would agree with your stipulation, but, since he's already cooked his own goose in this mess, the military seems way better than jail."

"It was interesting because Richard was here at the time, and he agreed with me."

She stared at him. "He did?"

He nodded. "We both have military backgrounds, and I was pretty happy to hear him back me up on that suggestion."

"I'm not sure that's something I would have expected out of him, but Brian's a pain in his butt too."

"More than that, with no consequences, Brian will just get worse," Timber declared. "As you mentioned, it's a slippery slope from hurting animals to hurting people, and the last thing we want is for Brian to turn into a wife beater or something worse."

She winced. "Yeah, especially since one of those potential wives is my former receptionist, remember? The one who quit on me."

"She hasn't come back?"

"Gosh no. She's young, and apparently I insulted somebody she cares about."

Timber snorted. "When you're young, you may have ideals and yet not the best judgment."

"Been there …"

"But then life hits you, and all of a sudden you realize you need a job, and you don't care how much your ideals come into play. It's more about getting a paycheck and putting food on the table, particularly if it's not just you that you need to put food on the table for."

She nodded. "I don't think Kelly has that type of relationship with him, but I really don't know."

Timber sighed. "If not right now, it will be with somebody sometime, and that's not what we want to happen either."

"No, sure it isn't," she murmured.

"It was good to see you, but I do need to get back to work."

"Right, go ahead." She gave him a wave of her hand, already feeling as if she'd overstayed her welcome.

"Yet you came all this way," he added, "so the least I can do is get you a cup of tea or something. However, the delivery truck and the supplies have just arrived, and I need to get out there to help unload."

"No problem. It's not as if I gave you any warning."

He laughed. "No, and I didn't issue an invitation either." She flushed at that, and he winced. "And I didn't mean it that way. I just didn't realize you would be coming."

"No, I get it," she said and stepped back. "Do you mind if I go check on the doe?"

"Go ahead," he replied. "I don't know if she's around or not, since we've been making a fair amount of noise."

"I'll check." And, with that, she quickly exited and made her escape from him.

Of course he hadn't invited her, but then it's not as if he knew that she was looking for an invite.

In fact, she just felt foolish right now, and that wasn't doing her any good, but what was she supposed to say? She quickly looked around for the doe and the fawn but couldn't find either one of them. When she headed back to her small truck, she saw the loads of supplies being delivered. She stopped for a moment to watch, then realized that she was probably in the way here too. So she quickly got into her vehicle, backed out of the way, and headed back home again.

When she got home, she set about catching up on a bunch of her paperwork and then the laundry, all the while feeling foolish for having gone out there. It was stupid because she normally wouldn't do that. Yet it wasn't something she would normally *not* do either. She was a friendly soul, and sometimes it got her in trouble, like right now. She hated feeling embarrassed about overstepping some unwritten rule that she hadn't picked up on.

By the time early evening arrived, she was groaning, regretting having gone to the Haven. When the phone rang, she answered it without thinking it could be him.

"Hey," he greeted her. "Sorry about having to rush you today."

"Not an issue. I was just feeling foolish for having come out there, without even checking with you first."

"And that's not an issue," he said, with a chuckle. "At one point in time, you mentioned a dog or two needing a home."

"One for sure," she confirmed. "However, you're still in such disarray that I didn't want to bring him today."

"When I saw you, I thought that's what you were probably doing."

"Right," she muttered. "It would have made more sense, wouldn't it?"

"Then when you didn't bring him in, I presumed either he's not ready to come or you think I'm not ready to have him yet."

"Kind of both," she agreed. "I was checking to see how you were coming along, but, if a couple more weeks would make all the difference, then a couple weeks is fine."

"Where is he staying at the moment?"

"He's at the clinic now, and I'll probably just bring him to my place, so he can get out of the cage for a bit over the weekend."

"Why don't you bring him this weekend, just so he can get to know what it's like out here?"

She smiled at that. "He won't want to get back into the crate afterward. You do know that, right?"

"That might be okay too," he noted. "I'm serious about bringing more animals in. I just didn't realize that you were coming today."

"And I've apologized for the umpteenth time," she stated, "but I can do it again."

"No need, so please don't," he replied. "Honestly, it's getting kind of crazy around here. The guys are living here, so I don't really feel as if I can just invite you over for dinner."

"Oh, gosh. I hadn't even considered that," she admitted. "I guess they're staying in the house, aren't they?"

"Yes, and, until I can get the house in a little bit better shape, it's not as if I have any space."

She burst out laughing. "The good news is, I don't need space, so it's fine. … I'll take a look at how the dog's doing over the next couple days. You've got your supplies, and I don't know when Badger and his big crew are coming, but maybe I'll pop in and say hi to him, if he's around."

"Check in with Kat," Timber suggested. "I don't know whether she and the kids are coming or not."

"Right, that could maybe be a day trip for her, and I … I'll think about it," Tiffany shared. "Anyway, get back to work, and I'll check on the dogs here in a bit."

And, with that, he disconnected.

She smiled, grateful that he didn't seem too bothered by her impromptu trip out there, but he wasn't exactly running all over to set up another date. Which they hadn't had a date in the first place, so what was she even talking about?

Realizing she was making herself nuts over all this, she sat down and drew up a list of supplies that he would need for his animal shelter. It's not that she had too much in the *spare money* category, but she did have lines to quite a few people who liked to help out, especially if she told them about a new rescue taking in some of the dogs that needed recovery time—or even to be fostered until they were socialized, or maybe even fostered indefinitely. She didn't know how that charity angle would work with Timber, but she knew these organizations would be very interested in helping him establish and run his rescue.

And, with that, she drafted a quick email, explaining the situation, set up a GoFundMe page for his rescue, and then sent him the link. She didn't want him thinking she had done something inappropriate and getting upset with her, especially without his knowledge. So she had that all set up and the link sent to him, ready to go live, if he was okay with it.

She got up and took a couple of the dogs out for a walk. It was such a bright evening with a lot of light, but she felt an oddness to it, and even the animals didn't act the same way. They moved rather quickly and kept glancing behind. It was the *glancing behind* part that unnerved her. Frowning, she looked around and had that weird feeling of being followed.

So, by the time everybody had a chance to lift their leg, she was already half running back home again. The trouble was, even back home and inside, it didn't give her any feeling of true safety. She had the dogs for protection, but that was all she had. Plus, she lived alone, which anybody could find out very quickly.

Hating it and not knowing what to do about it, she locked up the doors, put on the security system, knowing full well that wouldn't be enough to stop anybody who was serious about getting past all that.

And she took that thought with her to bed, only to be haunted by nightmares.

CHAPTER 17

WHEN TIFFANY WOKE early the next morning, she felt the exhaustion already pulling at her, exhaustion and scary thoughts that wouldn't stop, thoughts that were not of the sort she wanted to have at night, or to start her day either.

As she headed into the office, Katie looked up at her and frowned.

"Just a bad night," Tiffany muttered, with a shrug.

"There are bad nights, and then there are bad nights," Katie noted, waving a hand at her. "It looks as if you had nightmares all night."

"Yeah, I kind of did, but whatever. Is everything okay here?"

"Yeah, it sure is," Katie replied. "I came in twice and checked on the two dogs here. And I'm sure both of them are more than ready to go back out for a run right now."

"They're certainly ready to go out for a pee." With that, Tiffany chose to take them out herself, rather than having her assistant do it. As she walked around outside, giving them a chance to rest and relax, she realized that the one dog really was doing much better. So it would be a good thing for him to be moved. Either he could come home with her for the next few days or could go to Timber's place.

As she came back in, Katie smiled at her. "He's looking

so much better."

"He is, isn't he?" Tiffany noted, with a smile on her face. "I was thinking about taking him home overnight."

"You think that's wise? He'll think it is his new home."

"It's not so much that he'll think it's *his* home," Tiffany clarified, "but he'll realize that there is something *more* called *home*. And I think that is important too."

"Right. I would absolutely love to see him go someplace special," Katie shared. "I would love that for him, but I feel that way about all the animals."

"Of course you do. That's why we do what we do," Tiffany declared, "because we come from heart."

"I talked to Kelly the other day," Katie shared. "I was at the grocery store, and she was there too. She was friendly enough but not terribly nice about you."

"Yeah, it's funny. I don't have a clue how, but it went so badly, so quickly. She was cautioning me about Timber for some reason, and I mentioned something about Brian hurting that donkey."

"She doesn't believe you even now. She thinks you're telling lies, and that's not good for anybody."

"And yet I didn't say anything wrong," Tiffany noted, with a sigh.

"No, but young love and all."

Tiffany groaned and rolled her eyes. "I get it. Young love and all, yet, if she's okay with that kind of animal abuse, we don't need her working here."

"No, and she'll go to the retail stores, looking for work."

"Good for her," Tiffany noted. "I'm sure she'll do fine in that. I had high hopes for her here though, and we could still use a couple more people."

"That's always the challenge, isn't it? We are getting busier and busier."

Tiffany already knew all that, but it was a constant reminder that additional staff was needed, and, if they didn't get good staff, they were in even more trouble.

"Anyway, I just thought I would let you know that Kelly hasn't changed her mind since leaving here."

"Is she likely to badmouth me around town, do you think?" Tiffany asked.

"I don't see how. I think most people are a whole lot more aware about Brian than Kelly is. I don't think she necessarily sees him for who he is at the moment. She seems to be quite infatuated with him."

"Right, … well, I don't know if he's even sticking around town though," Tiffany muttered.

"It wouldn't be a bad thing if he left, considering the trouble he gets into."

"I know, but dare I say that? Nope. … I'll be the one who's the bad guy then."

Katie laughed. "Yep, right back to that whole *young love* thing. And, in Kelly's eyes, you're way too old for any of it." When Tiffany stopped and stared, Katie burst out laughing. "I figured that would get to you."

"It's so strange to realize that everybody else sees me as old, considering I'm only thirty-two," she admitted, with a headshake. "I would never have considered myself old."

"No, … maybe not, but, because you are thirty-two, you're older than her age group."

"*Older than her age group*, goodness." Tiffany shook her head. "I'm only a decade older than her, I swear. I'm not old enough to be her mother or whatever."

"You might be right about that. I think Kelly's only about twenty-two."

At that, Tiffany shook her head. "Was I that clueless at twenty-two? I don't think so. I was neck deep into exams and labs at college. Too busy and too focused to even date around." It seemed so impossible to think of anybody at that age being so gullible, and yet that's what Kelly appeared to be, and there was nothing Tiffany could do about it. Back in her office, she checked her schedule and got started on her day. She didn't really have a chance to even breathe until she turned around and walked into her office, only to find Kat sitting there. "Oh my gosh," Tiffany exclaimed. "What are you doing here?"

"I was about to head down to Timber's place," Kat shared, "and I thought maybe you could give me a heads-up on what I was up against."

"I've been there a couple times," Tiffany noted cautiously. "The road is a little on the rough side, but it's not bad. We've certainly been on worse."

Kat laughed at that. "Isn't that the truth," she murmured. "How are things going with you and Timber?"

"I think okay. We're not setting the house on fire, that's for sure."

"And do you want to?" Kat asked, her tone thoughtful, but that gaze of hers was so intense.

"Well, … I wouldn't mind checking to see whether it goes a little further than it is," Tiffany replied, "but I don't think he has that on his mind at the moment."

Kat smiled. "He's male, so I would say yes."

"Yeah, … well, I'm not interested if that's the only draw," Tiffany pointed out, with half a laugh.

"I get it," Kat said. "Does that mean you want to come with me, or do you want to stay here?"

"I'm not sure I have a choice," Tiffany muttered. "I've

still got patients."

"I'm picking up a big load of groceries to take out there because we're prepping for a large crew coming in tomorrow, plus some heavy equipment."

"At his place tomorrow?" Tiffany asked in astonishment. "Does he know about this?"

"Yes." Kat gave her a wry smile.

"Wow, well, … that would be something to see."

"I would invite you, if only to see just how much chaos we can create in a short time."

"I would absolutely love to see the process," Tiffany said warmly. "I just don't know that I can take the time. I've got my own clients coming here tomorrow."

"Of course you do." Kat smiled. "I'll pick up the groceries and head out now and drop everything off. So why don't I call you tomorrow and see how your schedule looks?" she added.

"Sure." Tiffany nodded.

"Even if you come at the end of the day tomorrow," Kat suggested, "that would be great too."

"Are you sure?" Tiffany asked. "And I don't want you matchmaking."

Kat laughed. "That's not my thing, although my husband would disagree. He's always accusing me of matchmaking, but I just don't see it," she teased, followed by a chuckle. "I could be wrong."

"*No matchmaking*," Tiffany reiterated, shaking her finger at her friend.

"Okay, fine, no matchmaking," Kat muttered, with an eye roll. "But—"

"No, no *buts* either …"

Kat glared at her and then laughed. "No buts. If we get

there, we get there, and if we don't? … I guess we don't." At Tiffany's nod, Kat added, "But some people need some prodding to move things along faster."

"Sure," Tiffany conceded, "but sometimes things just need to happen as they're meant to be."

"In other words, no matchmaking?" Kat asked.

"Exactly. No matchmaking."

"Oh, *fine*," Kat grumbled. "Still, come out for dinner tomorrow, and we'll go from there."

"Okay, I can do that," Tiffany agreed, "as long as I know it's okay with him."

"In that case, I've already talked to him about it, and he said it was fine."

She stared at her friend and then sighed. Kat was a force to be reckoned with. "You wouldn't steer me wrong, would you?"

"Never." Then Kat laughed.

"Okay, fine. I'll see if I can come up for dinner tomorrow then. With these late summer days, it won't be dark, so I can see the road at least."

"You want someone to pick you up?"

Tiffany laughed. "*Nah*. I've already driven that road a few times. Besides, I did get a bunch of supplies in, not that he's asked for them. And I did want to set up a GoFundMe page for his new shelter *coming soon*, but he hasn't responded to my email about it."

Kat looked at her with interest. "That's a great idea."

"I know that he's doing all this with his own funds, and he won't ask for help, but, at some point in time, the community would offer some help, particularly for animal shelters coming in," she explained. "So I would like to do this, but I sent him a link to my draft, and he didn't exactly get back to me about it."

"Yeah, that would be Timber," Kat stated, with a snort. "He's not much for social media. He's not exactly the most social to begin with in person either."

"And is there a reason for that?"

"I think just because of the accident, where he lost friends at the same time," she shared. "The whole recovery process is pretty tough, and I'm sure he's looking at himself as less than whole."

Tiffany stared at her in surprise. "But he lived. It's just a leg."

Kat nodded at her with approval. "It *is* just a leg," she confirmed, "but, for a lot of people, that *just a leg* comment matters a lot more than you might think because it represents so much more. And honestly, people look at you differently, especially once they see the prosthetic. No doubt about it."

"That's part of the problem," Tiffany muttered, with a headshake. "It shouldn't matter to anybody. Honest to God, what's wrong with people?"

Kat smiled at her and repeated, "Meet us for dinner tomorrow."

"Fine, I'll come for dinner tomorrow, but, if he's pissed off that I'm there," she added, "I won't be back. I don't want to cause trouble for our working relationship."

"No, it won't cause trouble at all. You're trying to raise money to help him set up his rescue. We're all trying to help him get this animal shelter off the ground," Kat noted. "He's just a loner and was thinking he would do it all himself."

"Which he wanted to do," Tiffany pointed out, "and I'm certainly not trying to take that away from him."

"No, and doing it all by himself is one thing, but doing

it all by himself when there's the potential to have Max Killerman lurking around is a whole different story."

"True, I haven't met him, but honest to God he sounds horrible." Then she stopped and frowned, thinking about the weird sensation of being watched last night.

"What's the matter?" Kat asked.

"I'm pretty sure it's just because of the whole weirdness going on at his place, but I got a sensation of being watched last night," she admitted, again looking around. "I couldn't shake it, and it was so bizarre. It's not like me to get nervous or spun up, but the dogs were racing to get back home again, and I thought that was really strange."

"This was at your home?" Kat asked cautiously, but her gaze was intent.

"Yeah, at my house, which is nothing to write home about, but is home and normally feels safe," Tiffany added. "But last night? Not so much."

"Good enough," Kat noted. "As always, just keep yourself aware, and stay safe. Hopefully it was nothing."

"*Yeah*," Tiffany muttered, unconvinced. "Hopefully it was nothing." Then she frowned at Kat and asked, "But you don't believe that, do you?"

Kat shook her head. "And you don't either."

"One of the things I have cultivated as a vet is understanding what patients are trying to tell me, but not just patients, what their owners are trying to tell me—or trying *not* to tell me too. So I pick up innuendos and coverups very easily."

Kat smiled, a brilliant, brilliant smile.

Tiffany sighed. "No wonder Badger is all over you," she said, with a hard look at her friend. "That smile of yours is enough to knock anybody sideways."

Kat started to laugh. "It's not intended to knock anybody sideways," she stated. "But the fact that you are comfortable enough, happy enough, or confident enough to stand up to me about it is a really good thing."

"If you say so," Tiffany muttered, "but I still think you are procrastinating. Or you're trying to get out of something."

"I'm not trying to get out of anything," Kat declared, "but I will mention to the men that you felt somebody was watching you."

"I don't think it's important though," she protested. "Why would you tell them?"

"Because I don't want anything overlooked with Max on the loose. If he's bad news, and if he's hanging around, then we need to have a good idea what he's hanging around for. If he's not bad news, then it doesn't really matter."

Tiffany frowned at that. "But you do think it's an issue."

"I don't know whether it's an issue or not," Kat noted, "but I'm not willing for it to become one. So I will be telling the men, and, if they aren't worried, we'll let it be."

"What if they are worried?" Tiffany asked.

Kat raised one eyebrow. "If they are worried, then they'll need to do something about it."

"I don't want anybody coming here and feeling as if they need to look after me," Tiffany protested.

"*Right, of course not,*" Kat quipped. "*Makes no sense at all, right?* I mean, … you want to confirm Timber's looked after, but he's not allowed to confirm you're looked after?"

Tiffany blinked in confusion and muttered, "I feel as if you just set me up with that."

She burst out laughing. "It's not that I set you up, but I certainly left it open for you, and you did not disappoint."

"Yeah, definitely a setup," Tiffany muttered. "I don't know how you get away with that stuff."

"Oh, I'm good," Kat stated. "And, just like you, I also have to interpret what people say, versus what they're really trying to say. A lot of the men who come to my office are not in any shape—or with any awareness to be perfectly honest—because they no longer know who they are. They just see what their physical body has become, and they assume that's who they are now, and it's not even close."

"No, it isn't," Tiffany declared in agreement. "I can't imagine what the loss of a limb would be like, and I realize I probably sounded cavalier before, and I apologize. I deal with animals losing a leg all the time, and they have such an interesting way of healing and adapting, and they do it so naturally. Yet people?" she noted, with a huff. "I think that would be a whole different kettle of fish."

"It absolutely is, and, in many ways, it's not something easily definable either. People are"—Kat shrugged, then smiled—"they're just people. It's complicated and yet, at the heart of it, so very simple. They just want love. They want to live a good life. They want to live it with people who care, and they want to leave behind a legacy that they are proud of. So really, it's not hard at all." And, with that, Kat announced, "So I'll see you tomorrow night then. I'll do that delivery run right now, and then I will come back tomorrow night."

And, with that, she was gone.

CHAPTER 18

THE NEXT MORNING Timber hopped out of bed, thankful nothing woke him up last night but still knowing that the day would be crazy. In fact, it was the start of several crazy days, which, according to Badger, were necessary. Timber knew it was necessary, but he would have gotten there on his own eventually. It's just that the thought of getting some of this work taken off his to-do list, so he could get a start on all the other things that needed to be done, was massive. As he walked into the kitchen, Dwight was already scrambling a big batch of eggs.

Dwight looked over at him and nodded. "Breakfast in a little bit. Also found a bunch of rotting fish on the driveway outside this morning."

Timber groaned. "Max, of course."

Dwight nodded.

"Sorry you had to deal with that." Timber nodded his thanks. "You know you don't have to cook, right?"

"I like cooking," he stated in his brisk way. "Toby's out feeding Sparky and Danny, but he'll join me in the kitchen in just a bit. I figured we could make up a bunch of sandwiches for lunchtime, when the big crew gets here later."

"Good idea," Timber added, with gratitude. "I was trying to figure out how to handle the food, as the crew grew bigger."

"Kat dropped off a crap load of food last night, but it won't last long, not once we start divvying it up by a dozen men or so." Dwight turned to point the spatula at Timber. "And you're lucky if it's only a dozen men. Knowing Badger and Kat and the growing crew that's at their place, we need to plan on a lot more than just twelve extra mouths to feed. So we've got to be ready. Not just for breakfast but for lunch and dinner, as well. We do need to feed the crew."

"When Badger told me he was sending over a crew, I didn't even ask him how many guys he was talking about," Timber muttered, as he stared out the door.

"Wouldn't matter," Dwight replied. "Even if the number started at twelve, by the time they drove over here, another dozen or two could have insisted on coming too."

Timber frowned at the possibility of thirty or so guys coming to help. He shook his head at the generosity of veterans working for Badger. Timber glanced at the front door. It was wide open, and he could already see Toby coming back from the barn. "You guys have been a godsend."

"And in a way you've been a godsend for us," Dwight shared. "Don't ever forget it's a two-way street. We all know the power of helping each other out because it comes back to help heal us as well. We're happy to help."

"Even if it's not over with Max?"

"Absolutely. However, it would be the best if he never showed his face again," Dwight noted. "Regardless, I won't back down from a fight, but I'm not here to look for one."

"I'm glad to hear that," Timber said, "because, for me, it'll always be about the animals first."

"I can see that," Dwight replied, with a gentle smile. "And you can do a whole lot worse than that lady vet you chased away."

"I didn't chase her away," Timber protested.

"You might as well have," Dwight grumbled. "I get that it was crappy timing, and I was serious about what I said about Max, but you really should have set up another date with her."

"That wasn't exactly a date, and, according to Kat, Tiffany's coming tonight."

"Oh, so there we go, even more mouths to feed," he quipped, pulling on his scraggly beard.

"Yeah, something else I hadn't thought about," Timber admitted. "Maybe burgers would be the easiest."

"Burgers would be easier," Dwight agreed, "but maybe we should make something else to fill their stomachs too."

"Like what?" Timber asked, turning to look at him.

"Maybe a potato salad. We've got load of spuds," Dwight muttered. "I can bake them right now, then turn them into a really good potato salad to go with the burgers."

Timber nodded. "You want to do that, fly at it. I do like to cook, but I am a little bit lost at the idea of cooking for that many people three times a day for … quite a while."

"I'm not," Dwight declared. "I've got this." He plated up breakfast for Timber and put it in front of him. "You eat this, and I'll be out to help you in a few minutes."

"What will you do that will get you out of the kitchen in a few minutes?"

"I'll throw forty potatoes in the oven to bake. I'll handle them later," he explained. "We've got lots of hamburger defrosting for the burgers, but I need to check if we've got enough buns. If not, we can text Kat and ask her to bring some."

"Yeah, that we can do," Timber agreed.

Dwight frowned. "I can bake bread myself, but I should have started it already, if that were the case." He shook his head.

"I can bake bread too," Timber shared, "but I sure can't produce hamburger buns for a large crowd in twenty minutes."

"Me neither, not in twenty minutes anyway, but we've got a couple hours still," Dwight pointed out. "Yet it's more about where our time is better spent. So, right now, if Kat can bring buns, that's a better answer." And, with that decided, Dwight called Toby in for breakfast. Dwight hitched a thumb over his shoulder. "I'll go wash up those potatoes in the big utility room sink." And he was gone.

As Toby arrived, Timber asked him, "Everything okay?"

"Yep, that donkey is quite the character, isn't he?"

"Yeah, Danny is that."

"He seems to be getting along just fine with Sparky."

"That's good to hear," Timber replied, with a smile. "Sparky has been a little on the lonely side."

"I don't think anybody can be lonely with that donkey around," Toby declared, laughing. "He'll be a noisy pain, but a refreshing pain."

"He's here and has a home for life, as far as I'm concerned," Timber declared. "It was Andy's wife's pet, making Brian hurting him on purpose even more of an asshole move that hurt his grandfather."

"Jesus," Toby muttered, with a headshake. "I sure hope that kid goes into the military, as you suggested."

"I do too."

"I don't know if his grandfather's got the will to pull it off for him."

"It's not even about that," Timber stated. "I think it's

partly from seeing what the military may have done to his son that has Andy afraid his grandson might come back the same way."

"And he might. It's definitely happened before. But that end result can't be all put on the military. Look at us. None of came back as serial killers."

"No, we sure didn't," Timber confirmed, pushing his hat back and looking out into the distance. "Are you guys okay to stay here for a while? My to-do list isn't a short one. In fact it just keeps growing, no matter how hard we work."

Toby looked over at him and nodded. "I'm staying. Something is very healing about being here." He winced as he moved his arm to grab a plate.

"How are the ribs?" Timber asked.

"I didn't really expect to have metal in my rib cage at this point in my life, but I guess … it is what it is. We don't all expect what else is happening around here either."

"No, we sure don't. But you take it easy when you need to and don't injure yourself more."

"Yeah, not planning on it," Toby replied. "I'm here to heal, but I have to heal in more than just a physical way. So I'm doing the best I can to heal my soul while I'm here too. You're lucky that you've got this piece of land, Timber. Honestly, I would say it's pretty special."

"It is, and I know that Andy was talking about selling off more pieces of it, which is why I'm really hoping to get some more. I just hope he is alive and well enough to see it through."

"He's got quite a place here, doesn't he?" Toby asked.

"He really does, and for the longest time it was a success-ful working ranch. However, when the family doesn't want to keep it up, and it's all left to Andy to handle, then it becomes more of a burden than a joy. Seems the younger generation just sees dollar signs and wants to sell it, then take the money and run," Timber explained.

"So, you're looking to buy more acres?" Toby asked Timber.

Timber nodded. "I'm looking to buy more, if Andy's willing to sell more."

"I wouldn't mind a piece, just a small piece," Toby noted, "big enough for a little house and a veggie garden, maybe some chickens. I wonder if Andy would be interested in selling parcels like that."

"He might," Timber noted. "When we get down to talking about it, I can mention it, if you want."

Toby smiled and nodded. "Yeah, I would, Timber. Some place a little closer to town, a little closer to the road. And, if you're looking for somebody long-term to help you run the place, that would suit me to a tee."

At that, Dwight returned to the kitchen, carrying a bucket of washed potatoes. "I only heard a part of that, but I could use a piece just big enough to put up a cabin, maybe grow some food. And the same goes if you're looking for somebody to help out long-term. I would really like to work just with the animals though. I've got no tolerance for people, but animals? ... Absolutely. Count me in if there comes a time you need full-time help."

Timber stared at both of them. "Wow, that's not what I expected, but I'll definitely need help."

"You absolutely will," Dwight declared, "and, if nothing else, you'll need somebody to cook. You cannot live on burgers alone."

"Are you sure?" Timber asked, as he dug into his scrambled eggs. Still, he smelled garlic toast and God-only-knows what else. "Is that bacon?"

"Yeah, it's bacon. I've got it warming in the oven," Dwight shared. He pulled out a big platter of it and the garlic bread, along with more scrambled eggs. "Let's eat before Badger's crew arrives and chaos ensues."

Toby laughed. "Funny how you think it'll be all chaos."

"It will be chaos, but it'll be a good chaos," Timber pointed out, with a smile. "So, let's put our heads together to confirm we're ready to maximize not only this day but the next few weeks."

"It'll be crazy," Dwight insisted, "but I can't wait."

Timber smiled, nodding. "Guys, I can't thank you enough for all the help and support."

And, with that, they gathered together and had breakfast.

They had just barely finished breakfast when Timber heard the trucks arriving. He looked over at the two men who had quickly become his friends and asked, "Are you guys ready for this? For building whatever is needed? For cooking for however many men show up? For keeping an eye out for Max?"

"Oh, yeah," Dwight declared, as he stood up. "When it comes to this shit, I was born ready."

CHAPTER 19

IT HAD BEEN a long day at the clinic. Coupled with the poor sleep she got the night before had Tiffany beyond tired and wondering whether she should go to Timber's or call it off. Running almost every scenario through her head, she decided there was no point in *not* going because she was expected. So, if she didn't go now, it would cause more of a stir than being there.

As she drove toward his place and entered the turnoff, she could already see that the roadway had taken quite a beating. Even as she arrived, empty trucks were pulling out. It seemed they had been running steadily all day here, beating down the ruts in the dirt road, making it a whole lot easier to travel on now.

As she drove up to the main cabin, she was hard-pressed to find a place to park among all the other vehicles, where she would be out of the way. Kat saw her, smiled, and waved her to an approved parking spot.

Kat approached Tiffany as she exited her truck and said, "Come on into the kitchen. I could sure use a hand."

Tiffany laughed and asked, "Okay, what are we doing?"

"Everything," Kat declared. "I've got Dwight in there helping, or maybe I'm helping Dwight," Kat clarified, with a smile. "A lot of people are here to feed."

Tiffany followed Kat inside and quickly walked into the

kitchen. Dwight was there, manhandling a massive bowl of potato salad. "Good God," Tiffany muttered, as she raced over to help because the bowl could flip off the table at any moment. She braced it while Dwight's big strong forearms dug in there, tossing it rapidly, and the potatoes didn't seem to break down. "This looks fabulous," she noted.

"Oh, you wait and see. It will be fabulous when I'm done," Dwight added, with a bit of a gasp. "I forgot what it was like to cook for so many though."

"You've got experience doing this?" Tiffany asked.

"Yeah, some, though it doesn't seem to be quite enough for this moment in time." He looked over at Kat and grinned. "But Kat is always helpful when it comes to cooking for a crowd."

"Cooking is one thing," Tiffany noted, "but cooking for a big crew like this is something else altogether." She wanted to take a head count, but she decided to focus on keeping the potato salad bowl upright on the counter instead. She was aware of various noises coming from various directions. She heard hammering, drills, other unknown machinery. "Wow, I'm not even sure what's going on, but it sure is a hub of activity around here today."

"Oh, it's insane," Kat murmured, and then she laughed. "But it's all good, and it's exactly the way it should be."

"If you say so," Tiffany muttered, glancing around now that Dwight had dismissed her. "This is pretty amazing."

"It is."

Tiffany stepped out on the deck with Kat, who pointed out where fence posts were being placed all along one section of the property.

Kat explained, "They're working on fencing as much of the sixty acres as they can, and then cross-fencing to mark off pastures and paddocks, plus putting in access gates as well. We've got one barn here currently and a crew of a dozen men over there, trying to get that barn fixed up structurally. Still, the barn needs to have water and electricity before housing any of the animals coming here eventually. Plus, we've got another crew of plumbers, electricians, and masons, all working on their assigned tasks in the barn and in the house. I even hear we're running a security crew, what with Max on the loose. To tell you the truth, I don't even know how many guys ended up here or what all they're up to," Kat admitted, with a laugh. "I heard most of the guys brought tents and bedrolls and were looking forward to camping out in the woods."

"With a bear on the loose?" Tiffany asked, frowning.

"I think bear spray is a pretty usual component of back-packing gear," Kat noted, with a shrug. "Besides, these are *our* guys. They survived being overseas in much worse conditions. Still, I've got some temporary housing coming."

Tiffany frowned. "Who's paying for all this?"

"Everybody is here on their own, volunteering, just to help out Timber."

"Jesus," Tiffany muttered, staring at her friend. "That is incredibly awesome."

"It is," Dwight agreed, right behind her. "I don't know whether Andy will come over or not, but he was invited for dinner."

"That would be good," Tiffany noted. "At least he would see the kind of people Timber is working with."

"Do you think that's an issue?" Kat asked, looking over at her.

"I don't know," Tiffany added, with a shrug. "But, with a grandson like Brian and a son like Max, I think it might do a lot of good for Andy to see what the best of people have to offer instead."

"Sometimes you just don't know what people are thinking—about these construction projects or just about themselves." Kat sighed. "One minute it all looks workable. Then it seems absolutely nothing can be salvaged."

"Maybe," Tiffany conceded, frowning. "I prefer to think that Andy would see us as the kind of people who are just like him, trying to step up, making homes and businesses, carving out a life for ourselves."

Kat looked over at Dwight. "I heard from Timber that you might be looking at buying a piece of land out here too."

"I don't know if Andy is willing to sell me a piece of land," Dwight pointed out, "but I'm just looking to have enough for a home, just a small square. I know that's something Toby is interested in too."

Kat nodded. "Maybe Andy would be okay with having a few neighbors."

"At least we're good neighbors," Dwight declared, with a smile.

Suddenly a loud gong came from outside, and then a whistle was blown.

Tiffany looked over at Dwight and asked, "Was that a makeshift dinner bell? Does that mean that the barbecue is on?"

"Yeah, it sure is," he declared. Then he looked at Kat and asked, "Is the beer cold?"

Kat shrugged. "God, I hope so. Otherwise somebody's in trouble if it's not." And, with that, she bolted around to the back of the house, with Tiffany on her heels.

Tiffany muttered, "You guys are really pulling this off."

"Maybe," Kat noted, with a chuckle. "Lots of pieces have

to come together for this," she murmured, as she checked to confirm that coolers of cold beer were spread out everywhere.

Very quickly they were overrun as men came from all corners, sniffing for food.

"Is this the end of the workday then?" Tiffany asked no one in particular.

One of the men stepped up and replied, "Nope, not while there's still daylight."

Kat looked at him, and he shrugged.

"We talked about it and decided that there's a lot to be done and that time is short. So, we'll pull another shift after this meal," he explained. "At the end of that shift, we'll be ready for more grub."

The look on Tiffany's face had him burst out laughing. "Don't worry. More burgers would work. Hungry men don't care what is cooked. We just need lots of it."

Tiffany whispered to Kat, "Do I need to go to town and get more groceries?"

She frowned back at her. "I have no idea. I wasn't expecting them to pull another shift."

Badger came over a few minutes later, the sweat rolling down his back. As he reached in, grabbed a beer, tossed back half of it, he closed his eyes in joy and murmured, "God, I'd forgotten what it was like to pull a twelve-hour day like this. I need to get out of the office more often."

"Yeah, and at the risk of sounding like your wife," Kat began, "don't hurt yourself."

He grinned at her. "Something is so inherently good about doing a job like this," he shared, a smile on his face. "Not only are we helping a great guy for a great cause, but it's physical labor that is great for the body as well as the soul. So, aside from the sore muscles, I have a feeling all this hard work will do a lot more healing than hurting."

"You're not kidding," Kat muttered, kissing Badger on the cheek. "Dwight and Toby are practically unrecognizable. Not their normal grumpy selves at all, and they both want to stay."

"There is definitely something special happening here," Badger declared. "As for me, I spend way too much time at a desk nowadays. And every single one of these men are here, not only volunteering for the assignment but also taking no pay." He bent closer to the ladies and added, "What you may not know is that every one of them has also decided that they are pulling a third shift tonight too. As long as we have a backup generator and trouble lights or headlamps, we can keep on working."

Kat frowned, but nodded. "That makes sense because they all want to work hard and then go home. Plus it's summertime, and we have a few more hours of daylight. So I can see the wisdom behind it. So it's burgers and beer all around on repeat, so the men can go back and can get a hell of a lot more done tonight. I also need to get home to the kids tonight. I set up a babysitting plan for a few days of back and forth but this is getting big now. I just didn't want them here with so much traffic coming and going, and their loving to get into everything," she finished laughing.

Just then another truck came rolling down the road.

Badger looked over and nodded. "Here come the sleeping cabins."

"Sleeping cabins?" Tiffany asked.

Kat nodded. "These were custom built for us, and each one of them can accommodate twelve men. This expanded crew will all be here for at least the next few days, up to a week, and they need some place to sleep since Timber doesn't have it, and this was decided to be better than individual tents."

"Twelve men per sleeping cabin?" Tiffany repeated. "Wow. Wait. Two more trucks are behind the first. How many men do you have here, Badger?"

Badger tilted his head. "I was expecting about twenty-four," he began, as he looked around the place and shook his head. "Then more men showed up," he added, with a note of satisfaction. "If there's one thing we've cultivated over the past few years, it's a really strong sense of family."

"Yeah, but some of them have families they need to go home to," Kat pointed out.

"And those ones will head out with us later tonight, only to come back again in the morning," Badger shared. "The rest are sticking around, and they'll camp here, so …" He looked over at Kat and asked, "How much grub did you bring?"

She rolled her eyes and muttered, "Not nearly enough. We'll need to get a bloody refrigerator truck in here if that many showed up and they plan to work around the clock."

Badger laughed. "Let's do it." When Kat just shook her head, he smiled. "This isn't something we budgeted for, but it seems to have taken on a life of its own. This is one of those times where we go with the flow and just see what happens."

"How long is this team planning to work here?" Tiffany asked.

"A week," Badger stated. "A week to see how much we can get done and then to reassess. Some of the men have to go back to other scheduled jobs. Some have families who are a little farther away and will need to go home occasionally. Others came for the whole week, and they'll stay as long as they're needed. For all I know, at the end of that first seven days, Timber will have a crew of a half dozen guys sitting here, thinking it might be a good place to spend the summer."

Tiffany smiled. "I have never seen anything quite like it," she murmured.

Badger nodded. "No, and I'm not sure you ever will again. It's pretty special."

Kat agreed, "I think both Toby and Dwight are hoping to each buy a piece of land from Andy and have a spot to call home here for themselves, while working full-time for Timber."

Badger nodded and then murmured, "That's not a bad thing. I've always tried to pay them wages for regular jobs, but they always refused. So I just put it in the bank. I don't know if it'll be enough to buy the land, but it might be enough to help throw up a cabin for each of them."

Kat smiled. "I gather that's what we'll be doing now for a lot of our old-timers."

"Considering they won't let us pay them," Badger noted in frustration, "it's not a bad thing if we can find a place for a lot of them to settle down and to own their home. That would be huge."

At that, Timber walked over, fatigue visible in every line of his body, and waved at Tiffany, a small smile on his lips.

Kat just looked at him and frowned. He shook his head and ordered, "No frowns."

She sighed. "It won't do you any good. I've just told Badger to take it easy, and he basically said the same thing."

At that Timber smiled and shrugged. "When these men come and volunteer to help me do the work on my own project, you buckle down and you work beside them. I can be sore tomorrow, but I sure as heck can't get this kind of help from anybody else." He looked over at Badger. "This is amazing, and I don't even know how to begin to thank you."

"Don't worry about it. You've got bigger issues right now," Badger pointed out. "You'll soon be out of grub and beer, if you don't have somebody to do a supply run. These guys are here for a week at least. After that, some may stay on longer. However, the bulk of them will likely leave over the weekend."

"Wow," Timber muttered. "At this rate, we can get a lot of shit done in a week."

"That's what the hope is, and that's why we brought tools and materials and food and beer, along with the manpower," Badger stated, with a smile.

"Thanks again." Then he sat next to Tiffany.

"Timber, I sent you an email about setting up a Go-FundMe for supplies for the animals," Tiffany pointed out, "and you never did answer."

He shook his head and then confessed, "Sorry, I haven't had time to check email. Plus, I don't even know what a Go-whatever-you-called-it even is."

Badger laughed. "Just say yes and leave it with her to handle."

Timber frowned. "That means I won't like it."

"No, it's just asking the community and other animal lovers to donate toward your animal rescue," Tiffany explained. "So, you may not like it, but the community often is looking for projects to help with, especially when it comes to animals. Even in the best of cases, running a shelter is really expensive, so I would suggest you keep your head down and accept the help. It may not be much. You never know. It might be a few hundred bucks, and it might be a whole lot more. I don't even really know, but it's something I do fairly regularly for a lot of the animals that come through the clinic."

He opened his mouth to say something, and she silenced him with a wave of her hand. "And I know you're not an animal, but you are dealing with animals in need, and that's just as important."

Timber sighed. "Fine, go ahead. Do what you want with your Go-whatever-it's-called." He shook his head. "Do what you have to do."

"Good." Tiffany smiled. "That's the best way to look at it."

"Is it?" he asked.

Kat laughed and agreed. "Yes, it absolutely is."

"Fine," Timber muttered. "In that case, go for it." He looked from Kat to Badger to Tiffany and added, "One of you will have to explain it to me later."

Dwight walked past him and interjected, "I don't understand either, but, if it's bringing in money, just say yes. You know full well that plenty of money is out in that world, but getting some of it to come your way to help the animals? Now that's a different story."

And, with that, Timber and Badger headed out to get a burger, before getting back to work.

Tiffany looked over at Kat and asked, "What was that about Toby and Dwight never accepting any wages?"

"Yeah, it's an atonement thing for them," she whispered, followed by a sigh. "So, maybe finding them a place where they can call home would be a really good answer for them."

Tiffany slowly nodded. "I think you may be right."

Dwight came up just then and handed them each a plate of food. "Remind Timber to ask Andy about selling me and

Toby a small plot of land. We were talking this morning about maybe each buying a small piece of land from Andy. Somewhere out closer to the road. Then, if Timber needs the help, maybe the two of us can stay on and can help him on a permanent basis. This place is huge, and he can't run it himself."

Kat looked at him in delight and nodded. "I think that's an absolutely fabulous idea."

"It depends on Andy though, right?" Dwight asked. "He's struggling apparently."

"He is," Tiffany agreed. "But part of the reason is because he doesn't want to see the land broken up into million-dollar homes, when the ranch was meant to be his family's heritage."

"He did build something beautiful," Dwight admitted. "This will be a different vision than what he'd planned, but still an animal refuge is better than some McMansion village. Still, that's where the challenge comes in."

"Challenge, indeed," Kat murmured, as she got up and pulled out her phone.

"Don't ask him now," Tiffany suggested.

"No, I'm not," Kat replied, "but it just occurred to me that, if we're doing a third round of work, we'll need a whole lot more food. I get that there's potato salad and burgers, but we'll at least need more beer," she noted, with an eye roll. Then she proceeded to call somebody in town.

When she got off the phone, Tiffany offered, "I can do a run into town, if you need me to."

She smiled. "No worries. I've got a delivery truck coming. I don't think your truck would hold it."

"Hold just beer?" she asked in astonishment.

"No, I'm afraid we don't have near-enough groceries for

this many people, especially when staying a week and working two to three shifts each day."

"Does Timber even have a place to put that much food?" she pointed out. "It'll take an awful lot of cooler space."

"Let's go take a look."

And, with that, the two women headed inside to sort out the logistics of feeding forty-odd men for a week.

CHAPTER 20

TIMBER GOT UP each day and carried on, no matter how much his body ached. One morning he found arrows in all the tires on his truck, courtesy of Max. A couple days later, a dead duck was on the front porch of Timber's cabin. He just dealt with each and didn't react. He had to conserve his energy for the work each day.

So four days later, sore and tired but with a huge smile on his face, he sat down to review his massive work list. So many things were crossed off that it amazed him. Another dozen had been added to the bottom, and some of those were taken off as well. He sat here, amazed, hugging a cup of coffee with a pen in hand.

Dwight came over and sat down beside him, noting, "We're getting there."

"We sure are," Timber declared, with a huge smile. "It's amazing just how much you can get done with people working together."

"It sure is," Dwight agreed, "and, as you know, you must have the right kind of pull with the right kind of people."

Timber smiled and nodded. "I'm still in shock that so many guys showed up for this."

"You and I both know that these men have totally bought into your animal rescue idea and are here and are happy to help."

Timber smiled. "That's one of the biggest parts of all this. The fact that they are here with such great attitudes and a real desire to help is massive."

"So, what's on the list for today?"

With that, the two men settled into a discussion about what to focus on today and how to maximize the assistance they had available right now. As they were about midway through today's plan, Toby joined them.

He was still yawning and rubbing his shoulders.

"Did you hurt yourself?" Dwight asked him.

"No, I'm just, … you know, … getting old."

Dwight laughed. "You don't need to tell me that," he muttered. "We're both feeling our age these days."

"Yeah, we are." Toby looked over at Timber and asked, "What do you and Andy think of our idea about looking at a couple small pieces of land close by?"

"From my perspective it would be a huge boon to have you guys close by. And Andy seems to be getting old before my eyes. So he may be more inclined to sell off those parcels with each passing day. I'll remind him the next time I see him."

"You can't run a place this size on your own."

"I know it. At the moment, it's fine because we don't have any animals—well, not any rescues that aren't mine. Although that might change soon enough. I did tell Tiffany to bring one this weekend, before I knew these guys were coming. So she should definitely bring her foster dogs around because some men here might take one or two home."

Toby laughed at that. "And that's yet another excuse to bring Tiffany back over here again."

"She's been here a lot this week," Timber admitted, "so I kind of hate to even ask her to do anything more."

"And yet she seems perfectly happy to help out," Dwight pointed out.

"I know, and it's been a godsend," Toby noted. "She's done trips back and forth for all of us, trying to keep things flowing, like the beer cooler packed full and the kitchen stocked."

Dwight added, "I've been keeping up, but, man, I forgot what it was like to cook for this many. We don't really have the big pots and things we need for bulk cooking," Dwight pointed out, as he looked around at the kitchen. "The outdoor kitchen setup helps, but we still need some more kitchen equipment to make life a whole lot easier."

Toby shared, "I think Kat mentioned something about that earlier today."

"*Today*?" Timber asked Toby.

Toby winced. "It must have been yesterday. I guess I'm a little tired myself."

"The men will be up soon, so I better get started on pancakes," Dwight announced.

Timber nodded and stood. "Yeah, I can give you a hand."

Dwight pointed. "You start cooking bacon by the yard, and I will make the pancake batter."

"I can help too," Toby offered.

"No worries," Timber said, raising a hand. "We can take care of the breakfast, but, if you're up for it, can you go feed the animals?"

"I can do that." Then he tossed back the last of his coffee and headed out.

Knowing that a lot of the men would be up soon, and

some of them already likely were, Dwight and Timber started filling huge coffee canisters with fresh brewed coffee, so, when the men got here, something would be ready for them.

Timber had set up an outdoor cooking area, with a big work table and a huge gas griddle that Kat had brought out. Then she added an outdoor Blackstone grill and a two-burner gas hot plate, complete with a huge stainless steel buffet server and lid. With Timber filling the grill with bacon, Dwight cooked pancakes on the griddle. By the time he had a good forty or fifty pancakes stacked up in a warming tray, the crew started coming out and loading up, then sat on the benches scattered around the yard. There weren't enough actual seats, but people made do with everything from five-gallon buckets upended to lawn chairs that some of them thought to bring along.

Timber felt bad for not having better accommodations for the men, but thankfully the cabins that Kat brought in allowed the men to sleep in shifts, now that they were working around the clock on the barn, which meant nobody could sleep in there. Yet now it had a good roof on it, which made it inhabitable for any incoming rescues that came before the proper facilities were set up.

Timber also had a rotating team of four who were out at night, attempting to keep extra eyes on the property except that was hard with everyone working. Even with all the work, the nighttime perimeter watches, and the one-star accommodations, so far there didn't appear to be any complaints, as everybody had a really good idea of what they were getting into when they had volunteered for this gig. Still no one could keep watch 24/7.

A few of the men sat around talking, while some came

over to speak to Timber. Jaxon pointed to the guys with him. "We've got some suggestions on some of this work-load."

"I'm open to hearing it," Timber replied, still flipping bacon, while Dwight continued to mix up more pancake batter.

"We've got a group of carpenters, a group of tradesmen, and a group of framers," he began. "We've got the lumber, and the fencing is well in hand, and we've already got a team working on that."

"Two teams," Timber corrected. "They are working from each end, so they should handle that this week and have the entire place fenced and cross-fenced."

Dwight looked over at Timber and raised an eyebrow. "Wow, do you realize just how huge of an accomplishment that is?"

Timber laughed and nodded. "Damn right I do, as I'm the guy who planned to do it by myself. So thank you, guys, for taking that off my plate."

Jaxon nodded. "Seems the expansion on the old barn is done structurally, so time to get people to do the electrical and plumbing. While they're doing that on the existing barn, we wondered what you thought about us building another barn beside the old one or at that other location we dis-cussed?"

"Is it necessary right now?" Timber asked.

"I know it's not on the plan for this year, but you have the wood, and you've got the framers, so that's probably putting our skills to the best use," Jaxon suggested. "We've also got a couple guys building gates, and you'll need a ton of those."

"I know," Timber nodded, listening attentively.

"Once the fencers are done, they'll come back here to help with the paddock work. We'll have to mark those off, get the post holes dug, before the fencing begins there." Unrolling a big drawing, almost a blueprint of the property, Jaxon added, "This is where you indicated adding a large animal barn over on this side, and I think that's a great spot for it. So, we should at least get the concrete poured and the framework up before this weekend."

Timber laughed and repeated, "A concrete foundation in my new barn?"

Jaxon nodded, with a wry smile. "You're laughing, and, because the barn's for animals, we don't want concrete in the stalls, *although* … you might want some concrete between the two buildings, around the buildings, even a center driveway through the center of the two barns, so you can drive in wet conditions and unload and load a trailer."

"Right," Timber muttered, "but I think rain is in the forecast, so we may have to delay any concrete pouring for a bit. We still need to address flooring in both the barns, including an estimate for materials needed."

So that started a heavy discussion, with the general consensus suggesting something that could be accomplished this week, meaning a dirt floor with rubber mats, topped by straw. Somebody went out and checked the inventory supply. When he returned, he stated, "We're close to having enough to finish the flooring on both barns. But can you get this list of stuff brought in today? I know that might be an impossibility, but I think we can get it done."

Timber frowned. "Not sure if Badger is coming here today, but let me check on that. If not, I still think I can arrange for a delivery today." He looked at the men around him, then at the drawings for the second barn. "I do appreciate this, guys. Getting that second barn built would be absolutely massive, if we could get this far."

Jaxon added, "Not only this far, but let's get the water running too. That's a hell of an artesian spring you've got here, and you've got a good watering hole, so it shouldn't be too hard to tap into that either."

Pleased and seriously stunned to see how much work was being done, Timber also needed to take a serious look at his bank account, but that wasn't happening today. No matter what it looked like, it was game on. Today was all about making sure that the work continued as much as it could.

The next time Timber looked around, they had all headed out.

This was the difference when dealing with people who knew what they were doing versus people who had to be guided. This team of Jaxon's had figured out where they could put their skills to the best use, and they were already up and at it.

Even Toby looked over at him and said, "That would be massive."

"I know," Timber said, with a headshake. "The changes to the house we can do on our own," Timber noted, as he looked around. "But a big barn like that? ... It would be amazing."

"It's not even that you need many changes done in the main cabin," Toby pointed out. "A new roof, of course, but if these guys can help you update the plumbing, that's a big part of it. We need more electricity run through the place, but I don't even think that's as much of an issue as you're thinking it is. Not with all the skilled tradesmen you've got here."

Timber nodded. "Yeah, having all you guys to get me

totally set up in weeks, instead of years, is freaking amazing. It's all about getting the animals set up right now, before even worrying about my house," he shared. "I'm afraid we'll end up with some livestock a whole lot sooner then I'd planned."

"You've got some coming?"

Timber shrugged. "Part of the deal with Andy was that I would take over some of his horses that he's had for a long time. He's afraid that if he leaves it up to his family, they'll just end up at the meat market or the proverbial glue factory."

"That's shitty," Toby snapped.

"Andy has some idea of what we're doing here right now, so I don't know when he'll pull up with a trailer and say, *Here's your part of the deal, Timber.*"

"Right. We may need to be ready just in case, but surely he's a little more reasonable than that," Toby said, looking over at him.

"I'm not sure about that. I had some pretty hard words for Andy the last time we spoke, and who knows what kind of a shit show he's got on his hands over there."

Toby nodded. "Right, with that son and grandson of his."

"Yeah, but that son of his," Dwight noted calmly, "is a wanted man, and nothing about him is nice and decent."

Timber added, "I can't really blame Andy if he's upset over the way things are working out. It's got to be hard, awfully hard on him to see things turning out so differently than he'd always planned."

"Still, giving his horses to you is a good solution for him," Toby pointed out, "and one that he's probably okay with, if he cares for his animals."

"I think so," Timber agreed. "He was happy about that aspect."

Toby asked, "So, how many head of horses are we talking about?"

"I think six in the first run. That's one of the reasons for getting fences and cross-fences up and pastures laid out. Thankfully we already had a plan all mapped out."

"That's one good thing. You had a huge amount of the planning for this already done." Toby laughed. "At least in your mind."

"Ever since I started talking to Andy about buying this property," Timber shared, "I started working out how to make it all fit together," he murmured.

"And what will you do if you get the extra 120 acres from him?"

"I'll just keep expanding," he said. "There'll never be a problem with having too much land, and, where water is still one of the prime directives as to whether the land is usable or not, we'll see how much land has water on it and keep an eye on it. So, if we find an extra watering hole, which I happen to know there is one on that 120-acre piece, that's something that I definitely need and want."

"Right," he agreed. "So, let's just keep hoping that we get some pastures done, because otherwise where would you put that many horses right now?"

He shook his head. "I don't know, Toby. Badger offered to go talk to Andy and see what kind of mood he is in these days. He and Kat are worried about his health. And you know Brian and Max are taking a toll on Andy's well-being. Anyway hopefully Andy will hold off for a little bit before bringing over the horses."

"Would he just come here with the horses unannounced?"

He winced. "I don't know. He's a good man, but he's also strapped in many ways right now. I would hope he would give me a little bit of time to get the corrals and stuff up but"—he shrugged—"it is what it is, and I'll make it work no matter what. That was part of the conditions of sale for the land I already bought. It remains to be seen what will happen with the other deal, selling me more land and his grandson not going to jail, though I still feel like shit over that deal too."

"You would feel even shittier if this Brian kid goes off and hurts somebody."

"I would," he agreed, "but so would Andy."

"Yeah, nothing like knowing your grandson is an animal abuser. We all know that grows into deeper psychoses of serial killers and psychopaths and such."

"He says his son Max is a large part of that, but I don't know if I actually believe it or not."

"Meaning?"

"It's easy to turn around and to say everything is your dad's fault, but, in this case, it sure as hell could be. I don't know," Timber muttered. "We don't have any way to know if it's just Brian choosing to act that way, which isn't cool either. Still, he's old enough now to bear some accountability for his own choices, no matter how he got to be that way."

"That's true enough," Toby agreed.

Just then, another truck came down the road. "I don't know what this delivery is," Timber admitted, with a laugh, "but let's hope it's supplies." And sure enough, it was groceries, sent out by Badger and Kat.

Kat called him just a few minutes later and stated, "I just got a notice saying that something was delivered."

"Yeah, groceries," he confirmed, "and I don't know that

I have very much space to store any of this."

"I know," she murmured. "This is only part of the load. And your part comes with a walk-in freezer too. I checked that you can handle it in that laundry room of yours. I had the rest of the food delivered to Tiffany's clinic. She's got a big walk-in cooler, so she's storing supplies for you as well. She's coming up later tonight with a truckload."

"Oh, good God," Timber muttered, turning to look at Dwight, who just smiled and nodded. "I really hate to put her out like this."

"I hardly think she believes she's being *put out*," Kat stated, with a laugh. "And she does consider you a friend, so you might want to keep that in mind. You'll end up insulting her if you argue too much."

He sighed. "She is a friend," he agreed warmly. "She's also a hell of a vet."

"And having a vet on your side right about now is not a bad thing."

"No, it sure isn't. Fine. … I'm working on this whole *accepting help* thing, in case you hadn't noticed."

"Oh, don't worry. You'll be getting a bill for some of these groceries," she warned him, with a laugh.

"We had no idea what we were looking at for food," Timber noted. "So I appreciate your help, Kat. Of course I also never dreamed we would have a crew this size either."

"My fault. I should have considered that when we first started ordering stuff in."

"No problem. It's working somehow," he noted. "We still need the food, and we still need to feed everybody, so I appreciate Dwight's and Toby's help in the kitchen. Between the two of them on cook duty, with me helping as needed, we're handling it all so far. Still, we're keeping it easy and pitching in to give Dwight a hand, but all the cooking is basically falling on him."

"Right," Kat muttered, "that's something else that maybe I can find some help for."

At that, Dwight yelled into the phone, "I'm fine."

"Yeah, you say that," Kat replied in exasperation, "and then you get really, really tired."

"That's what life is all about," he declared, "getting really, really tired."

She laughed. "We'll see. Anyway, expect Tiffany later tonight, as you work your way through some of that meal planning. She'll be calling to see what you need from her storage."

"Will do," Dwight confirmed. "We can also send somebody in to get a load."

"Maybe, but every man you send her way is a man who could otherwise be working."

When she disconnected, Dwight looked over at Timber and admitted, "She's right. Every time we take somebody off a job to pick up groceries or something else, it's men away from work that could have been done."

"I know," Timber muttered in frustration, "but I've seen Tiffany's cooler, and it's not all that big."

"Have you seen the inside of your fridges? They're not all that big either."

He winced, then nodded. "But remember that Kat is sending us a walk-in freezer too."

Dwight nodded. "Good point."

Timber added, "I still don't know what all is coming here with our part of the delivery." as they all stood up and walked outside to help unload the truck.

Timber had to laugh at the delivery. He saw big cases of

strudels and cases of fresh veggies and fruits, cases of milk, cases of coffee. "It's almost like Kat's done this a time or two."

"I would say so. She's handled how many guys in Badger's corner?"

"Who knows?" Timber replied. "Yet I think she's finding this logistical support for us to be a little bit new."

"It is, and that's okay," Dwight said, as he turned to him. "Nobody here will get upset because the menu isn't as diverse as they'd hoped it would be."

Timber shrugged. "Agreed, but I don't want anybody to feel as if their assistance isn't needed, wanted, and appreciated, so the least I can do is to feed them well."

"I don't think anybody will have an issue with that," Dwight stated, pointing at the kitchen. "Breakfast was a complete clean-out."

Timber nodded. "Just four pancakes are left. Make that two," he corrected, as he snagged them in his hand, on his way out to work. "Dwight, did you even get any breakfast?" Timber asked him, as he stared down at the two in his fingers.

Dwight laughed. "I didn't, but I am totally fine with one or two more," he said, snagging the last ones.

"Oh, good, because otherwise I'll feel like crap."

"You're good," Dwight replied, with a smile, "you go work. I'll clean up."

"Oh shit," Timber muttered, staring at him. "There's still the clean-up."

"And I've got it," Dwight claimed comfortably. "Besides, my shoulders are pretty sore today, so if I ease up on some of the physical labor while I'm doing kitchen duty, I won't argue."

Timber walked over to him. "Are you okay though? I need to know that you're not setting yourself back through all this."

"I'm fine," Dwight said.

"Yeah, I know you say you're fine, but that doesn't always mean the same thing as you're okay."

"I'm fine. I'm okay. We are good."

Timber gazed at the older man directly, then smiled. "Okay, just so you know …"

"I'm fine," he repeated, his tone hard. "Go get some construction work done, and then I don't have to do it."

Timber laughed. "I hear you there," he muttered and walked out.

CHAPTER 21

TIFFANY OPENED UP the rear loading dock to her clinic, as the delivery truck backed up. She'd already told her staff that some supplies would be coming in and would be stored in her walk-in cooler. She had the cooler cleaned out just recently, so that was a good thing. What she couldn't have was the bodies of animals they had put down stored in there with fresh or frozen food. At the moment she was lucky in that area. Absolutely nothing in here could be crossed over in terms of products, and so it went for the rest of the week. Every day, she spoke to Timber or Dwight, getting a list of what they needed and then loading it up, sometimes needing the assistance of her own staff, as some of the boxes were fairly hefty, and then she drove it out every night.

When she arrived the next day, she pulled up to the house, and this time Timber came out to help her.

He smiled at her. "You have no idea how huge of a help this has been."

She laughed. "Not exactly what I expected to do with my week, but I'm happy to help. I'll be looking forward to my weekend though." When he looked at her in concern, she waved it off and added, "I'm fine, honest."

"I know you're fine," he said, shaking his head. "Of course you'll say you're fine."

She laughed. "And I am. It's just that coming out here

every night wasn't among my plans. I will say I'm grateful you don't live farther away."

"Right," he muttered, with a sigh. "Sometimes I think I'm too far out, and then, other times, it seems as if I'm way too close."

She laughed. "It's all good. We just need to get through some of this right now." When she looked around, she gasped. "What the heck?"

He nodded and smiled. "Right, when you think about what's been done in just a matter a days, it's pretty amazing."

She whistled. "Holy cow, this is massive." She was absolutely stunned at the amount of work that had been accomplished.

He nodded. "And remember that a lot of the work you can't even see from here." When she frowned at him, he added, "We've got the entire sixty acres fenced."

"What? How in the hell—"

"Two teams have been working on just that all week, and that's been a job I can't even contemplate what my man-hours working alone would have been. Come look at this," he suggested, as he brought her inside and showed her the drawing, revealing everything they'd managed to get done. She just stared in shock.

He added, "Now these men are not just any men but men quite capable and quite comfortable seeing what needs to be done, forming teams, and getting at it. I think that's been one of the biggest parts I wasn't really expecting.

"They also," he began, as he nudged her out the front door again and pointed off in one direction, "have this going. It's not finished, … but we have a second big barn going up over there for more animals," he shared, with a sense of joy and contentment in his tone.

"The old barn has had all its timber reframed, a new roof, the water system repaired and hooked up," he shared, "which is huge. There's always been water, but the pipes had rusted out, and now they have all been replaced. The plumbers have been in the main house as well, since they were here," he noted, with a laugh, "so the plumbing has been updated."

"Already?"

"In the process of being updated," he clarified. "I'm not sure that it will all get completed right now, but it's definitely way better than it was."

She just stared at him. "This is like …"

"I know. Believe me that I know. Which is also why any foodstuffs, anything that could be brought in to make these guys happier and their jobs easier, I'm more than happy to provide. I know I have a huge bill with Badger to take care of, but I'm more than happy to pay that because they're the ones who have been organizing all this food. They also organized all the people."

"All this in just one week?" she asked.

"Absolutely, and for just one week," he confirmed. "We will reassess on Sunday. It's shocking how much these guys have done."

She stared at the new barn and shook her head, speechless. "This is one of the most incredible gifts anybody could have ever given you."

He looked at her, and she saw the almost helpless awareness, when realizing that somebody had done something so incredibly good for him that he just didn't even know what to say.

She smiled. "And you deserve every bit of it." Startled he looked at her in shock, and she nodded. "I can see it. You're still thinking that you need to do something to pay all these people back or to somehow come up with wages for them or something."

"They're doing it for nothing," he stated. "They all took time out of their lives to come and help."

"And they did that because they wanted to," she pointed out.

"I know that, and I hear you. I hear Badger's and Kat's comments on that as well, but it's such an incredible thing for people to do, and for so many to do."

"And yet what did you do when you worked with Badger?"

He frowned. "That's different." Her lips twitched as he glared at her, and then his shoulders sagged, and he nodded. "Yeah, we did something like this, but I've never been on the receiving end of it."

"And now you are, and I think it's unbelievably awesome. Can we go see the barns?"

"Sure."

They went to the older barn first, and, as she walked in, she noted that the big support beams had been fixed, new hinges were on stall doors, new framing was up, more water troughs with water were already installed, plus a big concrete walkway had been added through the center, complete with drainage. She just stared at it all. "This is unbelievable."

As she looked up, she saw a big hay storage area at one end of the loft. At the far end on the ground floor was a big tack room and also grain storage and other needed supplies. "You'll need some equipment for moving this around."

"I know, and that's in the budget, or at least it was," he admitted, with half a laugh. "That might take a little longer to pull together, considering what this is likely to cost when all the bills come in," he noted, with a shrug.

She turned to look at the second construction project close by, and she asked, "Did you say a second barn?"

"Well, I call it a barn, but I suppose it's also an intake room, treatment center …"

Her eyes lit up. "May I see?" she asked eagerly.

"It's still in the very basics of being put together."

"Of course," she said, but she was already eagerly walking toward it.

Timber laughed. "So, what you're really saying is this is the building you care about."

She stopped and looked at him intently. "Not so much." She shrugged, feeling self-conscious.

He just laughed, slung an arm around her shoulders, and said, "Come on. Let's go have a look."

Smiling as they walked up to the group of men who were working, one of them came over and greeted her. "Hey, Doc."

She smiled. "Hey, I heard you guys were helping Timber get a second big building up, and, I must say, it's already looking fabulous."

"I guess it's a good thing you're here because we had some issues with where to put some of the electrical, since our electrician does not like some of these ideas."

"And what kind of problem is there?" she asked. "Because, for any kind of an examination room, treatment center, and surgery, power is critical."

"Yeah, that's what we were telling him, but he didn't quite get the whole picture."

"I got the picture, just not right off the bat, that's all." Somebody off to the side came over, hitching up his tool belt as he came across, a big grin on his face. "Hey, Doc."

"Hey," she replied, wondering how everybody knew who she was or that she was a vet at least. She glanced over at Timber, but he was talking to some of the other men.

"So, I know that this is still kind of rough," the electrician began, "and we'll certainly get in as much as we can and get it done as fast as we can, but it's at this stage that we really want to get in as much of the groundwork as we can."

"Right." So, she found herself dragged into a discussion about individual exam rooms, how to set it up, from moving animals from one room to the other, and she answered a lot of their questions on the fly because she didn't know what kind of animals they would be looking at. And the problem was, it could be any and all species. When she finally stepped back out again, she blew strands of hair off her face.

Timber walked over to join her. "Thanks for helping out George, the electrician."

"Wow," she muttered, "I wasn't expecting all that."

"Yeah, sorry. Nobody has too many answers yet. We're trying to do the best we can, maximizing the opportunity to utilize the skilled tradesmen we have here, making fast and workable decisions about some of these things."

"Oh, I hear you, and it's fabulous. You do need a drainage system, depending on what you'll be doing here at this level. Then there are security systems, cameras, heat, water in every room, that kind of thing."

He nodded. "We've got the water in and set up for four treatment rooms." She stared at him in surprise. "I wasn't sure if we needed to hold the animals here," he explained. "I've thought about this a lot over the years, but thinking about things a lot doesn't necessarily mean I have a really good idea of how it should work in reality." He shrugged. "My brother was a veterinarian and—"

"Will he come join you?"

He looked over at her. "He passed away a few years ago."

"I'm sorry," she muttered.

He smiled and nodded. "Thanks. So am I. It's been a huge loss in my life, but this was also something that we dreamed up together, so I have a lot of his notes as to what could work and also pros and cons of different things. I'm just kind of going off that."

"And that must be a fabulous help."

"That's what I thought," he agreed, with a smile.

"Do you have any other family?"

He looked over at her and shook his head. "No. I think that's one of the reasons I'm so adamant about setting up this place and having a home."

"At some point I'm sure you'll want a family of your own."

He smiled at her. "I don't want to take that off the table at this time, but it's not as if I've really considered it, not ever having had a serious relationship before."

"I'm not sure you'll have time for it either now," she noted, as she stared around at the chaos going on around her. "This is an absolutely wondrous thing happening here."

"It is, and I am incredibly grateful. … I look around and still can't quite believe how much we've accomplished."

"It's amazing," she muttered, as she watched the men work.

"It'll be much calmer next week," Timber shared.

"How so?"

"A lot of the men will be leaving, but some—and I don't know exactly how many—will be coming back on Monday and staying for another week," he explained. "So that'll be a huge help too."

"I can't even imagine, and the fact that these men are out here doing this for you, for the animals …" She felt the tears choking her up.

He slung an arm around her shoulders. "Hey, you're not allowed to cry."

"Why not?" she asked. "If you won't let yourself cry about it, I have to."

He looked at her and then smiled. "My mom used to say something like that every once in a while."

She nodded. "My mom did too. She used to say that we were all such tough guys that if we wouldn't open up our hearts enough to be the people we needed to be, then she would have to do the crying for us. She was adamant that, somewhere along the line, there must be that emotional release. I tried to get her to understand that her releasing it didn't make it any easier on us, and she used to laugh and say, *Somebody has to, and apparently I am it.*" Tiffany smiled at the memory.

"And your mom now?"

"She died of breast cancer a few years back," she replied. "About three years ago, I guess. It was kind of at that point where I was deciding, do I buy the business or do I not? Do I go home, or do I accept I have nothing to go home to?"

"No family left?"

"No. … I guess I'm kind of like you in that way. It's such a weird thing when you realize you are now an orphan and all alone in this world."

"I hadn't considered it from that point of view," he noted.

"Yet it is the point of view of truth," she declared. "Just … such a weird understanding when you get there, that it's you against the world." She looked down at her watch and winced. "Oh, gosh. I've already stayed way longer than I expected to tonight."

He nodded. "You look a little tired."

"Yeah, I had some difficult surgeries today. I'm hopeful on the one but the other one? We had to put the other one down, and it's never easy to do that."

"Right, and I think that's always the hardest part, particularly if it's one you've been working on for a long time."

"Exactly, and I've been keeping this one alive for a long time," she said.

"I was hoping maybe you would bring some dogs out if you had some looking for homes," Timber mentioned. "Maybe some of these guys might take a liking and adopt some."

"I was wondering about that, and we did discuss it. I just didn't want to add to the chaos, and God knows there's a few—I say *a few* with facetiousness in mind."

He laughed, then nodded in agreement. "There is no such thing as a few rescues, but if you have a couple good candidates, you are welcome to bring them out."

"I do have a couple," she stated, "and maybe more than a couple that could come out. I could always bring a truckload tomorrow and see. It's Saturday, and I don't have anybody staying in the clinic needing care, so I could come out a little earlier."

"And you'll just wither away and get completely worn out because you'll go right back and do surgeries on Sunday."

"Not on Sunday," she stated. "I'm free and clear on Sunday."

At that same time, George, the electrician she had been speaking to earlier, walked over and added, "If you're coming back here tomorrow, I could use a hand refining some of the details as I get into it."

She immediately nodded. "Done, I was thinking of coming back tomorrow anyway. I might even bring out a few dogs that need to be adopted."

He rolled his eyes. "Don't tell my wife you're doing that. She feels the need to pick up every damn stray she comes across."

"And that's because the strays need women like her," Tiffany pointed out, with a smile.

"I know, but, if I tell her more animals need adopting, she'll make a trip out here herself," he grumbled.

She laughed. "So, does that mean you don't want to see them?"

"We're kind of partial to pugs," he admitted, "but I'm as much of a sucker as she is. So, I'm listening to you with both trepidation and hope because, well, we love animals too." With that, he shook his head, muttered something about his wife, and left again.

"So, I guess I am coming out tomorrow, but where would I put the animals though?" she asked, as she looked around. "We ought to figure that out before I haul them here."

"We have a temporary enclosure over here, and a couple guys brought their dogs," Timber added. "So maybe we can work something out."

She walked over, took a look, and nodded. "Yeah, these are all healthy animals, so that would work."

CHAPTER 22

WHEN TIFFANY PULLED up to Timber's place the next morning, feeling a little bit better but still tired, with six dogs in tow, she got up to the house to find Toby standing there, shaking his head.

He heard the dogs yipping in the back of her truck and teased, "Just a few, *huh?*"

"Well, … yeah, just a few." She scrunched up her nose. "If nothing else it will be good for the men's morale," she noted. "I don't expect to get all these adopted but thought it would be nice to at least give these dogs a chance to get out of their pens and the small runs and to get some real exercise and socialization."

"You're right about that." Toby walked over and took a look. "Oh my." And there, right in front of him, … was a basset hound.

She laughed. "His name is Toby too."

He looked over at her and shook his head. "I've always had bassets."

"Toby, … meet Toby," she announced.

Little Toby, who was still lying down in his crate, looked over at Big Toby, and an immediate interaction began between them. Tiffany watched it happen. She started to smile. "*Uh-oh*, you do know that this is a case of love at first sight, don't you?"

But Big Toby wasn't even listening to her, as he was already opening the crate and helping Little Toby out.

"He's young," she shared.

"How young?"

"Probably two and a half."

"How did he come to be in your care?"

She frowned. "We're probably better off not to go into too many discussions about that." When he turned to her with a glare on his face, she nodded. "Sometimes it's better to just start them fresh with a clean history."

"That bad, *huh*?"

"Yeah," she agreed, "that bad, but I've had him for a couple months now, and he's doing a lot better. He has learned to trust a little, as you can see. Still, he's certainly got a way to go."

"Of course," Toby replied. "The minute there's been any kind of betrayal at that level …"

"Particularly by the owner," she interjected, "so trust has to be earned again."

But it didn't look like it would take much trust because Toby, the dog, had already gotten out of his crate. Instead of jumping to the ground, he put his paws up on Toby, the human, and started licking his face.

At that, Toby just picked him up and hung on to him, taking him a few steps away to have a little private time with the dog.

She watched them bonding faster than she'd ever witnessed before. When she turned back around, Timber stood there, his hands on his hips, staring at Toby with the dog.

"Wow," Timber muttered.

"Yeah, wow is right," she murmured. "It's also kind of funny because the dog's name is Toby too."

He grinned. "Looks to be a match made in heaven."

"I would think so."

With Timber's help, she unloaded the five other dogs, then asked, "Have you had any trouble at all this week? No extra visitors?"

"Max made his presence known," he admitted. "Yes, everybody is aware of what the potential issues could be, but I suspect, with this many people around, Max won't cause any major trouble—at least until they're gone."

She nodded. "That would make sense to me." He looked back over at what she already thought of as the clinic building. He smiled and pointed. "You want to take a look at the most recent progress?"

"Yeah, I sure do," she stated.

As she walked over, she passed George the electrician. He was muttering to himself, as he unwound what appeared to be miles of electrical wire. She asked, "Do you need a hand?"

"Yes," he snapped, "it's definitely not a one-person job."

"I'm a good helper, if you want one."

"Of course I want one," he grumbled, now frowning over at her, just in time to spot the pug she carried in her arms. He cried out, "That's dirty pool, Doc, and definitely not allowed." But George was already up off the ground and reaching for the pug in her arms. She just laughed as she held out the baby. "I wasn't sure if I should bring him or not because I figured you would say I set you up."

"You *did* set me up," he declared, but his hands were eagerly cuddling the dog in his arms.

"It's a girl," she noted. "We call her Sheila. She's fixed, and she's young, we figure six, maybe seven months. I've had her for about six weeks," she explained.

"And how did you come to get her?"

"Let's just say the owners couldn't keep her in a quality way," she replied. When he frowned and faced her, she nodded. "Yeah, since no rescue or shelter is here yet, I tend to wind up collecting a few at my clinic."

"Right," George muttered. "This little girl, Sheila, is absolutely perfect." Laughing, he grinned and pulled out his phone and started taking selfies of him with Sheila, as he danced around with her.

Behind her, Timber laughed. "What is it about animals that turn otherwise rough-and-tumble grown men into *this*?" he asked, grinning at the electrician.

"It's called love," she declared. "That's all, just love."

He smiled and nodded. "That's a heck of a good answer because I feel as if you have completely halted the work for the day."

"Oh no, we can't have that." As she turned around, George pulled a jacket out from somewhere and put it around Sheila, placing her into a little designated cuddle corner.

"Now, you just stay right there and have a nap," he ordered the little dog. "We'll finish this up, look at this clip, and then we'll take you for a little wee somewhere. Then we'll come back and get after the other part of this job." George just kept up a continuous ramble, joy and love in his tone, while Timber and Tiffany looked on.

She turned to Timber. "So, is it a good thing I came?"

"It seems to be a *great* thing that you came," he noted, staring at the electrician. "I wouldn't have seen this one coming at all."

"I know," she murmured. "That's two now. Toby and Sheila have found good homes," she stated, with a smile. "I hope the decision is to keep them longer term than just today."

At that, the electrician turned, shot her a hard look, and declared, "Oh no, this one is mine. You can go now. If you've got other dogs to deliver, that's fine, but nobody gets anything to do with this little one but me." He reached down and chucked his finger under her chin, and her tail started wagging like mad.

Timber sighed happily. "You're right, Tiffany. That appears to be two adopted."

"At least two," she added, laughing. "Nobody even knows about the other ones yet."

But, as soon as people found out dogs were here, looking for forever homes, some of the men came from all corners of Timber's property to see the new arrivals. Nobody else went as crazy as the first two men had, but Tiffany still saw lots of interest in the others.

Joe came closer and asked her, "Are they available for adopting?"

She nodded. "They certainly are. They are animals that I have at the clinic, or that I take home to help socialize and to get out of the pens while they heal from surgery, or whatever trauma they had been through," she shared. "So, these are ready for adoption, but I also figured some socializing would do them some good."

"And if you can adopt them out?" he asked, with a wry look in her direction.

"And if I can adopt them out, it's good for everybody," she replied, as she pointed out Toby, who was still cuddling his dog.

Joe shook his head. "It's not that I don't want an animal at all, but I'm just not set up for it."

"That's fine," she said, giving him a smile. "It doesn't matter in the least, but, while you're here, and you want a dose of puppy love, soak it up because there really is nothing quite like it for both the human and the canine."

He eyed her and nodded. "I've always been kind of a cat person myself."

She laughed. "I've got a bunch of those too. I just didn't think I should bring everybody today."

"You've got cats?" At her nod, Joe hesitated. Then asked, "You got any of those huge Maine coon things?"

She laughed. "I've got something the size of a Maine coon, but his true heritage is up to his daddy's mysterious origins," she added. "Very typical of all cats, of course."

"Yes, of course," he muttered. "It's not gray, is it?"

She smirked. "You've got a preference for grays?"

"I had one growing up," he shared. "I kept talking about, you know, … one day, … but somehow one day never happened."

"No, one day doesn't happen on its own," she stated. "You have to make it happen." And, with that, she pulled out a picture of the baby kitten she had at home. "He's just under six months, as far as I can tell, and, in case you can't gauge the size of him alone in this photo, let me show you another." She pulled out another picture of two cats together, one a standard-size full-grown cat and the other a kitten. She laughed when she saw it again. "The cat beside him is fully grown, and he's only six months old and already towers over her."

Joe grinned. "Yeah, that looks very familiar." And there was a little break in his voice.

"If you're interested in him, or you're interested in seeing him," she added, "I'm just in town. I can also bring him with me next time, but a cat out here might be a whole different story." She looked around at the dogs that were now being thoroughly adored by everybody coming by.

Joe nodded. "I'll think about it." Then he turned and quickly escaped.

She laughed to herself at that.

Timber came over to her and asked, "What's so funny?"

"Joe's a cat person, so I showed him a picture of a Maine coon mixed kitten that I've got back at the office," she shared, with a smile. "I think he's more than a little smitten."

Timber's lips twitched, and he nodded. "And I can see how that might be a problem."

"It might be a problem for him, but it's not something I would pressure anybody into because, if you're not ready for an animal, it is just not the right time," she noted.

At that, George, the electrician, waved her over and called out, "Hey you, we've got some discussions that need to happen."

"You know I can't make all these decisions," she replied. "Some of this stuff needs to wait."

"No time to wait. I'm here now," George stated. "I can put in a rough sketch for use here, and we can fine-tune it later," he suggested, "but some of this stuff needs to be done now, if we can."

She sighed. "Okay, fine, I hear you. I just don't think you're listening to me."

"I'm not," he admitted, as he cuddled little Sheila in his arms.

Tiffany snorted. "How will you work with this little gal in your arms?"

"But I won't be holding her," George added. "That's why I need you. *You* hold her."

"Sheila can walk, you know?"

"Doesn't matter. This gal needs some love and attention. You brought her, so that means you're it." He quickly passed Sheila into Tiffany's arms and proceeded to get to work, but every now and then he would stop to confirm Sheila was doing okay, then smile and keep on going.

Tiffany sighed. "You're really addicted to this puppy, aren't you?"

"I showed the wife, and she's wondering if you have a second one."

"A second what?"

"A second puppy so Sheila won't be lonely."

Tiffany smirked. "I did bring a few others over."

"I know, and I haven't gotten over there to take a look, so the wife's a little mad at me right now."

"She doesn't need to be mad. I do have other animals back at the center, as well."

"Yeah, what kind?"

She shrugged. "You know, the four-legged kind."

He rolled his eyes at that. "We might need to get a puppy for Sheila because we don't want Sheila to be lonely."

"No, of course not," Tiffany deadpanned, her lips twitching. "We can't have that."

He looked at her in outrage. "You don't get to laugh at me. Our pets are family."

"And that's how they should be," she declared. "They absolutely should be family." And then she went off on a discussion as to what animals she had available, and that was just the start of her day.

Soon she was fielding questions on electricity for a treatment center, questions from several of the men on the six dogs that she brought with her this time—well, make that four since two were claimed immediately. By the end of the day, the other four had been claimed as well.

George, the electrician, was adamant that she bring a couple more on Saturday. Otherwise he would swing by the clinic early on Sunday, before he headed home to the family—only if somebody was at the clinic on Sundays. Tiffany agreed to show him a few pictures, so he could see the animals she had. They then made arrangements for the weekend, then got back to work on Timber's clinic, going through a list of things this building needed in terms of the wiring.

CHAPTER 23

B Y THE TIME Tiffany arrived at the Haven—very early Sunday morning, as agreed—George was here, his vehicle already running, with Sheila sitting in the front seat. George came right over and took one look at King, who was a pug crossed with something else, and smiled.

"I don't know King's parentage," she admitted, "so we could have all kinds of bits and pieces in there. Yet he has the definite look of a pug."

George had the most incredible light in his eyes, as King wagged his curly tail and stared at George. "Yeah, he'll be just fine." He picked him up and cuddled him a moment, and instead of barking or doing anything defensive, King just tucked his head under George's chin and, with a heartfelt sigh, visibly relaxed in his arms.

The electrician looked over at her and muttered, "Wow, okay. Driving with King *and* Sheila in my arms will be a challenge, considering I'll be on the road for a while." He cleared his throat and added, "I'm coming back in a couple days, so be prepared for more questions on the medical rooms inside the clinic building." And, with that, he drove off with both King and Sheila.

Joe came over and pointed at George's truck, heading out toward town. "I see you brought another animal."

"Yeah, I did, and I also brought that cat for you to meet."

He looked at her, then hurried around to the back of her truck. There, under the canopy, not even in a cage, Tiffany had the Maine coon kitten sprawled out. He had a leash on, something she'd been working with him on for a while now.

"A leash," he said in delight.

"With a big cat like this, when we want him to have outside exercise, I figured a leash wouldn't be a bad thing to get him used to."

Joe just stared at the cat. "I'm heading home to pick up some more clothing and stuff. I'll be back but not before next weekend."

She just nodded, not sure what she was supposed to make of that.

Then he groaned. "Do you think you can hang on to him until I get back, until I'm ready to leave again? Because then I'll be staying home to go back to school pretty soon. So I won't be traveling. I just don't want this guy to be alone the first few days I get him home."

"That's a very good point," she said, "and absolutely he can stay with me for a while longer."

He sighed happily. "Thank you." Then, in a surprising move, Joe crawled into the back of her truck and stretched out beside the cat, getting to know him.

With a small headshake she left him to it. She turned toward the main house, and Timber stood nearby on the gravel driveway, watching her.

"I see George left with another dog in his vehicle."

"Yes, he took King with him," she said, with a smile. "I didn't really expect that, but I'm grateful."

"And so are those animals," he noted.

"Absolutely," she murmured. "The thing is, all of this *is* for the animals, so ..." She just smiled and didn't say anything more. "It is really nice to see it happening," she murmured.

"Yeah, it is." He faced her, then asked, "Coffee?"

"Yes, please. I would love some."

"And did I see Joe crawl into the back of your truck?"

She smiled and nodded. "You did. He's interested in the Maine coon mix that I have, but he's leaving today and will apparently be back in a few days, staying for another week."

He looked at her and then nodded. "Good to know. I haven't really heard who's coming and who's going yet. It's been a little bit difficult to keep track of everybody. I don't want to push anybody, yet I really want to push all of them."

She burst out laughing. "I just can't believe how much has been done."

He nodded. "And some of the men don't want to leave a job unfinished, so they're coming back. The guys who did the fencing have been helping the other guys making all the gates and the stiles, which aren't quite finished, so they're staying for another day," he shared, "until it's done. They told me that they can't leave it any other way because that is just the nature of the beast."

"Of course." She chuckled. "And what about the deer? Can they come and go freely with all the fences and the gates?"

He nodded. "They'll jump them, and the stiles will allow them to climb, if they get smart enough."

She laughed. "I don't know if that's a good thing or a bad thing. Will you wind up with horses that can climb them too?"

"Who knows? Speaking of which, apparently Andy is coming by today."

"Is that a good thing?"

"I hope so," he muttered. "We left things a little rough last time, and I don't particularly like that."

"Of course not."

Big Toby came over just then with Little Toby trotting at his heels. Tiffany bent down to say hi to the little dog, and he gave her a greeting and then immediately took off after Toby.

"That's lovely to see," she noted, with a big smile, "happy dogs."

"Yeah, are you kidding? This place will be overrun with dogs soon."

"Dogs and horses," she added. "What about cats? I have a few that need homes too."

He nodded. "Cats too."

After they had coffee, she was prepared to head back into town, mostly because she had laundry and housework to take care of. Plus, she didn't want to impact Timber's ability to get work done. Just then she heard another vehicle coming in and stepped outside.

It was Andy. He stepped out at the front of the house, took a look around, and whistled.

She walked over to him with a smile on her face and greeted him, "Hey."

"Hey yourself," he replied, smiling at her. "You a part of this chaos too?"

"To a certain extent, where I can be of help."

He nodded. "Anything to do with animals, isn't it?" he teased.

She was happy to see that he appeared to be in a good mood and that everything was potentially good between him and Timber. When Timber came out, the two men shook hands, and it was almost as if all the animosity was long gone.

Andy shared, "I know we talked about six horses the last time, but I brought eight because a little birdie told me that you had room now."

"Yeah, I sure do."

Andy looked over at Tiffany. "You want to give us a hand?"

"Sure thing," she replied.

And, once he backed up the trailer to the first paddock, they opened the doors and moved all eight horses out to the holding pen, with the help of Toby and Dwight, who came to join them. She worked through them all, taking off halters and checking them over, one by one, with Timber keeping notes, as they identified any deficiencies in each of them and worked up a list of things to focus on.

Timber and Toby and Dwight set about checking the water troughs and the fencing, just to be sure, plus letting the horses get acclimated to their new place and to these new people. Meanwhile Tiffany and Andy headed back to his truck.

"They should be in fairly good shape," Andy noted. "Though honestly, we just haven't had the time and energy to do much with them. I don't have very much knowledge of them either. Horses were more my wife's thing, and these were all hers," he shared.

"And that's fine and dandy when you've got your wife there to help you," Tiffany pointed out, "but—"

He nodded. "But time happens, and you're just not in the same shape and condition to keep riding anymore. It's been a couple rough years."

"And the cancer?" she asked, looking at him closely.

He hesitated, then nodded. "It's back."

She felt the pain coming off him in waves, as she muttered, "I'm so sorry, Andy."

"I am too," he said. Then he sighed. "And yet I'm really not too bothered because ..."

"Because you get to see your wife soon."

With tears in his eyes, he nodded. "That's exactly it, and though I know that my son"—he stopped and then bravely forged on—"he would say that was a cop-out, but I'll be pretty happy to see her again."

"Of course you will," Tiffany agreed, "and everybody processes death in their own way. You certainly get to do what's right for you."

"I would just as soon not process it at all," he admitted. "I just want her back again." She smiled and nodded at him. "Hey, at least I'm being honest."

"You are, indeed," she said, "and I get it. I absolutely get it."

"It's a good thing you do because a lot of people don't."

"Doesn't matter about a lot of people," she murmured. "It's all about doing what's right for you."

He sighed. "I really, really didn't want to see some massive subdivision go up on this land, so this is kind of a good option."

"I know a couple men here are hoping that maybe you would sell them just enough to put a house on. Maybe somewhere closer to the road because they want to stay and help Timber here, since he can't run something this big on his own."

"No, he can't. I wondered if he had thought about that because it's pretty easy to have that expectation and then have it get too big on you," Andy shared. "That's kind of what happened to me when I first started farming, then ranching, then family, and suddenly ... it just skyrockets.

You need more help in order to get the bills paid. You need more land to put more into seed and cattle and …" He shook his head. "It leads to even more. At some point you turn around and realize that you've created something so big that it's no longer yours anymore. … It can be hard."

She gave him a gentle hug. "It can be hard, but it can also be hard to hand off a big responsibility to somebody else. It can be hard to see another stage in life come and go—but that doesn't mean any of it is wrong. It just means that it's all there and happening, and that's good too."

He gave her a bright smile. "Maybe I just needed to hear somebody say it was okay to let go."

"It's definitely okay to let go," she declared.

Then Timber and Toby joined them, Dwight still with the newly arrived horses for now.

Timber announced, "Andy, we've got the horses unloaded. Do you want to stay and have a cup of coffee? Or see where we've got them settled and say goodbye to any of them?"

Andy laughed. "No, they're probably more than happy to say goodbye to me. I haven't had the time or the energy for them these last few months," he admitted, sadness in his gaze. "So, it's all good. It's kind of like saying goodbye to my wife all over again when I say goodbye to these guys."

"No," Tiffany countered, "not now."

He looked over at her, his eyes bright with understanding, and he nodded. "You're right." He turned to Timber and said, "I also brought the paperwork for the acres you wanted."

Timber's eyebrows shot up, and he grinned. "That's perfect. So, do you want to go inside and talk?"

He shrugged. "I kind of figured if I gave you a good

price, you might take all of it," he said hopefully. "Would you take it all?"

"If I can afford it, I sure will," Timber declared.

Andy nodded. "I know that, very quickly, this refuge could grow into something that might require a whole lot more land. If not, at least if you keep it all intact, you could do something with it yourself."

"How do you feel about letting a couple of the men here buy a piece of land, … maybe a little bit closer to the highway?"

"I've got another plot on the other side," Andy replied, "and I wasn't quite sure what to do with it. It's not very big, probably be enough for, … I don't know, maybe eight single homes."

Toby immediately perked up. "I would really like one," he stated, turning to face Andy.

At that, Andy nodded, then looked over at Timber. "I don't know what to charge for them. They're just bare land. Nothing is there. I don't even know if there's water."

"Water would be an issue," Timber noted, giving Toby a sideways glance. Then he shrugged and added, "I'm pretty sure we could dig wells."

"You can certainly dig wells," Andy agreed. "I just don't know how deep you'll have to go."

Toby smiled and interjected, "That's okay with me. I'm good with that." Seeing Dwight heading toward them, Toby asked him, "Dwight, how do you feel about a piece of land down the road a way?"

"How much land?"

"Andy's got a piece on the other side that's about eight houses' worth."

"It was supposed to be split off," Andy explained, "so it's

already been delineated into housing sections. I just wasn't sure what to do with it."

Dwight replied, "Depending on how you feel about it, me and Toby want to buy two of them."

"And if you wanted to hang on to some of them a little bit longer," Timber suggested, "we could potentially find a few other men who might very well want to have one section to live on."

Andy studied Timber, then asked, "Do any of them have families?"

Toby looked over at him and replied, "Not me, not anymore. That's the thing. Some of us just want a place to call home."

"I get that too," Andy murmured. "I'm happy to sell you a lot if that's what you want."

"It's absolutely what I want," Toby declared, and he looked at Dwight. "You too?"

"Yes, please. … How much are you looking to charge?"

Andy pondered it for a moment. "Are you guys all military?"

"We're all ex-military, either retired or out with medical injuries, one or the other. Some both, and we are all associated with Kat and Badger, one way or another. I swear to God, Kat is a full-time prosthetics designer just for us," Toby said, with a laugh.

"All of you?" Andy asked, frowning.

"All of us. Everybody who came here this week to help out is a part of Badger's group in some way," Toby explained. "Some with more skills than others, some with more labor-intensive muscle, and some with experience in the trades." Toby smiled, as he shook his head. "It's been pretty amazing. So, yeah."

"Good God," Andy muttered, as he pondered that. "Let me think about what kind of price to charge, and I'll get back to you. I didn't come prepared for that."

"And that's okay too," Toby said. "We'll get this place set up for the refuge, and, when we get that done, we'll look at what we need to do to get the land livable and to put a house on it for each of us who want a section." And, with that, Toby nodded to Timber.

Andy stayed a few minutes longer, but then he left as well, saying he would be in touch to discuss the other property set aside for homes.

She looked over at Timber, clutching the paperwork. "You need to look at that paperwork." She saw the worry in his expression as he looked down at it.

"I know. Yet I hesitate. It's like having something you really want right here, but it might not be possible."

"Or it might be just fine," Toby added. "You go on and take a look at it and see if you need to make some changes. I gather the prices are negotiable."

"We had talked price before everything turned upside down with all the trouble with Max and Brian. And now Andy's offered more property than the 120 acres we were discussing before—and that's not even talking about the eight individual housing sections—so I don't really know if I'm able to swing this or not."

Tiffany nudged him. "You won't know until you look."

With a deep breath he flipped open the paperwork, studied it carefully for a moment, then looked up with a big smile on his face. "Yeah, this is doable."

The men just grinned at each other and nodded. "Now we're talking," Toby exclaimed.

CHAPTER 24

ARLY THE NEXT morning Timber had already contacted Andy, saying they had a tentative agreement. Timber had also contacted his lawyer to get things started. Timber wanted it processed as quickly as possible, particularly considering the fact that Andy's son was likely still around. Although Andy hadn't mentioned Max—or his grandson Brian for that matter—Timber still figured that the sooner he could get this sale locked in, the better.

That good news was spoiled when Timber took a post-breakfast walk around the new construction and found a dead rabbit nailed to the main door of Haven's new clinic building. With a sigh, Timber took care of the poor animal. "Damn you, Max." He would tell the guys of yet another Max visit to vandalize and terrorize, just to keep them all alert. Then Timber brushed all thought of Max from his mind. He chose to fix his thoughts on all the good things happening here.

And the fact that a couple men from the crew wanted to stay close and to help out long-term was also a boon, but Timber certainly didn't want to depend on them permanently, in case they needed to move on with their life. Still, the idea that they would stay and would live out their lives in this peaceful place was an absolutely lovely thought. As he stood here for a long moment, he smiled as he realized just how much land he would have here, and very soon.

On his way back from a supply run in town, he stopped in at the vet clinic. Although Tiffany was with a client, he waited for her to be free.

When she came out after saying goodbye to the one patient, she turned to him and asked, "Hey, how was it?"

"It's great," he said. "I just finished with the lawyers, and they're working on sealing the deal right now."

She smiled. "That's wonderful news."

"I know," he declared, not able to stop smiling. "It's huge. Anyway, I just"—he shrugged—"I wanted to invite you out to the center for dinner one night this week."

"Have you not noticed that I've been out there for dinner every night this past week?" she asked in a teasing note.

He winced. "You probably have, but I thought maybe this time there would be a whole lot less people around."

"Well, that depends. How many people do you still have?"

"I don't know," he admitted with a frown, as he thought about it for a second. "So, maybe when I say, *out for dinner*, it could still end up being a bunch of people eating with us at my home," he clarified.

"And that's fine too," she replied, now laughing. "I think a celebration dinner is definitely in order."

"I would like to think so," he said, "but I'm still waiting until the paperwork is processed though."

"Of course," she noted. "Do you think that Brian or Max even know about it?"

"I don't know," Timber stated. "I wanted to ask Andy about that, but there's always a chance I could be opening a can of worms that could get pretty ugly."

"And yet the law is on your side," she added.

"You also know that won't make a damn bit of differ-ence to somebody like Max Killerman."

Within seconds, after saying their goodbyes, Timber was back in his vehicle. After making one more stop to pick up some materials, he was soon back home again, happy with this turn of events.

He spent the rest of the day working at the center, haul-ing some materials to the guys as needed, he'd just started up the engine to hit the road again when Andy called. As soon as he picked up, Timber heard a wavering tone in his voice that made him pause. "Are you all right?"

He gave a shaky reply, "Yes, … but my son—"

"I know. He's gone off the rails, but that's not your fault."

"Listen," Andy muttered, the pain evident in his tone. "Max has Tiffany, and he's holding her captive."

"What?" Timber asked. brought his truck to a halt, the tires screeching.

"He just called me."

"What did he say exactly?" Timber asked, alarm in his tone.

"Max told me that he's got her somewhere on the prop-erty. She's safe at the moment, but … he *wants to have some fun with her*. Oh my God, he's so sick."

"He is sick, but why does he have her? She didn't do anything to him."

"No, but …" Andy gulped. "But you care for her and getting to you is what matters to him."

"I get that, but he's not up against one young woman when it comes to me," Timber snapped. "Andy, you need to know this won't end well for anybody."

"I understand," he replied, his voice shaky. "And I hate

it. I absolutely hate that this is what it's come to, but something's wrong with him, something is broken, something is sick. He's absolutely loving the prospect of inflicting pain. He's always been like that though." Andy was in tears now, sobbing. "When Max went into the military, it was the first time I was able to breathe. I never knew what to do with him," he cried out. "What do you do when you have a son like that?"

"I don't know," Timber admitted, "but right now I need you to think, Andy. I need you to think about where he'll have her."

"How would I know?" he cried out in that still-shaky tone of voice. "He said he's on the property,"

"But where? The new piece you just sold me?"

"I don't know."

"You better find out, Andy, or I swear to God—"

"Timber, we need to find her. He's … he'll hurt her. He'll keep her as a toy. Oh my God," he cried out. "She's such a sweet girl."

"Doesn't matter what she is right now. He's just out to torture her to get to us, and we can't let that happen."

"No, no, no, no," he cried out.

It was obvious that this was far more than Andy could handle right now. "I need you to stay in control, Andy," Timber snapped, stilling his own nerves. "I need your help. Listen to me, and think. Max has a place on that property that he goes to, has always gone to. It's been his safe place, and, with you selling it, or even if you didn't, when he's feeling threatened, he goes there. I need to know where that is, and that's got to happen before he hurts Tiffany. Do you hear me?"

"Yes, I hear you. Really I do," Andy muttered, pulling it

together somewhat. "I'm trying to think. We've had all this land for so long, and he's never cared about any of it."

"Maybe he did care, but he didn't let you know about it."

"Maybe," Andy conceded, the shakiness in his tone giving way to a bit of strength. "But he was never one to go out there. He doesn't ..." Then Andy stopped. "He didn't like being out on the land. He told me how he just wanted his creature comforts."

"Does he have a house out here, a trailer, a camp, anything at all?"

"No, not now."

"How about before? Did he have a place at any point? All we need is somewhere to start from."

"There was, but ..." Andy sighed.

"But what? Come on, Andy."

Andy groaned. "He had a house at one time. A cabin, and he burned it to the ground in a fit of temper, but that was a long time ago."

"Is anything left of it?"

"No, nothing. ... It's down to dust and dirt. Nothing's there."

"And you're sure he hasn't rebuilt anything there?"

"I don't think so because he hated it so. It was a place his mother loved, and anything to do with her he hated."

"What the hell? That's a conversation for another day," Timber muttered. "Right now I need to know where he would take Tiffany, and it'll be somewhere close by."

"You keep driving," Andy suggested. "The old house was by a creek."

"Oh, don't you worry, I've got other men coming too, and the sheriff's office has been contacted as well."

"Oh God, you need to tell them that Max's armed. He's likely armed to the teeth."

"That's not cool either," Timber noted, with a heavy groan. "He'll hole up somewhere, and it'll become a bloody manhunt."

"I'm so sorry that it's come to this."

Timber heard the fear in the older man's words.

"I've never known what to do with him. He's just gotten worse and worse."

"Right, and I knew it," Timber admitted. "I think I always knew it would come to this. He probably held off when I had so many men here, but still, I'd hoped he would have time to cool off, and that nothing would happen."

"You can only hope," Andy replied, "but things are looking pretty bad now."

"I get it," Timber muttered. "I really do. Now, Andy, I want you to stay put. I don't want you going out after him."

"But I'm the one who can probably talk to him the most."

"But you might also trigger him the most, getting him so completely pissed off to the point of doing something drastic."

"Yes," Andy muttered, "that's true. It might, but, if I can hold him off or can distract him from hurting her, at least it could buy some time for you to get there."

"And how will he respond to that, when he finds out what you're doing?"

Andy gave a broken laugh. "He'll kill me without a second thought. He's wanted to for years." At Timber's shocked silence, Andy added, "I'm not kidding. Something is very wrong with him. At this point, I don't think he cares anymore."

"Yeah, I agree," Timber muttered. "I think he knows he's done for anyway, and he'll just take out as many as he can with him."

"But he's not done for yet, is he?" Andy asked, ever hopeful.

"It doesn't look good for Max," Timber shared. "Now that everybody knows he's here, it's only a matter of time before the authorities catch him. He won't go down easy. And you don't understand. Not just the local sheriff's deputies are after Max. The military has been looking for him too. They've apparently had an investigation going into some of his prior actions."

Andy was crying again, breaking up his words, making it hard for him to continue.

Timber added, "He'll never see daylight again."

"Shit," Andy muttered.

"Exactly, and he knows it. And you know how he feels about being in prison. There's no give in him."

"No, … there isn't. There's no give in him, and all he wants is to cause chaos and pain."

Timber sighed. "And to go out in a huge mess of firepower."

"Shit, shit, shit," Andy wailed. "I don't want that sweet girl to end up being a casualty in all this. She's done nothing. I don't want to think Max would hurt an innocent woman, but—"

"But he's apparently done it before," Timber added, thinking about Dwight's wife.

"There may be a few animals around too that he's hurt."

"What do you mean?" Timber asked.

"I don't know for sure, but I heard some shots earlier. I just assumed he was out hunting."

"And yet hunting implies hunting for meat, for a meal."

"He hunts for the pleasure of killing things," Andy snapped. "Something's wrong with him, and I don't know how to fix it."

"I don't know that there is any fix anymore for Max, and you need to prepare yourself because I don't know that your son's coming out of this alive. I'm sorry to say this, but I can't see it."

"No, he's not, but that will be by his own choice. However, if there's any way you can save him—"

"Shit, Andy, don't do that to me. He's holding a woman right now, a woman he's already told you he'll hurt and make suffer. She's done nothing to deserve it, but he'll make her pay for everything that's gone wrong in his life. I can't stand by and let that happen, and I know you wouldn't want me to."

Andy started crying, great big ugly sobs, as if he realized his son was already as good as gone. "I'll go try to help her."

"No, you need to stay where you are."

"No," Andy argued. "I should stop him from hurting her. It's the least I can do. I should have killed him myself years ago."

"What do you mean?"

"He's been wrong for a long time, long before he joined the military," he whispered. "I just wasn't able to stop him, but now? … Now he's gone too far." And, with that, Andy ended the call.

"Shit, shit, shit." Timber pounded the steering wheel in frustration as he drove as fast as he could to the nearest road. When his phone rang, he answered, "Toby, is that you? Talk to me."

"No, it's not Toby. It's Richard. What the hell is going on?"

"Max Killerman has taken Tiffany hostage," he snapped. "And he's bound and determined to punish her for whatever transgressions he thinks I've made. I've just talked to Andy, and he says Max is likely fully armed, as in heavily armed, and he won't go down easy. He probably won't come out alive."

"Shit. So, this will be death-by-cop, unless we can beat him at his own game."

"It'll still be that way," Timber snapped, hardness in his tone. "The military has opened an investigation into some crimes that were committed while Max was in the service. Everybody is basically saying that he committed a fair number of his own atrocities while he was over there and thoroughly enjoyed himself."

"I know," Richard replied, "and that could well be what is triggering this right now. Anything else I need to know about this mess?"

"His dad just sold me the rest of the property we were talking about. Andy told me that Max once had a place out here, but he burned it down in a rage years ago, supposedly never rebuilt it. The trouble is, Andy was so upset, I couldn't get a good location out of him, other than by a creek. Max apparently told Andy that Max and Tiffany were somewhere on the property. Andy didn't know where but says I need to get there or she'll be hurt in some way. I can't even believe I'm saying this, but everything he says about Max is just sheer ugliness."

"I am on my way now."

"I'll meet up with Toby, and we're heading into the woods together."

"Are you armed?"

"Of course. Toby is meeting me there, and we'll have the horses."

"Just be aware that Max will likely take down the horses, just because that's who he is."

"Right, so he'll kill the horses, put us on foot, and try to take us out that way."

"You know his file?"

"I know enough. He's always preferred ground maneuvers, and he doesn't like horses, according to the military. He's got an unreasonably angry attitude about them. Probably because his dad loved them so much, and so did his mother. Maybe that's what is setting him off. I don't know," Timber admitted.

"I don't know what kind of twisted-ass story Max's got going on, but I can tell you that he is not somebody to play with, and I need you to stay out of it."

"That's not happening. You're not here. You're not in position, and Andy has already headed over here because he's got some cockamamie idea that he can stop his son from hurting Tiffany."

"Do you think he can?" Richard asked.

"I don't know, but Andy sounded as if he'd already taken a hell of a beating from his son."

"Well, shit," Richard muttered. "If we didn't already know what kind of man Max was before, we do now."

"Exactly, and I just can't handle the thought of him toying with Tiffany."

"You two have become quite close, and somehow Max must have found out."

"It wouldn't have taken a whole lot, since she's been back and forth on the property while we've had a large crew of men working here all last week."

"I heard there was a ton of traffic your way."

"Yeah, a ton of traffic and a ton of building going on,"

he stated, bitterness in his tone. "I've got men all over the place."

"You better have those men heading to town because this confrontation with Max will be worse than anything they've seen."

Timber snorted. "These are all trained men, ex-military. I've warned them all, and no way in hell will they run away from trouble. Plus, you can bet every veteran on my property is armed with more than a gun."

"Well, shit. … I don't need a whole team of your men going out there yet, not when I'm trying to round up my men here."

"Richard, it might be a whole lot better if you stay in town," Timber suggested. "You won't like anything about what's coming." And, with that, he disconnected, as he swung into the yard to find the horses already saddled and weapons all about, but they weren't limited to just two horses and two riders. Between Timber and his crew, they had motorbikes, quads, and trucks, with a whole mess of armed men setting up an operation right here in front of him, with military precision.

As he raced in, Toby looked over and nodded. Dwight just glared.

Timber got close and shared, "You all need to know that Max's armed and digging in and not planning on getting out of this alive. He has Tiffany. I don't even want to go over what he's planning on doing with her," he shared, his voice stiffening by sheer will alone. "The deputies are planning on coming. Some of you may already know Richard, and, as a good man, he's still trying to round up a team."

"That's fine," Toby stated calmly. "Yet we're here right now, and we're not waiting, and we're not letting Max get his hands on Tiffany."

"He's already got her stashed somewhere nearby. According to Andy, Max had a place somewhere on the new land that we just bought," he explained, "but he burned it down a long time ago. It was near a creek back then."

"What's the problem then? Let's head out."

Timber grimaced. "The problem is, the new land with Max's burned-down cabin covers 160 acres." The men exchanged glances, and some whistled. "Max knows the land, and we don't."

All the men just nodded, and not one of them had a word to say differently.

Timber sighed. "I don't want anybody going into this and getting their asses shot. That will not help the situation."

"Don't matter to me none," Toby declared, "except that there's a new puppy to be looked after—in case I don't come out of this."

Timber swore at that.

Dwight nodded and added, "I'm going in. You don't get no say in that. I've been waiting for this asshole for a very long time."

"Dwight ..." Timber began, putting a hand on his shoulder.

"I know." Dwight shrugged off his hand, nodding. "I hear you, but it ain't changing shit."

Toby raised a hand. "You also need to be aware that one of the tactics Max is well known for is shooting the horses out from under you." Toby shared, looking from Timber to the men at large.

"That's what I was about to mention," Timber noted. "He'll cripple them and leave them there. If that happens, we need to put them down. I hate to say it out loud, but you know what I mean. If we can save them, that's better, but if not? … Put them out of their misery."

At that, every one of the men nodded. "Agreed."

"Now, let's start, nice and easy," Timber began. "We're all from different parts of the service, but we all know exactly what we're up against right now. I am not expecting any of you to go out there, and, if Max sees too many of us, it will just cause us more trouble."

"We've already got it worked out," Dwight stated. "Stealthy all the way—except for you, Timber."

Timber nodded. "Yep, I distract him."

Toby patted Timber on the shoulder, giving him a big fat grin. "So quit your jawing, get your ass on that horse, and let's get going." The other men had quickly distributed the weapons they had gathered.

"I need more firepower," Timber announced. And, with that, he kicked the sides of the horse he was riding and turned toward his main cabin. "Follow me to the house, and let me get armed up. Have you got any idea where we're going next?" Timber asked the men.

"I do," Toby replied. "We've already gone over the plan, while we were waiting for you to show up."

He stopped at his house, hopped off his horse at the front door, and quickly went inside, then holstered his rifle, grabbed the sidearm he kept at his bedside, then ran outside and hopped up onto the back of Sparky, who immediately shifted, almost as anxious to go as the rest of them.

The other men were loaded up, awaiting the final *go* order.

Timber added calmly, "Be aware that Andy is heading out there too. He's hoping to stop his son from hurting Tiffany before we get there. However, he also realizes he's likely to get killed by his son. Yet Andy's hoping to save his son's life, but I told him that would not likely be the outcome."

The men nodded, and, with that, they all split up and moved out.

Timber turned to Dwight and Toby and asked, "You guys want to let me in on the plan?"

"Yeah, if you ever quit jawing and get your ass in gear."

He gave a bark of laughter and followed Dwight and Toby out.

"There's one spot," Dwight shared, as they set the pace. "We had drones out today looking at the land."

"When did we get drones?" Timber asked.

"That's not the point. One of the guys brought drones back with him and thought maybe it would be something you could use in terms of keeping an eye on things."

"And?"

"So, we decided to check out what you might be working on next," he explained, "and we found one spot. It's got a creek alongside what looks to be a lean-to cabin. As soon as we saw that, I knew that's where Max was."

"How far away?"

"Probably about twenty minutes out," he estimated. "The men will take up positions all around. A couple of them will block the main paved road to confirm nobody is coming or going. Badger has been contacted, and he's rousting up some assistance too. He's contacted the military and a few other people, trying to pull some additional resources together for you."

"Yeah, but by the time he gets all that, we'll have a real shit show on our hands."

"Chances are it'll be all over with by then." Dwight gave

Timber a cold smile.

Toby laughed. "And you know I won't back down on this one."

"I don't want you to die, as you have one a hell of a needy puppy at home," Timber reminded him.

Toby laughed. "Yeah, well, that might be the case." Then he frowned and added, "If I don't make it, confirm Little Toby will be fine," he stated calmly. Dwight snorted and walked away.

"I will, but you damn-well better make it back because, if not, I'll cross over myself just to kick your sorry ass back home where you belong."

Toby snorted at that. "I've got a big ass, buddy, so consider what you're taking on."

"I've got a good idea," Timber muttered, then frowned as he realized Dwright had disappeared from sight. "As for Dwight…"

Toby looked over at him and smiled. "He's gone ahead to the cabin. … He used to be a tracker, so don't you worry about him none."

Timber swore at that. Dwight had every reason to kill Max on sight. Max had killed Dwight's pregnant wife, the psycho who killed Dwight's family. Max tried to kill Dwight, but he survived. Max got away, probably perfectly willing to kill other people's families too.

"Everybody here will do what we can do to make this come out in a good way," Toby declared, "so don't you worry about that either."

"I'm not worried about that, but I don't want Dwight hurt. And I understand he's already got a history with Max, so Dwight has it in for this guy."

"I know that very well, and there wouldn't be any stopping Dwight, so I figured it was best to just let him be."

"Jesus. Dwight and Andy will both get themselves killed."

"We can't let that happen," Toby stated. "We need Andy alive long enough to buy some land off him."

Timber barked out a laugh, appreciating the gallows humor to relieve the tension. "Isn't that the truth. I can't believe any of this has gone the way I thought it would just a couple weeks ago."

"Life never does. It absolutely never does," Toby noted, with a frown, "and that's okay too because right now we've got other things to worry about. At the top of the list is making sure you get Tiffany back. There are very few people out there I would go to bat for at this point in my life," Toby admitted, "but she's good people. Besides, you'll need a veterinarian for this place."

Timber snorted at that. "You're telling me that's the only reason we're going to save Tiffany?"

"Nope," he snapped. "Mostly I just want to get my hands on Max. Dwight and I have been friends for an awful long time. If I can take down the one serial killer who ruined Dwight's life, then I'm game."

Timber looked over at Toby, worried doubly so now, but Toby was stoic and riding solid, calm, and quiet. "You know you could be riding to your death."

"Yep. ... Been there, done that a time or two, just like you." He snorted. "Nothing's killed me so far, and I'm not heading into death in a lighthearted way either," he declared. "However, you and I both know Max has to be stopped."

"I do know," Timber muttered. "I was just hoping that we wouldn't have Andy around to see his son die."

"Nobody should have to see their son gunned down, no

matter how deranged that son may be," Toby stated, "but this son of his might just up and take his own life too. If he doesn't do it himself, he'll go with death-by-cop. I figure Max is not strong enough to off himself. Yet he might be pretty damn sick of everything he started and is just looking for an easy way out."

"I won't say I wouldn't welcome that," Timber admitted, "because it sure as hell is looking to be a bad deal right now."

"It is. It's a bad deal all around, and we've got to get Tiffany out of there. She doesn't deserve to have any of this thrown on her."

"I know it," Timber spat. "I'm just hoping we can finally finish this right now."

"You and me both."

As they moved cautiously forward, Timber got a jolt as his phone buzzed in his back pocket. He'd turned off the ringer. As he answered it, he heard Dwight's voice.

"He's got her where we thought he would be," he began, his voice calm and quiet. "He's heavily armed, and he's already on the lookout. You're about two miles to the west."

Immediately Toby nodded, having overheard.

"Keep going strong. You should be coming up soon," Dwight said. "I would give you maybe fifteen minutes. I say, ride for about ten, then take the last ten on foot. He's a mean son of a bitch, and I don't think anything left in him is good right now."

"How is he acting?" Timber asked.

"He's shooting at anything he sees that's alive and moving, and that's from a grouse to a songbird. So, any animal will go down first."

"Good enough," Timber noted. "We'll send the horses

back on their own."

"Hopefully they won't need to be pushed in that direction," Dwight replied, "because otherwise we'll need someone to move them along."

"I don't know," Timber muttered. "Sparky and I have been together for a very long time, so he won't take kindly if I try to send him home alone."

"But he needs to be sent home. Otherwise you'll need that vet in a big way."

"We'll need her in a big way anyway," he stated, "I just didn't realize how much."

"Yeah, you had your eyes working a little too hard on everything else."

"Yeah? What else was I supposed to do?"

"Not much. I think you were well on your way to including her in everything you wanted her in," he stated calmly. "And that's why we're doing what we're doing. We've just got to keep focused, to stand strong, and to confirm this asshole is contained," he spelled out. "This time he goes down, and he stays down." With that, Dwight disconnected.

Timber looked over at Toby, who was moving ahead ever-so-slowly. They stayed in formation for a little bit longer. Then Toby slid off his horse and moved over, so Timber could come up to his side. He quickly dismounted and looked over at Hilton, Toby's horse, and told him to go home.

Hilton had hopefully been at Haven long enough to understand what *home* meant. But he didn't want to leave, and when Toby gave him a slap on the back, the horse just turned and looked at him.

"Dang," Toby whispered, "I don't see a whole lot of

obedience in that."

"No, what you're seeing is loyalty," Timber muttered, as he pointed to Sparky, who hadn't budged either. "We need them to move, and we need that now because they are a dead giveaway and will get us or themselves killed." Timber turned and smacked his horse hard across the rump. Immediately Sparky jumped up and moved out, heading back the way they'd come. Hilton followed him gingerly. Toby and Timber both watched them go, their hearts heavy, silently urging the horses to go faster and faster.

"They are on their way," Toby whispered. "Let them move out. If you keep looking back at them like that, they'll both return to us."

"Yeah, I know," Timber muttered, "damn it."

"It's all good."

"Says you."

Toby gave an almost silent laugh, then tapped Timber on his shoulders and began speaking to him in sign language—a method developed over many years in the military. They were going forward just a few feet and then turning.

Timber nodded, following quietly. He remembered this area from some of his earlier scouting trips around this land. He recognized the creek, and all of a sudden he knew just where they were, just how far away they were, and just what he needed to do. And, with that, his whole awareness of the scenario shifted.

It had been a little slow in coming, and he felt a deserved fury at his own rustiness, but he was here now, in the full sense of it. As he came up beside his partner, he tapped Toby on the shoulder and stepped in front of him, moving ahead, cautious but steady, letting him know in no uncertain terms that Timber was taking the front position. As he turned around once to check on his progress, he noted that Toby had already moved out, slipping away into his own search of the surroundings.

Timber found the lean-to, with a little bit of smoke coming out of the edge, but saw no sign of her, at least not visibly, which also meant that there would be no sign of Max. He would be hidden in the shadows somewhere, waiting for Timber. He had no choice but to flush out Max, and that meant making his own presence known.

He let out a whistle and then shifted quickly to the side, just as a bullet slammed over his head and into the tree trunk. Even though Timber had already moved, Max had been nearly on him. Timber half smiled in the semidarkness, didn't say anything, and zigzagged very, very quickly and as quietly as he could. Then, using an old tried-but-true technique, he threw his voice to the side and whistled again.

Immediately another bullet slammed, but this time Max's aim had been way off, so Timber's trick made all the difference. He kept approaching in an indirect manner, getting a little bit closer and closer, knowing that he wouldn't get close enough to make a difference.

Suddenly Max called out, "Quit playing games. I know exactly where you are."

Timber didn't say anything.

"Get your ass over here before I hurt her." Then he appeared, stepping out of the shelter, holding Tiffany in front of him, his free hand on her neck, prodding her forward.

As Timber studied her closely, he saw the tears in her eyes, but he also saw the defiance in her expression, and he realized just how much this moment would matter. He couldn't afford to make a mistake.

Hesitating, considering his options, another noise

sounded off to the side behind him. Max shifted ever so slightly and fired immediately into the bush. Yet he didn't fire once; he fired multiple times, which was an interesting reaction. Either that was fear or a sign that he didn't give a shit. He just wanted whoever was out there to know that Max was here and was in charge. Timber didn't say anything, trying to figure out what was going on in this man's twisted mind, all the while knowing time was short.

He suspected Max was done with everything and wanted this over with, and maybe taking Tiffany was literally just that, a chance to bring this to an abrupt end of some kind. But, in the end, that would have Max going out in a blaze of glory, with no actual glory involved at all. A blaze of fury most likely was what it would be. Max wanted to go out, wanted something to spike his temper enough that he could do everything he needed to do and just shoot until nobody cared anymore, that *nobody* being him—and not caring anymore because he would already be dead.

"Come on. Stop screwing around. I can wait around all day, or maybe I can't. I don't give a shit," Max bellowed, then turned and put his handgun up against Tiffany's head.

She closed her eyes and didn't say anything. She just stood firm.

"Look at her. She thinks somebody here is coming to her rescue. Little does she know that it's just bringing you all to your death."

Just then came a wavering voice from the side, and Andy stepped out of the shadows. "Leave her alone, son. She hasn't done anything to you."

"Oh, look at that, good God. The bleeding-heart old fool is here," Max announced, spitting venom.

"Haven't you done enough, Max? I can go talk to Timber again, if you think that's what you need. We can sort this out peacefully."

Max laughed. "Peacefully, *huh*? You should have thought of that before. What do you think, Timber? And what kind of fucking name is that, asshole? You think I should go beat up the old man … again?" Max looked around to the exact area where Timber was. "Andy's the one who sold you that property, after all. I told you that I wanted it back, not for you to go get a bigger chunk. That's my land. That's all my fucking land, you asshole."

"No, it was my land," Andy snarled, some of his own temper coming back. "And you ain't got no business treating your old man like that."

"Why not?" he asked, turning to him. "You're useless. You always have been, always will be. I've got no use for you when you're like that."

"You've got no use for anybody," Andy declared to the shadows around him. "That's the problem. You came back even more damaged than when you went away."

"Yeah, … well, I'm not damaged. I'm just fine. You're the only one who seems to think I'm damaged," he said, followed by a laugh. "I'm just me, same as I've always been."

"And that's the problem," Andy cried out. "There's something wrong with you. It not normal to be so hateful like you are."

"Doesn't matter whether it's normal or not. It doesn't matter at all. What matters is that I get everything I'm supposed to get," he snarled. "Go home, old man. I don't want you here."

"Why not? You afraid to let the old man see just how far you've slid?" Andy asked, with a quiver in his tone.

"I already know how far I've slid," Max declared, "and I

don't give a shit about you anymore. You sold off my land, and for what?"

"I sold the land I don't need because I'm dying," Andy admitted. "And because you've got both the MPs and the civilian cops looking for you, you'll never get free of them. They'll lock you up for life, and you'll never work the land like you were supposed to."

He looked over at him. "The military ain't gonna find me." But his tone was weak and faint at that.

"You know better than that, son. You absolutely know better than that. They won't give up until you're hunted down, and they'll take you back for whatever it is that they feel you've done."

Max shrugged. "They're probably right in whatever they think I've done," he stated, "but I really don't give a shit because those sins aren't sins as far as I'm concerned. Everybody I ever killed or hurt deserved it."

"Everybody?" his father repeated, his voice quivering. "I highly doubt it, son. I doubt it greatly. You like to hurt things. You always have."

Max shrugged. "Sure, what do I care? None of it matters. I don't feel any pain like they do, so I can't really see what all the fuss is about. Besides, it doesn't really matter because you won't be here much longer either."

"No, I won't," Andy agreed in a shaky voice. "Whether you shoot me or not," he added, "I won't be here much longer because the cancer will take me."

"So, the property sale hasn't gone through yet," Max decided. "I'll just reverse that. Even if I sit on it in jail for twenty years, it'll still be there for me."

"Except you can't," Andy cried out. "The deal's already done. The land has already been sold."

"Then I'll just shoot him and take it back."

"You can't," Andy cried out again. "You can't take it back. It's legally Timber's."

To Timber, Tiffany seemed to be holding her own, thank God. Yet Andy seemed to have gained a certain amount of strength, only to start fading ever so slightly, and that was a concern. If he was fading, he would look weak in the eyes of his son, which could trigger Max to take an unfair advantage over the old man.

Timber stepped forward. "So now what?" Timber asked in a conversational voice. "You got your dad here. You've got Tiffany, who doesn't even know who you are, or what you're up to. Plus, you've got me. I'm right here."

"Look at that. You must really like this piece of ass, *huh?*" he asked, as he twisted Tiffany's hair.

Timber watched Tiffany cry out in agony, only to stiffen ever so slightly against the pain sent her way.

"She's got spunk." Max laughed, maddeningly. "I kind of like that. Too bad you didn't move a little faster with her though. She really needs some taming."

"She's not a horse," Timber replied calmly. "And none of your insults will make any difference."

"No? That's too bad because I was thinking that maybe I could make her life a whole lot nicer, you know, spend some quality time with her." At that, he laughed uproariously.

She turned to stare at him but managed to keep herself quiet.

"Oh, you see? Now look at that. That look in her eyes. If you could see it there, she's ready to murder somebody," Max declared, with a howl. "Too bad she doesn't realize that she won't get a chance to do anything."

And he held her just firmly enough and close enough

that Timber didn't dare take a shot, couldn't do anything, and Andy was also fading. "Your dad needs a hand," Timber said. "He's too old for this shit."

"He was too old for this shit from the day he was born. What do I care if he needs a hand?" Max asked, with a cold stare. "The old man sold me out."

"No, you sold yourself out," Timber clarified calmly. "You're the piece-of-shit son Andy couldn't hand the land over to because you wouldn't work it."

"Of course I wouldn't work it, but I would have stayed here, and I would have loved the place," he cried out, passion in his tone. "Because, at the end of the day, everybody needs a place to come home to."

"And since you've come home, you've done absolutely nothing but torture Andy. The man can hardly even stand."

Max looked over at Andy and shrugged. "So what? As if I care."

"I've not been here for long, but I know that what you're doing to him isn't fair and that you're just crying out to be killed this way."

"I'm not trying to … Oh. Oh, God, you think I'm trying to get shot? As in death-by-cop or something? *Nah*, … that's not happening." He chuckled. "I'm totally okay to just shoot her dead right now." And he put the handgun right up against her head, a smile on his lips. "And don't worry. I'll find those horses of yours and make them pay too."

"I don't doubt that you would," Timber replied, his tone hard as he realized just how far gone Max was. "You do realize that there's no way out of here for you. This is a one-way ticket. You say that's not what you were planning, but it's obvious that it is."

"What do you mean, it's obvious?"

"You're done for. You're washed up, cleaned out, and nobody can help you anymore. Not that you want help, but you can't get out of this. So, as far as you're concerned, it's time to just take down as many as you can."

Max shook his head. "I already told you that I don't need that kind of an out."

Dwight's voice came from the shadows. "Obviously you do because that's the kind of out you're taking, and, if you didn't need a bunch of armed men surrounding you, … then you wouldn't be doing this. You wouldn't be reduced to such a sad wailing, crying scenario that you're putting in right now. You know that these men aren't alone, and you also know that there's no way you're getting out of this alive."

"Where are the cops then?" Max asked, followed by laughter. "Of course you guys don't want the local yokels, and you know why? Because you're the same as everybody else, the same as me. You're all just killers. Everybody who goes into the military is a killer. Everybody just wants to get their kills recorded properly."

"No," Dwight countered, "all of us went into the military and had opportunities to kill, and most of us—not you obviously—did our best to avoid any situations where it was necessary. Only assholes like you came back and enjoyed it all too much and then continued to take out more people."

Timber pointed. "I believe you know Dwight here, *huh*?"

Max looked over at Dwight, who stood up and appeared at the sound of his name, both guns pointed at Max.

"Well, … well, well, that was a different scenario entirely. Dwight and I go way back, don't we, Dwight?"

"Yeah, we sure do," Dwight agreed calmly, his gaze never leaving the snake in front of him.

"You really want to be the one who takes that shot, don't you? I killed your wife and unborn child. I killed your family but never was caught. Yet, you kill me now, in front of all these witnesses, and you would go to prison for my murder."

"Sure, absolutely," he confirmed, with a nod. "Don't have an issue with it at all."

"And you've been busy hurting animals in this area too," Toby added, now stepping forward a bit too, spaced out far enough from Dwight and from Timber to keep Max's gun moving from one to the other. "I wouldn't be surprised if one or two of them were hanging around, wanting to have a second chance at you."

"Jesus, Toby. Welcome to the party, pal. I should have known, if Dwight was here, you would be nearby too." Max laughed. "And, yeah, I'll pop any animal that comes my way." Then he looked at Tiffany. "I can't believe she's a fucking veterinarian. Like seriously, why do you want to help the animals for anyway?"

She looked up at him and even through the glaze of pain in her expression, she answered him. "I would help any four-legged animal, but there are some two-legged ones I would be happy to see die."

He turned to Timber. "See? She's got gumption. You should probably marry this one, but, *ooh*, sorry, you won't get a chance to do that." Then he burst out laughing, as if it were the funniest thing he'd ever heard. Then just as suddenly the laughter shut off, and he threw her down in front of him, holding the gun against her cheek, and said, "Don't ever fucking talk to me like that."

Another man spoke up from the far corner. "She can say whatever she wants. You pop her, and you're dead."

Timber added, "Max is dead anyway."

"Yeah, … I know I'm dead anyway," Max replied. "So I don't give a shit. In the meantime, I'll just cause as much chaos as I can." Then he laughed and laughed. "And I'll start with her."

"If you shoot her, it's still all over for you," Timber declared. Max hesitated, staring at him. "Come on, Max," Timber added. "You know that. The minute you take out your hostage, you'll go down. It's as simple as that."

"Yeah, but don't you want me to go down *before* I kill her?" he asked, followed by a mocking laugh. "After all, the only reason I went after her was because it's obvious you are sweet on her."

"So, you saw her come and go?"

"Sure did. And why the hell were all those men helping you all week?" he snarled.

And damn if there wasn't a hint of jealousy in his tone, as if Max never really understood what *help* or *camaraderie* or even *community* meant. For a fleeting moment Timber almost felt sorry for him.

"It's called friends," Dwight stated calmly from the side. "Something you wouldn't know about."

"Ah, that's you whining again. That bitch of yours, … I should have killed her a long time ago."

"You killed her when you did, so presumably that's when it was time."

"Yeah, and you ever think about her? You could still be married, have had more kids, that whole happy little fantasy that everybody talks about." Max shook his head. "You want to know something funny? I did it deliberately."

"I know you did," Dwight said. "I also know that I couldn't convince anybody that's what you'd done. Back then nobody seemed to think you were that twisted."

"But you knew."

"Of course I knew," Dwight stated. "I watched you all those years. I told her to stay away from you, that you weren't healthy, that something was wrong there, but she always seemed to think she could fix you."

"Yeah, she was a sweetheart." Max laughed. "On the other hand, you've been a pain in my ass this whole time."

"The only reason I've been a pain in your ass is because you've been afraid of retribution coming down, always looking for it to find you."

"You never did get there, so I guess I don't need to worry about it now because, even if you shoot me here, there will be so many bullets, nobody will know who did the actual shooting."

"That's fine," Dwight said. "As long as your ass never walks again, I don't really care."

Max stiffened and glared at him. "You weren't supposed to come, you know?"

Toby added from Max's left, "Of course not, but you also knew there was a good chance that somebody would come." Toby shifted ever so slightly.

"I didn't think anybody would come with Timber. Why would you guys come and take a chance of getting your old asses shot?"

"Feeling the heat now, Max?" Dwight asked.

"No, that's not normal what you are doing here. Nobody here does things like that," Max declared, his gaze going around to the shadows, looking for more people he couldn't see. "This isn't fucking normal."

"To you it's *not* normal. However, to us *normal* people, it is," Toby stated calmly. "It's called being friends, being like family, helping out, being a decent person."

"You don't even know what that means, Max," Timber called out. "And you can't even blame your dad for it because he's a damn fine man."

"Oh, that son of a bitch. You don't get to say that about him. Perfect old Andy was one mean son of a bitch. You have no idea what my life was like. Oh my God. Just sing me a song of sorrow already," Max wailed in a mocking tone. "I'm really fucking fed up with this. I don't care if you do shoot me, but I'll tell you one thing. You won't stop me from shooting her, so that will be the satisfaction I get out of this."

Timber noted Max was practically spitting saliva all over the place, waving his gun, his madness front and center.

"It might be the only thing I get, but that's okay." Then he looked down at Tiffany one more time and said, "Sorry, sweetheart. They're the ones making me do this." And with that he pulled her head back, put the gun tighter up against her chin, and muttered, "Say goodbye."

Instead she grabbed his testicles with her right hand, and squeezed as hard as she could, all the while twisting them for good measure. He screeched, loud and pain-filled, in such a way that every man in the bush winced. Then she dropped and rolled, knowing a bullet would likely still come her way, but, as Max pointed the gun at her, ready to fire, swearing and cursing her out all the while, bullets hit his body from all directions, making him do a manic dance before he dropped.

She sat on the ground, pulling her knees to her, as she stared at Max in horror, even as Timber raced toward her. She looked up when he reached her, tears in her eyes.

He wrapped her up in his arms and held her tight. "Oh my God, sweetheart. I'm so sorry."

She shook her head, but she couldn't talk. The tears came, and her body trembled, completely consuming her.

When Toby arrived, he checked first to confirm Max was dead. Then he walked over, bent down to face Tiffany. "Are you okay, honey?"

She nodded, whispering, "I'm fine."

"That was a mighty good move," he stated proudly.

"Balls, *huh?*" Dwight grinned as he came over as well. "We were hoping you had some ninja move that you could make to get yourself out of the firing line," he said, smiling but still looking concerned.

"You had me worried, as you took a fair bit of time to get there." Toby laughed. "But you got there." And, with that, he stood, then whistled, and both Timber and Tiffany watched as every man stepped out of the cover of the forest and walked slowly toward them.

She looked up at Timber. "Good Lord."

"I know," he said, with a smile. "That's the thing about teams. We don't have to do everything alone."

"I've never seen anything like this," she whispered.

"I haven't really either, not since I left the military at least. It was pretty damn nice to have these guys and others just like them watch my back while I was out saving the world back then," he added. "But this was way better."

"I am incredibly grateful to all of you."

Each one of the men came up and shook her hand and confirmed she was doing okay. One of them muttered, "I sure hope I never get on the wrong side of you, ma'am."

Another one added, "That was a mighty good grip you gave him."

"Yeah," she agreed, as she looked down at her hand. "People never seem to realize how much hand strength a vet needs to wrangle some of the animals that we work with," she explained. "I guess I'm stronger than I look."

"I'll keep that in mind, ma'am," he added, as he tilted his hat her way and then walked slightly off to the side to join the others.

She looked up at Timber, who was smiling down at her.

"This isn't exactly how I thought the evening would go," he muttered.

"Oh my God," she cried out. "What about Andy? Where's Andy?"

Timber stiffened, bolting to his feet, and turned to find Andy, looking down at his son, tears in his eyes.

Tiffany stepped away from the others and walked over to give Andy a gentle hug.

He looked up at her and nodded. "I'm so grateful he didn't hurt you." And then he looked at her closely, tears streaming down his face. "Or did he?"

"No," she replied, "you got here in time."

His shoulders sagged, and he nodded. "I was hoping I could do something, but ..." His voice trailed off as he looked back at Timber. "You were right. Max didn't even put up that much of a fuss, did he?"

"No, he was definitely looking to go," Timber confirmed. "He could have shot her many times. I think he was just done and didn't want to face a tribunal, didn't want to face any investigations, didn't want to sit in the brig or some jail in the meantime. He just wanted this over with."

Andy nodded slowly. "It won't be easy to recover from this though," he admitted, his shoulders shaking.

"Do you have family in town?" Tiffany asked him.

"I don't know," he muttered. "It seems as if I don't even know what *family* means anymore."

"Where is Brian?" Tiffany asked.

"Right here," a shrill voice shrieked harshly from nearby. "You fucking shot him. You shot my father."

Andy turned and looked at him. "Now you just calm down here, son."

"Calm down? Fucking calm down? You let them shoot him. They just gunned him down right in front of you. Did you see how many bullets hit him?" Brian held a rifle even now aimed directly at Timber, but it wavered between Timber, Tiffany, and his grandfather.

Andy looked at him and added, "This is really not the time to decide that you need to do this, son."

"No? I should have decided it a long time ago. He was a mean son of a bitch, but he was still my father."

"Yes, he was, and he was also my son, but he was damaged, and he had been damaged a long time ago. He came that way. I swear to God, he just never seemed to care about anything or anyone."

"He was still my father," Brian cried out in pain.

Tiffany walked toward him, her hands out, and said, "I'm so sorry. I know he was your father, and nobody needs to see that."

He just looked at her and snapped, "You're the bitch he was after but why? Why you?"

"Because she's friends with me," Timber declared, catching up with her, not letting her get too close to Brian. "That's all your dad wanted. He was holding her captive in order to hurt me."

"Yeah, ... I can see why. I've got my own beef with you too."

"Maybe you do," Timber stated, "but you're also heading for a whole lot of misery if you don't put down that gun right now."

"Yeah? And what will you do about it?" Brian snapped, staring at him and refusing to move the rifle.

Another voice came from the shadows, and soon Richard appeared. "We missed a large part of this obviously," he noted, "but I know exactly what I'm seeing right now, and damn it, Brian. Put down that rifle right now."

"No," he snapped, "I will not. He needs to pay for what he did. He shot my father."

"Technically he didn't. I think probably a dozen of us did," Toby admitted, keeping his own gun aimed at Brian. "But I can see that you don't care about the fact that Max was trying to shoot an innocent woman."

"Women aren't innocent. They're just toys, things to be used."

Tiffany stared at him and asked, "Is that really what you think? Do you believe all the gibberish that's coming out of your mouth right now?"

He just glared at her, furious that she would talk to him like that.

"Maybe you are like your father. Maybe you're a lost cause, just like Max was," she declared. "You are sure breaking your granddaddy's heart right now."

"So what? He's just a loser too."

Andy looked at him and said, "That's enough of that talk out of you, young man."

"What will you do?" he snarled. "You already let them kill your own son."

"I didn't let them kill my son. My son got killed due to his own actions," Andy snapped. "Don't you even think about talking to me like that."

At that, Brian turned the rifle on him and yelled, "Don't you even talk to me, old man." And he pulled the lever action back.

Toby stepped forward, but his grandfather was there ahead of him. Andy stepped up to the gun pointed right at his chest and taunted Brian. "Then you go ahead and pull that trigger. If you think your father didn't deserve what he just got, and you think the whole world is out to get you, then maybe you better go ahead and pull that trigger right now. Then you'll spend the rest of your life behind bars as some nasty sidepiece for an inmate, but that's okay because you're something special, aren't you?"

Andy was on fire, red in the face, with tears flowing freely down his cheeks. "You think that everybody else is out to get you and that you're suffering so much?" he snapped. "You don't even want to acknowledge the problems that your father had, or the military tribunal that was coming up for him to address the various war crimes he committed while he was in the service."

"That's what the service is for," Brian snapped. "He already told me, if I wanted to go in, he could give me some pointers on how to make the most out of killing people."

"Is that what you really want to do?" Toby asked, staring at him. "Just kill people the way you like to hurt animals? Is that all you really want for your life?"

Brian shrugged, his gaze on Tiffany, who stared at him with such accusation in her gaze that he flushed.

Tiffany asked, "Starting with all the girls in town? Like Kelly?"

"I already heard about that. I heard she quit. It's kind of funny actually."

"Why? Aren't you sweet on her?"

"No, I'm not sweet on her, God no. She's definitely not my style."

"No, of course not, she's on two legs, not four."

He stared at her in shock. "You didn't just say that."

"It's what you like, right? What you're doing is hurting four-legged animals because you're too scared and haven't yet figured out how to hurt the two-legged variety yet," she declared, her tone beyond angry, "but you know it's coming because I can see that you want to."

"No, I don't fucking want to."

"No? But you do want to hurt the animals?"

"No, I don't want to hurt animals."

"So why do you do it then?" she asked.

"It was my father. He told me it would make a man out of me."

"It didn't work. It just made an ass out of you—an ass who hurts other asses."

He just blinked at her, missing the reference to the donkey. "That doesn't even make sense."

"Yes, it does to the rest of us. You'll finally understand once you're in prison. Meanwhile I'm looking after the donkey you tortured, and, believe me that I will never let you live that down." He stiffened, then glared at her. "Yeah, I know it was probably just to prove to your daddy that you were something special. But he just wanted you to be a sick son of a bitch like he was."

Andy still stood in front of Brian and asked him, "So, have you decided what you're doing? Will I die today too?"

"Granddad, it didn't have to be like this. You didn't have to let them shoot him."

"I didn't *let* them shoot Max," Andy reiterated, frustrated now. "He got himself killed through his own actions. What were we supposed to do? Stand by and let him kill Tiffany? I get that you don't want to believe these things about your dad, and I can't help you come to terms with it. I have my hands full dealing with it myself right now."

"What happened to your face?" Brian asked. He was looking at Andy now, as if seeing him clearly for the first time. He was all bruised and swollen, and one eye had a big purple mark.

"What do you think happened to my face? Your father beat the crap out of me," Andy spat. "Just like he used to beat you, he also beat me."

Brian's bottom jaw started to quiver.

Timber noted the change. "That's what happens when you live with abusers," Timber explained. "They beat you up, and that twists you up inside because you love them, and you'll do anything you can to have them in your life. Both of you were Max's victims, but you don't have to stay that way."

At that, Andy opened his arms and said, "Come on, son. Let's not go down that pathway if we don't have to. We're all we have left."

"You're trying to send me off to the military," Brian cried out.

"Maybe there's another answer. ... I don't know," Andy muttered. "Lord knows after what happened to your father, I'm not sure I want you in the military either," he admitted. "But you can't keep going the way you are."

Brian's bottom lip started to tremble, and Tiffany stepped forward and added, "You need therapy, and you need to get the hell away from here where all these bad memories are. You need a better life, but first you have an awful lot of owning up to do. You've hurt a lot of people, a lot of animals, and nobody around here has any goodwill toward you. So, you need to make some decisions about your life, and you need to make them soon."

At that, Richard stepped closer and repeated, "Put the gun down now, son. You put it down and keep it down. Otherwise you'll pay the consequences."

Brian looked at him and then at the rifle in his hands, throwing it to the ground. Then he snagged up his grandfather and just hugged him tight. "Why did he do all that stuff?" he cried out.

Andy tried hard to just hold Brian close, but he was shaking and crying now. It was obvious that the dam which had served as some kind of a defense mechanism for a very long time had suddenly broke.

Tiffany moved Timber away, and he looked at her in surprise as she shrugged. "He is entitled to grieve too."

Timber looked over at Andy and Brian and nodded. "Both of them are."

"You still want Brian to go into the military?"

"I don't know," he admitted. "I can see why Andy doesn't want that because of the way Max was, even after a stint in the military, but honestly, Brian could learn from a tour." He held out his hand to gesture toward the men who were still here, standing ever silent in the shadows. "Brian would find the benefit of friends, a team, and teamwork, and he would learn a whole lot about himself. It's not about going out and killing things or having a license to hurt others. It's all about working together toward a common goal. Brian needs something to give him some purpose and to help him to rebuild his self-esteem."

"That's not our decision," she muttered, "at least not today."

Timber smiled, wrapped his arms around her, and held her close. Then he looked over at Richard. "How long were you standing there?"

"Long enough," he said, with a sigh. "Max really wouldn't get out of this one alive, would he?"

"He didn't want to."

"Right, I saw that." Richard nodded. "It was a clean shooting. I'm happy to say that you guys are all off the hook."

"*Ha*, you just didn't want to do all that paperwork."

"No, I sure didn't," he agreed, with a headshake. "Guess I better get a forensics team headed out here."

"That sounds good."

"You'll need to contact the military too," Toby added. "You can let them know that the manhunt they were organizing can be called off."

When Richard frowned at Toby in surprise, Timber nodded. "Max was up against all kinds of charges for what he did during his military service."

"Crap," Richard muttered. "I guess it's a good thing that's all been circumvented now too. How the hell does somebody go this wrong?"

"I think he's been wrong for a very long time." Timber looked down at Tiffany. "Shall I get you home?"

"Yeah," she said, as she looked around, shivering still. "But how will we do that?"

In the distance, he heard a slight nicker. He looked over to see Sparky standing there, looking at him. "How do you feel about riding a horse?"

"All the way back to town?"

"No, silly, back to my truck, and then I'll take you to town." He stopped and checked her over, then asked, "Do you need to go to the hospital?"

"No," she declared, with a firm headshake. "I won't go

to any hospital." When Toby stepped up and glared at her, she glared right back. "I'll go when you go."

"That ain't happening on this side of hell."

"Exactly," she snapped.

Toby beamed at her and nodded. "You know, the sooner you get your ass over to the Haven, the sooner we can treat you better."

"Treat me better? What's that got to do with anything?"

"Yeah, we decided we'll help Timber on the wooing part because he's a little slow at it."

She blinked and muttered, "On the *what* part?"

"He's a little behind, probably a little rusty on the wooing, so we figured that Dwight and I would help him out, you know, and show you just how good it can be over at the Haven."

"Oh, you did, did you?" she asked, a twinkle in her eyes. "The two of you think that's something Timber needs help with?"

Toby nodded. "Yeah, I think so."

Timber just stared at them. "You did not just say that."

"Look at you. You're awfully slow. Even now you've got an invitation to ride the two of you together on one horse because Sparky is good with that, and you could get to her place and stay the night." Toby nudged Timber. "Jesus, man. You've rescued the damsel in distress. She obviously needs comforting tonight, and look at you? You're still slower than hell."

She burst out laughing, then came to Timber's defense. "I think he's got that part down just fine."

"You think so?" Toby asked, winking at her. "'Cuz he's still standing here."

"I am not," Timber growled, not sure if he should be

howling with laughter or embarrassed. "Jesus Christ, Toby, you are too damn much."

"This isn't too much *yet*," he declared, "and you better get used to it because we're sticking around long enough to confirm everything is kosher at your place."

"And what will that look like?" Timber asked.

"I don't know." He looked over at Dwight, who stepped out of the shadows, a big grin on his face. "What do you think?" Toby asked Dwight.

"I don't know about helping Timber do any wooing. I think we should just let him figure that part out. Still, I ain't too anxious to keep moving anymore. I really like this place."

"Damn right." Toby nodded. "What do you think?" He looked over at Timber and Tiffany.

Tiffany frowned. "Timber's got some big stuff planned, and he's definitely gonna need a hand, but that's up to you guys to decide."

"We already decided," Toby announced. "Timber needs us, so we're staying, and he'll also need a vet. So you're staying too."

Her laughter rang out free and clear.

Timber snatched her up and whispered, "I am so sorry. I didn't know Toby and Dwight would be so involved in our relationship."

"I get why you're sorry, but honestly it's pretty fun to even be wanted for a change."

"Oh, you're wanted," Timber muttered. "But I sure don't want an audience." Again her laughter pealed out free and clear, and he smiled as he heard it. "Something about that laugh of yours is very infectious."

"That's because I've just been saved, and I have a whole new lease on life," she declared, as she looked up at him.

"And honest to God, there's an awful lot to be said for being alive right now. I would really like to get going though."

He scooped her up, lifted her onto Sparky's back, then walked him over to a log and hopped up behind her himself. He looked down at Sparky and said, "Yes, we can finally go home now."

And with a neigh, a nicker, and a headshake, the horse moved forward at a good clip.

"Wait, does he even know where he's going?" Tiffany asked Timber.

"Oh yeah, he knows." Timber lifted a hand to the men still gathered around. "We'll see you guys later."

"Don't make it too early," Dwight suggested. "There'll be pancakes, but not exactly at the crack of dawn."

With that, the other men grumbled.

"What do you mean there won't be pancakes at the crack of dawn?"

"We've got to eat too, man," another man called out.

"Looks like that won't fly, Dwight," Toby called out. "Besides, Timber will need to keep up his strength."

Dwight howled. "Okay, fine. Pancakes at the crack of dawn for you guys but not Timber. He is staying in town." He turned with a sharp look at Tiffany.

Tiffany laughed and nodded. "Orders received."

"Good."

And, with that, Timber and Sparky carried her gently through to the homestead.

CHAPTER 25

"**I** NEED TO check that everything is okay at the clinic," Tiffany shared, as they were almost back to Timber's place.

"Yeah, that's probably not a bad idea," he agreed. "Just so you know, I broke into the place. That's how I knew for sure you were gone."

She looked back at him in astonishment. "What do you mean, you broke into the place?"

"Well," he winced and added, "I wasn't really sure I should tell you that part."

"I didn't think B&E into my clinic would be that easy to do. I do keep drugs here, and that can be a draw to the wrong element."

"It is kind of easy, so we'll have to work on upgrading your clinic," he muttered. "I was already headed that way because Toby told me that you didn't call him back. So I had to confirm that you weren't locked in the cooler or something. Then Andy called me and told me that Max had you."

"I just *wish* I'd locked myself in the cooler. Max attacked me before I ever got the door open," she replied.

"I'm so sorry about that."

"It's okay," she muttered, "and you'll have to stop apologizing for it."

"That'll be hard to do," he acknowledged. "I feel very

responsible for it. Plus, it's just been one hell of a day."

"It has, indeed."

Back at his place, he turned Sparky out into the paddock, gave him some feed, and then turned to her. "Come on. Let's hop in the truck, and I'll get you home."

"Yeah, and, if you don't, you know you'll hear about it."

"Good God," he muttered. "Do you believe those two?"

"I kind of do. It's very sweet."

"*Sweet?*" he repeated. "Are you kidding? They'll make our lives miserable."

"Oh, I don't know. I think they'll fill our lives with laughter and a whole lot of love. All they want is a place to call home, to be a part of something, kind of like a family," she explained. "That's why they want to stay on with you because you're building something, and that's what they need. Somewhere to be included."

He looked over at her and smiled. "How did you get to be so wise?"

"Ah, it comes with age."

At that he looked at her, startled, then burst out laughing when he saw the grin on her face. "I do love your sense of humor."

"Yeah, it doesn't come out all that often. I tend to be a lot calmer and quieter, but something about coming close to death changes your perspective."

"I hear you there."

They drove through the streets, quickly stopped by the clinic, secured it the best they could, then finally pulled up in front of her house.

She sighed as she looked at it. "It looks awfully lonely."

"I'm bringing you inside to confirm you're okay anyway."

"If you don't stay, they are so going to get you for it."

"I know." He groaned. "If I go back tonight, they'll be all over me, but I certainly won't take advantage of your hospitality because of those two knuckleheads."

"I was kind of thinking that they might be right, you know, having the best idea."

"What idea was that?"

"That you should spend the night," she stated, with a smile. "God knows I don't want to be alone, and, no, that's not the only reason I'm inviting you."

"So, why are you inviting me?" he asked, his gaze intent as he studied her.

She smiled. "Partly because I don't want to be alone. Partly because I want to celebrate being alive. Partly because I never did get the dinner I was promised, and partly … I don't know, but do I need any more excuses?"

"No," he whispered, as he leaned over, grasped her chin, and pulled her toward him, kissing her gently. She moaned in joy as his lips touched hers. "I was so afraid Max had already hurt you," he admitted, passion in his gaze, "and that I would never get a chance to do this."

"I had that same thought myself," she shared, pulling back. "How sad that it took something like that to get us here."

"I was just waiting until we didn't have a zillion people around."

"I know. I kind of was too, and then you invited me for dinner, and I thought that maybe all the guys were gone, but that sure didn't happen. There were still a ton of guys there."

"I'm beginning to think that it might always be that way to some degree. I don't really know."

She burst out laughing, "That's is a good point too. I

guess you could always use a few good men around on a permanent basis."

"Toby and Dwight are staying for sure, and I think some of the others are staying for a couple weeks. I don't really know," he said. "Honestly, I'm just trying to go with the flow, and that in itself is a challenge."

"Of course it is," she agreed, "and I think, for you, it's a bigger challenge than most of us are aware."

"When you're used to planning your own life," he noted, "having people around makes you stop and think about what is important and also understanding what's important to them."

"Good, then get your ass in the house. I'm so sore right now. I don't really want to go to work tomorrow."

"I understand, but you don't want to cancel a full day of appointments either, do you?"

"No, I sure don't," she said, with a smile on her face. "Hopefully I'll feel better in the morning."

"Look. I'm only coming in if you want me to."

"I do, and I don't know quite what this is I'm feeling now." She closed her eyes and added, "This feels more like panic, shock maybe. I've never seen someone killed in front of me before." She stared at him, tears starting to form in her eyes. "It's all just kind of hitting me."

He held her close and whispered, "You *should* have a reaction to something like that," he noted. "Feeling and seeing the horrors stirs up our emotions that keeps our humanity in touch, as we don't want to be desensitized to something like that."

He quickly unlocked the doors, came around, and helped her out of the truck. "I guess we should have brought your truck."

"That's okay. I'm in no shape to drive anyway," she muttered. "You can drop me off in the morning—or whatever. We'll figure it out," she muttered, with a headshake.

"Come on. Let's get you inside," Timber whispered.

"I don't even know how to feel all of a sudden."

"There isn't any right or wrong way to feel when it comes to this," he said in a gentle voice. "It's just that you need to let it out. You need to feel what you feel. You need to let go of the stress. The reality is, you spent hours in a traumatic and highly dangerous situation. You almost died tonight. You had to fight for your life, and you watched your attacker die."

"And yet I don't know that I'm as upset about him dying as I am hurt for everybody else in this scenario. I hurt for his son. I hurt for his father."

"That's what makes you so special," Timber noted, "because they were part and parcel of a lot of it. Unfortunately it'll be a long road to recovery for them, and hopefully there will be some therapy to help them."

"I don't know that Andy has a whole lot of time for that," she murmured. "His cancer is back, and I don't get the sense that he has very long."

"Which means Brian will be the one who needs an awful lot of help," Timber noted.

"Particularly if he's about to lose his grandfather. When it's all said and done, it might be a really good idea for him to go into the military after all."

"Maybe that was why Andy was reluctant to do that."

She looked at him. "Why?"

"Because Andy is dying. He didn't want to ship Brian off to the military, only for Brian's last living relative to die while Brian was away and alone."

She winced at that and nodded. "Yes, you're right. Andy would absolutely want to keep Brian close and maybe have a chance to heal some of the trouble between them," she pointed out.

Timber nodded. As they walked up to the front door, she looked around. "Oh gosh, I don't even have my purse with me or my keys."

"I gather that's at the clinic too?"

"Yes." She stared up at him. "I'm so sorry. I should have thought about it while we were there."

He asked, "Do you keep a key hidden somewhere?"

"Oh." She frowned, thought for a moment. "Yes, yes I do." She quickly retrieved it and sighed. "Jesus, I must be in worse shape than I thought."

"You're okay, and you're still dealing with shock," Timber noted. "And who wouldn't be? Stop trying to be everything you think you need to be."

She looked over at him and shared, "I've been alone a long time, and, when you're alone, it's all you really know how to be. You're not so different yourself."

"You're not alone anymore, and honestly, if Toby and Dwight get their way, you'll never be alone ever again."

She burst out laughing, "They really are sweet, aren't they?"

"I don't know that they would accept that." Then he shrugged, shook his head, and added, "Who am I kidding? They would absolutely accept it from you. Now, if I were to call them sweet, I would probably get a fist in the mouth, but if you were to call them sweet?" He sighed. "It would be totally okay."

She grinned at him. "They really are though."

"Sure they are," he quipped, with a look in her direction, "but you're the only one who would get away with saying it."

She smiled. "I still think they're sweet."

"Good, I'm glad you do." He laughed. "But they'll also try to maneuver you into my life, whether you like it or not."

"I'm not against it and was kind of hoping we were heading in that direction anyway."

"There was no hoping about it. We obviously were. We just didn't get the chance to get very far on our own because of all the chaos of trying to support the huge work crew who showed up. Now, we're still not getting very far on our own because the two of them will be checking to confirm that I'm doing everything right."

She giggled. "I've never really had anybody around to do something like that. I didn't have a father most of my life."

"Tell them that, and they'll be all over you." Timber groaned. "It'll make them even more impossible."

She burst out laughing. "Maybe I won't tell them that just yet."

"Please don't," Timber pleaded. "I can't imagine what my life will be like if they think they have to step into the daddy role too."

"Oh gosh." She giggled and quickly had the door unlocked and stepped inside. Taking a quick turnaround, she noted, "It wasn't even on my radar that I might not make it home tonight as I have two dogs but I'll text my neighbor and ask if he can take them out and feed them considering the circumstances. I have to admit there's something very special about it."

"Absolutely, there is," he agreed. "Now let's get you upstairs, into the shower, and off to bed."

She looked over at him and nodded. "A shower would

be good. Getting knocked out and manhandled makes me feel especially grimy."

"I also promised Toby that I would check that head of yours. It was either that or take you to the hospital," he shared, with a wicked grin.

"*You* can check it," she muttered. "That hospital visit is not happening."

"Yeah, I think they knew that. So you wouldn't fight me on checking your head wound."

"Right. I'm not really picking and choosing, as they already made that decision."

Timber snorted. "That was pretty smart of them. … And tomorrow, we'll have an awful lot to deal with."

"I know," she muttered, "not to mention the sheriff's office. Is it wrong of me to be grateful that Max's dead and gone and that there won't be a trial or much of an investigation?"

"No, it's not wrong at all," Timber said, as he led her upstairs, and nodded at the master bedroom. "Where are your clothes for tonight?"

She walked over to the dresser, pulled out a clean nightgown.

"Now, let's take a look at that head wound before you go in for a shower, and then we'll see about getting it shampooed."

When he took a look, he wanted to kill the asshole Max all over again, and was shocked that she was doing as well as she was, but he knew that as soon as she collapsed after cleaning her wounds, her head would really start hurting.

"I don't even want you to touch it," she said.

"I know, and I can see why, but I need to confirm that you don't need stitches because it bled quite a bit. It's mostly dried up, but I need to see what's under there."

She turned and looked at him. "Really?"

"Yeah." He nodded. "You did get knocked down."

"That wasn't very nice of him, was it?"

He just smiled and let her keep talking as he closely examined her head. "I think it's probably fine, but it's likely to bleed some when you get in the shower."

"Then it can bleed because a shower is absolutely on my to-do list right now." She got up gingerly, and he frowned at her.

Watching her closely, he asked, "Do you feel faint at all? I don't want you passing out in there."

"No, I don't feel faint." Yet she turned to study him intently. "But you can always come in and help me anyway."

He rolled his eyes and muttered, "That is playing with fire."

"We've been playing with fire for a while now," she said. "This is just making sure I'm good enough to play again some other day."

His eyes widened, and he nodded. "That's not a bad point." He quickly shucked off his clothes and walked into the shower. He adjusted the water and waved her over. "Come on. Let's get that head of yours cleaned up."

CHAPTER 26

T IFFANY STEPPED IN the shower, right in front of Timber, completely lacking even a hint of self-consciousness at being nude. She felt a sense of, not relief but safety with him. She didn't have to worry about him because she already knew who he was inside and out, and that was something she couldn't put a price on. As soon as she stepped in and let the warm water pour over her head, she was half crying from the painful sensation.

He took the soap and began cleaning her back and then asked, "Are you ready for this? It'll probably hurt like hell."

She nodded, and he started in on her hair, gently building up the soap suds, probably hoping to give her less pain, then letting the warm soapy water slowly dissolve the dried blood that had accumulated on the top of her head and throughout her hair. She cried out a couple times, then tried to still it.

He whispered against her ear, "No, … release the pain. Absolutely no point in hanging on to that right now."

"It just hurts," she whispered.

"I know, yet it probably feels really good too."

"Yeah, how does that work?" she murmured.

"It's life," he said, with a laugh. When he was done shampooing her hair, he picked up the bottle of conditioner, held it up for her, and she nodded.

"Yes, please."

He gingerly rubbed that into her hair, working it into the roots, and, when he was done, he asked, "How is that now?"

"Perfect."

"Okay, then I'll scrub myself up really quick, or do you want me to help you out first?"

"No," she muttered, as she leaned back against him. "I'll stay right here."

"Okay, it might be a little hard for me to do *me* though."

"That's okay," she murmured, her eyes closed, just letting the water sluice down her face and her back. "You do *you* right now because I can't stand here for too much longer."

He quickly grabbed the soap and took care of his own head. She handed him the shampoo, and he washed his hair. Then when he was done, he prodded her along. "Okay, let's get you to bed." He turned off the water and very gently, if a little awkwardly, helped her out of the shower and wrapped her up in a towel, then he half carried her to the bed.

"You need to be taking care of that leg of yours." Then she stopped and asked, "What the hell?"

"What?" He looked at her.

She pointed at his leg. "You went in there with your prosthetic."

"Yeah, it's a special one that Kat made me," he noted, "and it's got a special joint cover that stops them from getting wet."

She stared at him. "That is amazing."

"You can look at it in greater detail tomorrow," he suggested, "but, right now, you're too exhausted."

"I am, but that's fabulous," she said. "Yet I didn't even

consider it, so, what does that say about me? I never gave it a thought."

"You know what it says about you?" he asked. "It says that you're very comfortable, and you're not treating me like I'm handicapped. You've treated me as if I were completely normal, which is awesome because I'm fine."

"Okay, good," she muttered, with a small smile, "because I'm way too tired to even work my way through that or anything else."

He chuckled. "That's good because I don't want it to be an issue."

"Good," she muttered, "I don't either." She moved toward the bed, then picked up her nightie, looked at it, tossed it onto her dresser. "Why bother?" Pulling back the covers, she asked, "Do you want the left side or right?"

"I'll take whichever one you don't take," he replied, with a note of amusement.

She yawned, slipped under the covers, then patted the bed beside her. "Sorry, but I need to sleep."

"You go to sleep," he said. "Do you need something for your head?"

"No, it's better if I don't," she muttered.

He didn't say anything to that as she closed her eyes. He made himself comfortable on the bed. He had his phone with him but wished he had a charger. Then he spied hers and realized it was the same kind of outlet and quickly plugged his in. He hadn't asked her where her phone was, then realized it was probably still in his truck, unless it was back at the clinic. That was something he probably should have thought about before he came inside, but he wouldn't do anything about it now.

When he got under the covers and rolled over, she immediately tucked herself into his arms and, with a happy sigh, drifted off to sleep.

♘

TIMBER HADN'T IMAGINED Tiffany being quite so open, quite so honest, and nowhere near as accepting of his prosthetic. She hadn't even thought of it, which he had to admit was a huge boon in his mind. It had always been a bit of an issue for him, as it was still a relatively new issue to deal with in terms of relationships, but, for her, it was nothing. She didn't even seem to consider it, except when it hit her that she might have hurt him, which was a nonissue anyway. But he was happy, and, with his arm tucked around her, he drifted off to sleep, only to be awoken by the phone about an hour later. He checked and realized it was Badger.

When he answered in a low tone, Badger asked, "You okay? I really hesitated to call but wanted to check in."

"I'm fine. Tiffany is sound asleep, and I'm about to do that myself."

"Good. We'll talk in the morning." With that, Badger disconnected.

Timber smiled, absolutely blessed to have the friends he had. Even as he went to sleep again, his phone buzzed with a text from Toby, asking if Tiffany was okay.

Timber sent a thumbs-up and texted that she was asleep and that he was heading there himself. He got a thumbs-up back. With a smile, he fell off into dreamland himself.

CHAPTER 27

IFFANY WOKE TO a furnace. She rolled over, saw Timber lying beside her, apparently sound asleep, then collapsed back down.

He whispered, "Go back to sleep. You still have plenty of time."

"I don't think I can," she muttered, with a yawn. "I've always been an early riser."

"Doesn't have to be this early, not today."

She smiled, curled up in his arms, and nodded. "That's a good point. Yet I'm still so tired, but I'm awake and not sure what to do about that." She wiggled up against him and then wiggled again.

He grabbed her and muttered, "You're heading for trouble."

"I hope so," she whispered in a teasing tone.

"Not exactly sure that should be on the agenda or that it would be that good for your head," he stated hesitantly.

"I'm sure. I've waited long enough. And it's just the two of us who matter here." She reached up to kiss him. "Besides, if we don't decide …"

"Oh my God," Timber muttered, "I'm sure Dwight and Toby will be texting us next, deciding for us."

She laughed and snuggled closer. He lowered his head and kissed her again and then again. She wiggled up against him, her lips twitching at his moan.

"Nice to know that all the important body parts work," he muttered, and she laughed.

"I can see that for myself," Tiffany noted, "or can feel it myself."

He nodded, "Yeah, … you sure can. I'm surprised I'm even still in bed, considering all the thoughts that crossed my mind overnight."

"Ha, you're too honorable. No way you would have gone there at that time."

He shrugged. "Yet I've been thinking about it for a long time, but I was a little busy at the center."

"You were, indeed, and, according to the men, you were too busy. You were supposed to be looking out for your future too, a future with me."

He smiled. "They'll be the death of me, you know that."

"Yeah, they sure will try," she said, with a grin. "I kind of really like it though."

"Yeah, me too," he murmured. "I'm half scared to say that they'll end up being major parts of my life, but it sure seems they will be. Guess I better get used to it."

"You will." Then she pulled up against his neck. "It's been a long time," she whispered.

"Me too," he muttered, nibbling at her ear. "My last relationship was before the accident."

"Ah, and of course, you've been worried about that, haven't you?"

He lifted his head, looked down at her in all seriousness, and asked, "Wouldn't you?"

She frowned, then nodded. "Yeah, I probably would. But the good news is, you don't have to worry because I really understand about missing limbs. If ever anybody would know, it would be me. I deal with animals, amputations, and prosthetics all the time, so the fact that you are missing part of a leg is nothing to worry about."

"I'm glad to hear that because I was kind of hoping you would say that."

"Absolutely," she murmured, as she wiggled up against him. "Besides, everything else is in working order."

He chuckled. "That is very true." As he lowered his head, he offered, "Unless you want a demonstration, just to be sure."

"Oh, I absolutely want a demonstration," she declared. "A gal can't be too sure, and I don't really want to just take your word for it now."

He lowered his gaze and smirked. "No, of course not. That would never work, would it?"

She burst out laughing, wrapped her arms around him, and pulled him closer. "Anything that works for you, works for me," she declared. Then he lowered his head and kissed her, a kiss that blew her away, made her breath catch in the back of her throat, and curled her toes. When he finally lifted his head, she murmured, "Wow, even if nothing else works, you can knock my socks off just with those kisses."

He burst out laughing. "I'll keep that in mind."

"You do that," she murmured, as she pulled his head down once again. "Believe me that I want more, so much more."

And the next few hours she spent absolutely loving every inch of his body, and he reciprocated with so much joy that she returned the favor. And so it went. They took breaks, making coffee, taking it back to bed, then made breakfast sandwiches and took those back to bed too.

At one point she looked at the clock and groaned. "I

don't want to go to work."

"I understand, but at least because we woke up so early we had lots of time together."

"And I loved every minute of it," she murmured. She leaned over and gave him a big kiss. "I absolutely loved it."

"Good. … So maybe we can do that again someday?"

"I sure hope so." She got up, had a quick shower, got dressed, and when she came back out of the bathroom, she noted, "I hate to say it but I'll need a ride."

"I know, and I have men at my place I need to deal with too."

"Right," she said, her eyes widening. "You've still got a ton of work to do, don't you?"

"I do," he confirmed, with a nod. "But that's okay, as a whole lot of good things are happening in my life right now."

She smiled, wrapped her arms around him, and sighed. "Mine too. So, can I come for dinner tonight?"

"I was really hoping you would," he said, as he gave her a long kiss. "Maybe pack an overnight bag too. I'll drive your vehicle in and pick you up."

"Oh, I like the sound of that," she murmured. "I can already see a lot of driving back and forth in my future, don't you?"

"Hopefully that won't be too onerous for you," he said.

"No, absolutely not. Besides, I get to see you that way."

And, within minutes, they were both in his vehicle, as he drove her to her clinic. He picked up her phone from the console. "Oh, good, I was wondering where this would be."

"I completely forgot about it last night," she admitted. "When I thought about it earlier, I figured that I may have lost it for good and would have to work on getting a replacement today."

Timber shook his head. "No, I picked it up from the clinic last night but forgot to bring it in. Sorry."

"No worries, I have a charger at work. It's all good."

When they got back to her clinic, he hopped out with her, checking the perimeter. Then she unlocked the door so Timber could check out the whole clinic inside. Everything seemed to be okay, and then, as he went to say goodbye, she wrapped her arms around him and gave him a whopper of a kiss. "I'll see you tonight."

He dropped his head down and gave her a kiss back and whispered, "Tonight."

And, with that, he left, bypassing two of her assistants who had just arrived for work. They took one look at him, one look at her, and muttered, "Oh my God."

Tiffany grinned and nodded. "Yeah, let's just say it was a hell of a night."

"We heard all kinds of rumors about chaos, but it wasn't that kind of chaos."

Tiffany laughed. "No, that kind of chaos was the good stuff. The rest? … I'll tell you later," she said. "We've got to get ready to open up." She smiled and waved as he drove past them, then turned back to the ladies.

And, with that, she focused on her work and her long day of patients she had ahead of her, but it didn't matter now because tonight she would have a long night ahead of her too, and that part would be fun.

Katie and Elizabeth were both grinning, and Tiffany suppressed her smile, adding, "Let's get at it."

CHAPTER 28

T IMBER DROVE HIS truck back out to his place, then parked out in front, and immediately was surrounded by dogs and greetings.

Dwight stepped out from the kitchen and asked, "You need breakfast?"

"I sure do, if you've got some," he said, with a nod.

"Hungry?" Dwight asked.

"Starving," Timber replied, knowing exactly what Dwight really meant.

Dwight gave a nod of satisfaction and said, "Damn good thing." And, with that, he headed back inside and added, "Flapjacks are coming, and you've got five minutes."

"You got coffee?"

"Of course I've got coffee," he snapped. "What kind of kitchen do you think this is?"

Timber burst out laughing and said, "It's my kitchen, so who knows on a day-to-day basis."

"Right now, you're not kidding," Dwight noted. "Everybody's been talking. … It seems the whole town is abuzz with rumors of all kind of shit. We've even got extra guys coming out next week now. Everybody wants to confirm you're set up and good to go."

"Is that because of what happened last night?" Timber asked.

"Yeah, and because it looks as if you're sweet on the veterinarian, and everybody wants her to have a good house, so we've got plans for that now too."

Timber frowned at him. "Seriously? I've got to have some money set aside for some of this."

"Yeah, you've got some money. I know you blew a whole load on land, but that's all good too. We can still get a shit ton of stuff done. You've got to give that lady friend of yours a nice place to come home to."

"And what if she's not too bothered?"

"It doesn't matter if she's bothered or not because you've got to make sure that whatever she's got coming her way is nice."

He laughed. "And you'll see to it, right?"

"Absolutely," Dwight declared. "We've decided we like her just fine, so we need her moving in."

"Really?" Timber turned to face him. "Isn't that a little hasty?"

"Sure, but we aren't getting any younger."

"Damn right," said a man from behind him.

Timber turned and looked at Toby, with little Toby right on his heels, greeting Lucy and the other dogs. "Seriously? You're in on it too?"

"Of course I'm in on it," Toby declared. "And there's nothing to be in on. The fact of the matter is, she's perfect, she's also got gumption, and we haven't seen a whole lot of that kind of woman in a long time, so she's handpicked."

"I would like to remind you that I handpicked her."

"Yeah, so she's handpicked, and now we've got a couple weeks to get this shit together for her. Besides, when is she coming?"

"Tonight. She's coming by for dinner."

"Perfect," Toby said, as he rubbed his hands together and looked over at Dwight. "What do you think?"

"I think it's perfect," Dwight agreed, with a nod. "Now we'll just have to work on making sure those two don't mess it up."

"What do you mean, mess it up?" Timber asked.

"You're so close," Toby said, "but we can't have you screwing this up now."

"We won't give you any pointers on it because, man oh man," Dwight muttered, "that would probably set you off. But we want that gal here, and we want the two of you nice and safely married."

Timber stared at him. "Aren't you—"

"No, we're not rushing things at all."

Both men were grinning like old coots, rubbing their hands together with glee. "You go off and get to work. We've got plans to make."

"Whoa, whoa, whoa." Timber raised a hand. "No plans and no rushing things, guys. Do not do anything to mess this up."

"Us? We're not messing it up. We're trying to figure out how to stop *you* from messing it up," Dwight declared, with a big laugh. "Now go on, get out, go to work. We've got things to talk about."

"What about my flapjacks? What about coffee?"

Dwight frowned. "Okay, you've got five minutes. Get yourself some grub, eat, and go."

Timber stared at them and sighed. "You two are unbelievable."

"Yep, we sure are," Toby agreed, grinning like a fool. "As we told you, we've got plans, so you need to get at it."

"I'm getting at it," Timber said. "Just make sure she feels welcome."

"She'll feel welcome. Don't you worry about it. This is our domain."

Timber eyed them suspiciously and asked, "What do you mean?"

"Nothing." They both looked at him innocently.

"No, stop. You've already done enough matchmaking."

"Are you married yet?" Dwight asked.

"No," Toby declared, and on they went.

"Is she living here yet?" Dwight asked.

"No," Toby replied again.

Dwight nodded. "So, apparently we haven't done enough yet."

Timber groaned. "You know that I will not be happy if you two chase her away with your nonsense."

They looked at each other, then frowned at him. "We won't chase her away. We're trying to stop *you* from chasing her away, so go, go on."

"For two grumpy old shits, you two are sure cheerful this morning," Timber stated.

Dwight nodded. "I agree. Now I don't know about Toby, but, speaking for myself, my load feels considerably lighter today, and the world somehow looks brighter."

Toby chuckled. "Yeah, and that sick rat bastard won't be hurting anyone ever again."

"Yeah, that too," Dwight muttered, with a gentle smile for his old friend.

Overcome with the realization that Max's death had relieved Dwight of a burden he'd carried for years, Timber reached out to shake his hand, and found himself pulled into an unexpected and heartfelt hug.

Warmed by the thought that Dwight could now live out his life in peace, Timber smiled as he headed outside, flapjacks in hand.

EPILOGUE

As Timber Woodland stepped outside, with the usual circle of happy dogs at his feet, a truck pulled in, and a man his age stepped out. Timber stared at him, confused for a moment. "Holy crap. *Burke?*"

Burke headed toward him, a big grin on his face. "I would give you a hug, but it looks as if you've got your hands full of—what is that, pancakes?"

Timber snorted, shoved the pancakes in his mouth, then reached out and grabbed Burke in an absolutely massive hug. "What the hell are you doing here?"

"I was talking to Badger and heard you'd gotten yourself into a big mess."

"Not so much now, but, honest to God, I feel as if I've just been released from a huge mess."

Burke nodded. "I heard that part too. Anyway, I'm kind of at loose ends, so I thought maybe … you could use a hand for a few days."

"Oh my God, I would absolutely freaking love it if you could stick around," Timber said. "We haven't had a chance to visit in a very long time."

"Not sure it'll happen now either. I've been told by more than a few people that you've got yourself a lady friend."

"Yeah, I do," he confirmed, with a beaming smile.

"Even with the leg?"

"Even with the leg, it doesn't seem to make a damn bit of difference to her."

"She's a veterinarian, I hear."

"She is a vet, and she's worked with Kat on some prosthetics for animals too."

"Dang, if she'd only seen me first," Burke boasted, "you would have been out of the running."

"I know. That's why I'm really glad that you didn't show up until now because she's already mine."

"Damn. She got a sister?"

"Nope, no sisters."

"How about a cousin?"

"I don't think so, but you can ask her tonight. She's coming for dinner."

At that, he slapped him on his head. "Man, I am so happy for you."

Timber smiled and nodded. "Thanks, buddy. It seems a long time coming."

"In so many areas," he agreed, "and I can't believe you've got all this."

"And so much more," he murmured. "It'll be a massive, massive sanctuary for animals."

"And what kind of animals have you got?"

"Oh, a few you may not expect," he replied, with a smile, "but that's okay because that's what a refuge is all about. It's a home for all. It's a safe haven."

"And is it just for four-legged animals?" he asked, his tone a little off as he looked at his friend.

"It can also be for two-legged animals," Timber stated, with a wry smile, "particularly ones in need."

"Yeah, I was kind of hoping you would say that. You got

a place where I could bunk for a day or two?"

"Sure do," he replied, looking over at him. "Troubled times?"

"Not so much troubled times, just maybe time for a rest."

"That's good enough for me," Timber said. "You know you've always got a home wherever I am."

"Thanks for that, man. I really needed to hear it." And, with that, the two men stood on the front porch, enjoying the bright sunshine. The dogs stretched out happily in front of them, Dodger the squirrel sitting contentedly on the railing close by. Birds trilled and flew by, cutting through the trees.

Timber looked out and smiled. "It really is a brand-new day."

"Amen to that," Burke replied. "I could use a whole new day."

"And if you need a hand with something …"

"Maybe, … I've got to work my way through it first."

"Good enough. I won't push."

"Yeah, you will," Burke countered, a knowing smile on his face. "Just don't do it today." And, with that, he slapped him on the shoulder and added, "I heard there's work to be done."

"Yeah, there's plenty of that."

"And you pay in grub." Then, laughing and joking, they headed out to join the rest of the men who were already swinging hammers in the wind.

Timber never thought he would see anything quite so fine. So he picked up a hammer and joined them, a smile on his face and his heart full. His life had never looked quite so good. This place, aptly named Haven, wasn't just for him, but for everybody else just like him, and that was even better.

From a short distance away, a doe with a spotted fawn by her side looked on, happily grazing.

This concludes Book 1 of The Haven: Timber.
Read about Burke: The Haven, Book 2·

The Haven: Burke (Book #2)

Burke, desperate for a fresh start, heads to Timber's place, hoping to exchange bed and board for some work around the refuge. He's trying to heal from a costly toxic relationship, but it seems the past isn't ready to let go. His ex has somehow secured credit cards in his name, determined to make him "pay" for the breakup.

The shocking details came to light when Shirley, his ex's sister, reaches out. She risks her own safety to warn him, putting herself on her sister's bad side—and, even worse, in the crosshairs of her sister's new boyfriend.

Amid the serenity of the Haven, Burke is caught in a whirlwind, trying to untangle this new mess while ensuring Shirley's safety. He's always had a soft spot for her. She is the shining light in that family, consistently proving her kindness and loyalty.

When the town becomes too dangerous for Shirley, Burke offers her refuge, knowing no one would dare trouble her here at the Haven. As they navigate these challenges together, a deepening bond begins to form between Burke and Shirley, a love that promises to heal old wounds and to offer a new beginning. Yet they both know she can't stay hidden forever ...

Find Book 2 here!
To find out more visit Dale Mayer's website.
https://geni.us/DMSTHBurke

Author's Note

Thank you for reading Timber: The Haven, Book 1! If you enjoyed the book, please take a moment and leave a short review.

Dear reader,

I love to hear from readers, and you can contact me at my website: www.dalemayer.com or at my Facebook author page. To be informed of new releases and special offers, sign up for my newsletter or follow me on BookBub. And if you are interested in joining Dale Mayer's Reader Group, here is the Facebook sign up page.
http://geni.us/DaleMayerFBGroup

Cheers,
Dale Mayer

About the Author

Dale Mayer is a *USA Today* best-selling author, best known for her SEALs military romances, her Psychic Visions series, and her Lovely Lethal Garden cozy series. Her contemporary romances are raw and full of passion and emotion (Broken But … Mending, Hathaway House series). Her thrillers will keep you guessing (Kate Morgan, By Death series), and her romantic comedies will keep you giggling (*It's a Dog's Life*, a stand-alone novella; and the Broken Protocols series, starring Charming Marvin, the cat).

Dale honors the stories that come to her—and some of them are crazy, break all the rules and cross multiple genres!

To go with her fiction, she also writes nonfiction in many different fields, with books available on résumé writing, companion gardening, and the US mortgage system. All her books are available in print and ebook format.

Connect with Dale Mayer Online

Dale's Website – www.dalemayer.com
Twitter – @DaleMayer
Facebook Page – geni.us/DaleMayerFBFanPage
Facebook Group – geni.us/DaleMayerFBGroup
BookBub – geni.us/DaleMayerBookbub
Instagram – geni.us/DaleMayerInstagram
Goodreads – geni.us/DaleMayerGoodreads
Newsletter – geni.us/DaleNews